His mouth crossed over hers. The heat simmered until she wanted to strip off his T-shirt. Throw off hers. Right as her fingers slipped down to his belt, he backed up.

His forehead rested against hers as he held her hands away from his body. "Yeah, that can't happen."

Disappointment slammed into her as her body switched from hot to cool at a rapid pace. She offered everything and he . . . Maybe she would never understand men. But she was starting to get how this one operated. "Because you still think I might be working with Benton?"

He lifted her hand and kissed the back. "Because you are a temptation I can't afford."

Her heart did a little flip. "What if I want you to give in?"

"Then I fear I'm doomed to disappoint you." He glanced at the bed, then back at her with regret shining in his eyes. "Get some rest."

And then he was gone.

By HelenKay Dimon

FACING FIRE

BAD BOYS UNDERCOVER

HELENKAY DIMON

AVONBOOKS

An Imprint of HarperCollins*Publishers*

AVON BOOKS
An Imprint of HarperCollins*Publishers*
195 Broadway
New York, New York 10007

Copyright © 2015 by HelenKay Dimon
ISBN 978-0-06-233009-3
www.avonromance.com

First Avon Books mass market printing: October 2015

Printed in the U.S.A.

10 9 8 7 6 5 4 3 2 1

To the writers and readers out there who love romantic suspense. You are my people.

FACING FIRE

1

JOSIAH KING reached for his gun and grabbed only air. Not that a weapon would do him any good. Shooting a wall-sized monitor wouldn't stop the bloodthirsty execution unfolding in front of him.

"What are you watching . . . Wait, where is this feed coming in from?" Mike Shelby asked as he walked up to stand next to his team leader. "Man, I hope this is some sort of training exercise because that guy looks like shit."

"It's real. A video. One-way, and I have no idea how were getting it." But this was personal and meant for him. Josiah knew that much. "I'm pretty sure it's live."

It had to be because Josiah would know if this horror had already happened. They all would. No, this hell played out in real time.

"So we can see this poor bastard but he can't hear or see us?" Mike got up close and squinted as his gaze scanned every inch of the screen. Even waved his hand in front of the monitor. "I don't get it. What exactly is this?"

Josiah feared he knew the answer. "A message."

"For?"

"Me." That's really all he could say. He couldn't wrap his mind around the idea of his personal life being beamed into a secure facility as spectator sport.

Mike glanced over, already frowning. "What?"

Josiah kept staring up at the center screen hanging right in front of him in the Warehouse, the de facto headquarters of the undercover task force called the Alliance. He blinked a few times, sure he'd fallen into a bleak nightmare he needed to fight and punch his way out of if he ever wanted to breathe again.

Somehow he spat out the right answer. "Uncle."

Mike shifted the whole way around and faced Josiah head on. "Uncle . . . as in your uncle?"

The man highlighted on the screen in front of them looked like a version of the very formidable 3rd Earl of Stonechase, Thomas Benedict Asher, a hereditary peer in the House of Lords. For Josiah, simply the uncle who taught him how to fish. Now a man tied to a chair, his white hair sticking out in every direction. His usually pristine white shirt ripped open to reveal the folds of pale skin around his stomach and spray of gray hair on his chest.

Blood ran in a line from his temple. More pooled in a circle near his heart. Yet more on his wrist. He'd been beaten and strapped down in a room painted gray with high ceilings and dramatic print curtains. Josiah couldn't see the bookcases he knew lined the wall, but he recognized the desk. Intricately carved, with a secret compartment used by his ancestors as they passed the secrets of the four-story stone manse down from generation to generation along with the title and the land.

It all looked familiar except for the bomb strapped to his uncle's chest and the obvious shake moving through him. Those were the parts that finally registered in Josiah's brain and kick-started him into action. This was no nightmare. He couldn't wake up, couldn't unsee the scene unfolding in front of him.

"Phone." He snapped his fingers and pointed to his cell on the conference table behind Mike. "Get me a phone."

"It's . . . it's too late for me. I will . . . die." His uncle's voice, usually perfectly smooth, held a rough edge as he stumbled over the words and his voice trembled. He stared straight ahead, probably into a camera, in a way that looked like he was talking directly to Josiah through the monitor. "No matter what action you take that will happen."

Mike froze as he handed over the cell. "Sweet Jesus."

Through the haze falling over Josiah he realized the clipped words coming through the monitor speakers weren't delivered in his uncle's normal style. That likely meant he read from a script or something similar. No question someone wanted to deliver a haunting message and decided to use an old man to do it.

"He says you caused this." His uncle's gaze darted up and to the right as he spoke, as if he were taking direction from someone in the room.

Josiah hit a few buttons and dialed to get through to his uncle's house. A beeping sound greeted him, so he tried again, desperate to hear the familiar voice.

"Anything?" Mike's gaze did not waver from the screen as he slipped his phone out of his back pocket.

"No." He was going to fucking fail again. Josiah could feel it. Be so close but not on time.

His heartbeat thundered in his chest. He'd spent a lifetime in the intelligence service. Seen people cut down by bullets and shredded by explosions. He'd stayed focused. Now, his mind took off on a wild rush and he fought to wrestle it back under control. Strategies bombarded his brain, none of them workable from his position on the grounds of Liberty Crossing, the modern complex outside Washington, DC, that housed the National Counterterrorism Center. Virginia had never seemed farther away from his uncle's London townhouse than right now.

"You and your team ruined everything." His uncle visibly swallowed as the trail of blood seeped down his cheek and his gaze stayed locked on the camera, which must have sat just out of sight. "Now you'll pay."

"He's being told what to say but seems to know he's talking to you." Mike didn't wait for agreement. He shook his head. "I'm calling everyone in."

No one else stood in the room with them. Bravo leader Ford Decker had his team practicing building raid maneuvers. Josiah had his Delta team muster for weight training earlier but they'd all moved out after showers, taking the rest of the day for some much-needed time off.

Somewhere the people who ran the Alliance sat in their offices across the Liberty Crossing grounds. Being people with access to everything they'd have access to this feed, as would other intelligence services, which were likely monitoring and mobilizing. Josiah knew in the next five minutes people would pour through the doors with theories and strategies. Later there would be questions about how this video beamed into the Warehouse with such apparent ease, about protocols and firewalls, but none of that mattered now.

He hit the emergency button and the metal doors clanked and locked with heavy precision as the Warehouse switched into lockdown mode, trapping them inside. The move would send a warning to the entire Alliance team. Bravo, Delta, and admin would get the call to come rushing back to assist. As he waited for that to happen he tried his uncle again, this time using private backdoor numbers.

The ringing in his ear echoed on the monitor in front of him. His uncle jerked at the sound but couldn't go far in his chair thanks to the cords binding him. Something in the room, something Josiah could not see, had his uncle's gaze shooting to that same corner spot again.

Then he looked directly into the camera. "You can't stop this, Josiah. Please don't try . . ."

The brief break in his tone. Josiah read it as a personal plea. One he had to ignore even as he knew to his soul no one could get to his uncle in time.

Phones started ringing in the Warehouse. Josiah could hear Mike relaying information, likely to team members. The other monitors lining the walls flickered to life in front of them and a steady hum filled the room as computers turned on and paper started spilling out of the printer. Lines of information filled one screen. Josiah knew his team had started working its magic but the gnawing in his stomach, the rolling bile, told him whatever they did would be too late.

Mike put a hand over the phone. "Where is he? Which residence are we looking at?"

The behind-the-scenes recon had flipped into action. The people Josiah trusted most in the world likely searched files and made calls to try to find a peaceful end to this. "Belgrave Square. London."

"Shit, nowhere near here." Mike repeated the information and listened for a second before disconnecting the line and going back to staring at the screen. "They're mobilizing MI5 or MI6 or whoever stops bullshit like this in your country other than us."

But Josiah knew it wasn't that simple. His uncle possessed resources. Serious resources. "He has security."

Mike shrugged. "We both know that can be broken."

He didn't get it. "He has guards, Mike. A damn militia within shouting distance at all times." Josiah rubbed a hand over his face as he started to pace.

"Who the hell is your uncle?"

He didn't wallow and never felt helpless. Right now both sensations raced through Josiah. "Someone hard to get to, which I'm assuming is the message here. No one is safe, no matter how well-connected or high up in government."

He was about to say more, to explain why this could only be described as surreal and impossible and how it shouldn't be happening, but the words fell away as he clenched the phone even tighter in his palm. He called the line that went directly into his uncle's home office again, hoping to get through to someone in power and reason with him.

The second after the private line rang his uncle started talking again. "He knows you're the one calling."

"Who is the 'he' leading all of this?" Mike asked to the monitor as a second screen filled with images of men in uniform, approaching vehicles on the way to the Belgravia residence.

One name popped into Josiah's head and refused to leave. The name of the same "he" the Alliance had been hunting across every continent, sifting through every lead and turning over every rock, waiting for him to slither out.

"There's only one person who knows enough background on us to come straight at us like this." Their nemesis, the enemy of every law enforcement and intelligence operation in the world. The man who hid under the radar until the Alliance had dragged him into the open seven months ago. They'd stopped a major international sale he brokered among some of the worst motherfuckers around, and then destroyed the delivery system he hid in Pakistan to spread a new viral weapon of destruction.

Mike's mouth dropped open. "It can't be. No fucking way."

"He wants you to know how this works . . . for . . .

for next time." His uncle closed his eyes and his head dropped. The rest of the words muffled against his chest. "Because he will not stop. I am only the first."

Josiah needed to walk, to hit. Much more of watching this and he'd crawl right out of his skin. Claw his own eyes out. "I can't believe this."

Mike grabbed the remote and zoomed in on the picture. "If it is him, he's smart enough to stay far off-screen."

"Goddamn coward," Josiah screamed at the screen even though he knew only Mike could hear him.

The minute he had this guy, whoever he was and whatever he called himself, Josiah would use more than words to eliminate the threat. Some people looked at him and saw a proper British businessman. Little did they know what lurked under the surface. The rage. The ability to turn off his humanity and get the job done.

"The bomb is attached to me . . . to my . . ." His uncle squinted as he looked away from the camera. "What did you say?"

A second later horror flashed across his uncle's face. What was left of the color drained away, replaced by an icy paleness that had Josiah dreading the answer.

"Heartbeat." His uncle coughed out the word as he faced them again. "As it accelerates, it triggers the bomb."

Mike turned to Josiah. "Is that even possible?"

He wanted to deny the possibility. They worked for an undercover group that answered to few and were bound by almost no laws or internal government rules. They saw fucking awful things on a daily basis. Women used as pawns and literally ripped in half. Men thrown off buildings and burned alive. And those were the lucky ones. But standing there as a mix of adrenaline and frustration pumped through him, Josiah knew the sick truth.

"Look at the incision." His gaze wandered over his uncle's chest, then down to his arm. "The blood. Even if making a human bomb isn't possible, someone wants us to believe it is."

"If my heartbeat stays even, he has a . . ."

"A what?" Mike leaned in, as if he were having an actual conversation through the screen.

Josiah watched as his uncle stared right into the camera, unblinking and almost still, and opened his mouth. "Kill switch."

"Fuck me." Mike answered the phone and hung up again without talking. "MI5 and SCO19 are moving in now."

"Firearms Command, like British SWAT." The words rolled off Josiah's tongue without even thinking them through first. He'd gone into operations mode. Heard everything around him, saw the battle unfolding on the screens in front of him. Only this time he would not be able to react in time. There wouldn't be a single defensive maneuver or offensive strike he could launch before death took his uncle.

Mike blew out a long breath. "These armed squads can get in there and—"

"I will be the first but not the last," his uncle said in a monotone voice, clearly parroting the message he'd been ordered to communicate.

The camera moved back and panned around the room. Men in dark suits, sprawled in lifeless heaps on the floor as blood ran from their bodies and pooled on the carpet that had always been his uncle's favorite. Worse, he was giving up. Surrendering to the end and letting the terror go. Josiah heard it in his uncle's voice, saw it in the now-determined lines of his body.

The calmer his uncle became, the more unraveled Josiah felt. He ached to do something—anything— even if it meant tearing the giant screen from the wall and smashing it into pieces on the concrete Warehouse floor.

"You will all pay. You will all watch as . . ." Fear morphed into sadness in his uncle's eyes as he continued passing on the information he'd clearly been kidnapped to tell. "You will all lose someone you care about."

Mike grabbed his phone and started punching in numbers. The yelling came next. "Where are these supposedly impressive reinforcements?"

"You need to . . ." His uncle leaned in.

Sensing his uncle was breaking from the prepared script again, Josiah stepped closer to the screen, desperate to hear any piece of intel that might help. Eager to keep his uncle talking until the gunmen had a chance to storm in.

His uncle's gaze darted around the room as he inhaled. Then his words came out in a rush. "About forty and scarred with burns. He said his name is—"

A sharp bang rang out, making Josiah jump back. He started to rush forward again but his knees buckled and he had to grab the corner of the table to keep from falling as the room on the screen in front of him blew apart.

"No!" But Josiah knew he was too late.

A static buzz sounded in his ears. The talking, the pleading cut off, and the heirloom desk vanished in an explosion of smoke. The room shifted on him as his gaze traveled over the devastation. Everything inside him stopped—his heartbeat, his breathing—as he looked at the splatter of blood and flesh on the screen.

Being thousands of miles away didn't save him from the pure brutality of the moment. Someone he loved, broken down to nothing more than bone and skin. Not recognizable. Not even human anymore.

"Holy shit." Mike grabbed Josiah, locked his arms around him, and wrestled him back. "Do not look."

But he had to. It was all so unreal and impossible. His uncle had people and prestige. *This could not happen.* "Let me go."

Mike held on as he stepped in front of Josiah, blocking the direct line of sight. "You don't need to see any more of this."

Just as Josiah broke free, the screen went blank. Completely black. He could hear a crunching sound and decided his mind had shut down as some sort of defense mechanism.

He stood there and rocked back on his heels. Buried his face in his hands and silently cursed a world where shit like this happened. As if blowing up another person were normal. "Fuck. I can't believe . . . fuck."

"Now what the hell is this?"

Josiah heard the shock in Mike's voice and looked up. The black screen had turned a smoky gray as the video snapped to life again. The crunching sound grew louder and Josiah could make out legs through the haze. Hear the crackle and thud as each footstep landed on unidentifiable piles of debris on the floor.

The figure turned toward the camera but the lens never strayed higher than knee-level from the floor. Bodies were scattered and shards of what looked like wood stuck up here and there. Papers littered the area and a ball of something—something Josiah feared was once his uncle—lay right between two black wing-tipped dress shoes.

A voice broke into the horrible silence. "The name is Benton, but then I think you know that."

That word. One name. It's all they had to go on. All any law enforcement agency in the world had of the faceless, seemingly invisible international terrorist who didn't pick sides and delivered death and destruction in the form of weapons sold to the highest bidder. A pure psychopath. One sick fuck.

"He survived." Mike shook his head. "We lit him on fire with a rocket launcher months ago and he lived."

But that was just it. They *did* hit him. Josiah knew that now. Gone was the smooth, cultured tone he remembered from their one meeting. Now Benton sounded winded, his voice scratchy. Josiah hoped that meant they'd done some real damage to the guy while in Pakistan. Nothing compared to what Josiah intended to do to him, but something he hoped hurt like hell, burned with pain, every day since.

"Your uncle was a hard man to reach, Josiah." A harsh laugh followed the line. "But I did. I couldn't get him to admit he knew you. So proper. So dedicated to protocol and keeping your identity secure. It's a shame your actions killed him."

Mike swore under his breath. "This guy sure does like to hear himself talk."

"I started with Josiah but you'll all get a turn." The figure they assumed was Benton shifted as he used the toe of his shoe to push the body at his feet to the side like nothing more than garbage. "Some of you will not be able to hold on to your secrets." He made an annoying tsk-tsking sound. "And you should know once I kill those you care about most I'll start again and keep going until the head of everyone you know is splattered in pieces against a wall."

"Next time I'm putting the rocket launcher right up his ass before I fire," Mike said to the empty room.

"See you soon." Benton delivered the line, then the screen blinked out.

For a few seconds they didn't move. Didn't talk. Alarms blared inside the Warehouse and monitors not already on sparked to life all around the room. Josiah heard a thunk as the lock on the main doors disengaged. The sound of voices as team members flooded in.

"They won't catch him." The police could surround

the house and lock it down, and Benton would get out. Josiah didn't doubt that for a second.

"No, but we will," Mike said, making every word sound like a guarantee.

"Right." Josiah stared at the dark screen. "We're coming for you, asshole."

2

SUTTON DAHL blinked but she still didn't understand the words swimming on the page in front of her. She'd been watching this office, the one next to the empty one where she'd set up her impromptu surveillance and hid out most days for the last two weeks. Marking every entrance and exit next door. Tracking the few people who came close to the entrance, in addition to the only two who ever went inside. Even arranging to "accidentally" run into the businessman who supposedly occupied the space.

Ryan Bane was a supposed reclusive bigwig in the pharmaceutical industry. That might explain his rampant paranoia and the overly intricate security for a small three-room office with little more than a safe and a desk in it. Would if Ryan Bane actually existed as anything more than an elaborate but fake paper trail.

Sutton didn't know what the guy really did for a living, other than scam and con his way through a cycle of identities, but he did not run companies. Every reference to him online traced back to empty shell companies and false leads that looked real on the surface but fell apart after a few levels of serious digging.

Not amateur stuff either. No, to track Bane she had to pull favors from an FBI friend and another in cyber security. People who knew how to investigate these things and not to leave digital footprints. Bane's identity, while full in terms of records, traced back to a carefully laid trail. It took her a year to find the right string to pull. When she did, a small piece unraveled. A fake pharmaceutical company. This one, at this address.

In the end, Bane turned out to be exactly who she always assumed he was. A pathetic creep of a man. A rabid liar. The same man she'd been tracking for years. A killer who got away with an unspeakable crime, then seemingly disappeared from the Earth to be reborn as someone new.

But he'd never been off her radar. She'd been tracking him through the only photo that seemed to still exist that tied him back to the man he was before. A partial of his face. She found the evidence in her mother's safety deposit box—the one she'd opened under an assumed name years ago—along with a handwritten list, half burned and in a man's heavy scrawl, that read like how-to directions on establishing a new identity. According to her mother's notes, he'd had slick answers back then for all her questions. Thank goodness her mom stayed skeptical.

Every week Sutton ran the photo through every database she used in her regular work as a private investigator in Baltimore, Maryland. Some through the front door and some through the back with passwords she wasn't supposed to have. But no luck. But when her target popped up in Paris, she'd moved in.

Now she shifted the papers around on his desk. The ones from the file she took from his safe. That's what happened when you trusted the safe that came with the place instead of having a new one installed. Very easy to pick, especially since Sutton had one just like it in her place next door and had been practicing for a week, looking for a way to get in it.

Not a mistake she'd expect from someone like Bane, but then again, he didn't act like he believed someone had sniffed out his trail. Though he did remain careful. He didn't use any kind of cleaning service, which would have made breaking in easier. No, she'd had to depend on new tech tools that deciphered security codes in seconds and some old-fashioned lock-picking ones. The tiny camera she planted in the fancy heating grate in the hallway helped with the rest.

After all that work and all that planning, the file in front of her didn't make any sense. It didn't connect to anything. Just a cover sheet with a random list of names. Pages with photos and what looked like lines of gibberish to her. Possibly a code of some type. But this was the same file he'd protected and hid in the safe. The only thing in there other than money, both dollars and euros, and keys to something. That pointed to the information being important.

She read through the first few lines, committing

them to memory, but decided that wasn't enough. She slipped the small camera out of her jacket pocket and snapped a few photos. Got a few more on her phone, because duplication helped to avoid surprises.

She'd hoped for something bigger. Sure, the idea of a diary of a madman outlining his crimes sounded more Hollywood than realistic. Still, a note that hinted as to his actual residence or the scam he was working on now would have been nice. He'd lost every tail she tried to put on him to follow him to the place where he slept. But his driver, or assistant, or henchman—whatever the actual job description of the big bald dude who rarely left his side might be—could give lessons in getting lost in a crowd or in traffic.

At least this gave her somewhere to start, which meant it was time to leave. She pocketed the small flashlight she'd been holding in her mouth and moved around in the shadows. The outside streetlamps provided a little bit of a guide, but she mostly maneuvered based on memory. First to the safe to dump off the file. Then . . .

She heard talking. The low hum of a man's voice. Only one, so maybe on a cellphone. She couldn't make out the words or even the tone. It all sounded so faint. But Bane could not be here. He never returned this late. The man stuck to a schedule and a late-night visit to the office wasn't normally on it.

Anxiety built and bubbled in her stomach, but she pushed it down. She had to get out without being seen. The one entrance proved to be a problem. So did the

small area. Her gaze flicked to the window, then back
to the door again. No way could she step out on a tiny
ledge. Heights were not her thing.

Her heart raced and a flash of heat warmed her face.
It took several beats before she could breathe again.
Panic. She recognized the sensation crushing her. She'd
dealt with the debilitating emotion in her regular job.
Had learned to push it down and hide it. Work around
it and keep going. But that proved a lot easier when collecting adultery evidence for some client's divorce than
facing the possibility of getting caught breaking into a
killer's secret office.

Looking around, she took stock of her options.
Sparse furnishings, an open room to one side and a
bathroom to the other. That was about it. So no real
place to hide. The closet, but that struck her as risky.

Her heart thundered in her chest. She could feel it
thump in her ears. She inhaled, nice and deep, trying to
get her misfiring nerves back under control.

The voice grew louder and she heard the jingle of
keys. In two giant but quiet steps, she slipped into the
next room. It took a second for her eyes to adjust to the
darkness. When they did, her gaze shot to the couch,
then to the window. The other door likely led to a
closet. The fear of heights and fear of being shot drove
her to pick that imperfect option.

The alarm chirped and the sound of the front door
echoed through the near-empty place. She didn't
waste one more second. She opened the slim door and
made out a pile of clothes and a stack of boxes in the

closet. She slid in the small space between the edge of the cardboard and the wall and ducked under the hanging bar.

Curled into a pretzel, she waited. Inhaled to fit as she pulled her knife out of her pocket. She couldn't bring a gun into France without questions and problems, but she'd use the knife if she had to.

Her heartbeat ticked up until she half expected to see it pump through her shirt. She'd spent most of her career dodging drug dealers and angry husbands. Once had a dead rat delivered to her office. None of that came close to the tension racing through her now. She was so close to revealing Bane for the disgusting piece of garbage he was. Her life's work could not end like this. He could not win again.

The footsteps clicking against the parquet floor told her what she needed to know. The slight slide of one side meant Bane. Something had left him with burn scars and an almost imperceptible limp. She liked to think one of his victims got in a good shot. She just hoped the person lived to tell about it.

The steps grew closer. He was in the room with her now. Close enough that she would have sworn she heard him breathing. Energy flowed through her, fueling her to fight off the potential attack. She tightened her hand around the knife's handle and felt it dig into her palm even through the gloves she wore.

He walked around the room. She could hear the moves but not see them. Being basically blind made her stomach roll. She pushed through the waves of doubt and terror. Focused. Called up every awful memory. Mentally paged through those photos from the long-ago crime scene, steeling her nerves for what could come next.

A light flicked on. She could see the shine under the door, watched it reach to the very edge of her shoe, and fought the urge to shift away.

The scraping sound rattled around in her brain. She tried to place it. The heel of a boot, maybe? A thump.

She inhaled and held her breath. Blood pumped through her and she couldn't believe he didn't hear the whooshing sound. Then the footsteps started again, only this time they retreated. Grew softer. The light clicked off. After another few sliding steps, the sound of the front door opening rang back to her. The alarm chirped again, as if being reset.

The air rushed out of her lungs in relief. She bit back a cough and a gasp. Rested her forehead against the back of the closet door as she tried to restart her brain and move it out of fight-or-flight mode.

Careful not to make any noise, she opened the door, just a sliver, to see if what happened in the room matched how she'd built it in her brain. The dark room greeted her. No sign of Bane. A quick glance around told her everything looked the same. She didn't question the noises or Bane's odd visit. She slipped out, keeping her back to the wall as she moved across the room.

A tingling sensation crept up her spine and she stopped in the doorway to look back over the open area. The couch seemed closer. No longer set against the wall, it was almost as if it had moved a few feet. But she didn't have time to assess. The need to get out of there drove her.

She nearly bolted for the front door. Only a quick flash of common sense had her peeking out the peephole first. No one stood there. Even through the distorted lens she could see parts of the hallway on either side of the door.

She entered the code and winced at how loud the alarm sounded as it bounced off the walls of the still room. Itching to be out and away, she stepped into the hallway and heard the door automatically lock behind her. She made it all of eight steps, almost to the edge of her doorway next door, when Bane appeared at the end of the hall. He ducked out of the elevator alcove and faced her.

Her heart dropped. She actually felt it go into free-fall as a breath jammed up in her throat, refusing to come out.

They stood maybe thirty feet apart and she could feel his intense, dark-eyed gaze from that distance. Those eyes narrowed as he headed down the hall toward her. With each sliding step her anxiety rose. She fumbled with the knife in her pocket, ready to stab. Absolutely prepared to scream.

He stopped right in front of her. A looming presence even though they nearly matched in height. "I heard my alarm."

Her brain raced to find the right answer. "That was mine. I just stepped out of my office."

"What are you doing here this late?" The strain in his voice made the words sound scratchy.

She skipped over asking him the same thing and forced a smile. "A late night working."

"What is it you do again?" he asked as if they'd ever had a real conversation before.

Her mind jumped to the first thing that came to her in connection with Paris. "Fashion."

That qualified as the worst response ever. She wore all black, pants to jacket. On a Parisian woman the outfit might come off as stylish. Not her. Some days she forgot to comb her hair.

He must have questioned the answer because he watched her. She refused to break eye contact. No squirming. No fidgeting. She just stood there and stared at him, careful not to let her gaze linger too long on the puckered skin to the right of his mouth or red patches on his neck that disappeared under the collar of his shirt. He kept his right arm bent at an angle and close to his body.

She wasn't clear about the extent of that injury, but the fake news trail included a tragic story of the house fire and losing his wife. As if any sane woman would marry this guy. Those cold eyes spoke to the lack of human emotion underneath. She could only hope whatever happened to him hurt like hell.

He shifted his stance, seemingly taking up even more of the hallway. "Did you hear anyone else out here?"

So something tipped him off. That certainly didn't make her happy. "Just me."

Then she waited. Wanted to see his next move. He simply nodded and gestured for her to pass by him.

The idea of letting this guy get behind her set alarm bells ringing in her head. Still, standing there would be weird, and he was weird enough for both of them. And now wasn't the time for a confrontation. She needed to figure out his plans. Find evidence that would convince the police back home to look into him. All of that required measured surveillance designed not to spook him.

She eased around him, careful to maintain eye contact to the last second, then zipped past him. She could feel his gaze on her. The heat of his unprovoked anger. She glanced back over her shoulder as she walked. Met his gaze and flashed him a big smile.

He looked away without returning it and went back to his door. Ran his hand along the doorjamb. Let his fingers linger over the alarm code keys.

The whole thing freaked her out. It was as if he could sense she'd just been in there. Either that or her cameras weren't the only ones trained on his place. The one in the hallway. The other one in the upper corner of his window, just outside. Both set up to beat any detection protocol he might run.

He was a savvy criminal. But she was smarter.

Her hands didn't stop shaking until she got to the elevator. Even then she didn't let up on the death grip on her knife. The bell dinged and she stepped inside. Tension made her punch the lobby button over and over until the doors finally shut, locking her in there without him.

As the car started to move, the names from that file in his office floated back through her mind. She had photos but she didn't take those for granted. She repeated the information over and over, making sure it stayed with her. Several were unusual names. Some were not.

She remembered the look of the page and the heading at the top. Delta something. The file also had contained photos and what she thought might be street names even though they weren't written as addresses, and lines that didn't make sense. Words that didn't match up but were strung together in what looked like sentences.

She lived ten minutes away. A quick walk, then the search could begin. She'd poke around, test a few names. Then she'd run them with "Delta" and see what came up. Not the most exciting evening ever, but it worked for her.

She'd come to Paris to find the man who'd killed her mother. Now she had.

3

THREE DAYS later Josiah stood on the grounds of his uncle's vast estate. Nothing but miles of open land, lush trees, and immaculate landscaping painstakingly tended by a staff of gardeners. Little had changed except for his gruesome death, news of which had been splashed in the press, from television to tabloids, all centered on the fable about a random gas explosion.

A "horrific accident that took the life of one of Britain's finest men," or whatever wording the few government and intelligence officials in the know agreed to say. The innocuous and untrue version meant to prevent full-scale panic over an unnamed terrorist attack. To Josiah the false descriptions stood as an echo of his failure to save his uncle.

Josiah walked into the maze of hedges and stared up at the pale blue sky. This part of the country, seventy miles outside London, had been rocked by the unexpected death of his uncle. Josiah knew the truth. His team knew the truth. His father knew the truth and placed the blame for it all squarely on Josiah's shoulders.

A shuffle of footsteps fell behind him. He didn't have to reach for a weapon or duck to avoid an attack. He knew these visitors. They'd arranged to meet here, now.

"I'm very sorry for your loss, Josiah." Tasha Gregory, former MI6 and current head of the Alliance, delivered the comment as he turned around.

He nodded because that's all he could manage before his brain shut down. The revenge? Now that he was ready to undertake. "What do we know?"

He looked from Tasha to Ellery Kimball. Where Tasha stood tall and lean with her long blond hair and smoking body as a shield to hide her lethal, kill-on-demand nature, Ellery was a cute, petite redhead. The size fooled most people. Josiah had stood next to her at the gun range often enough to appreciate her dedication to the team and impressive kill shot. She chose not to work in the field but Josiah would have welcomed her—either woman—on Delta team.

But Ellery had other skills. Impressive skills. She was downright spooky when it came to her ability to find and track information. She watched over them all, provided necessary intel, and searched down every angle. If Tasha had Ellery out in the field now, that meant Ellery had found something.

He turned his attention to her. "Well?"

"It could be a coincidence but—"

"I doubt it." He didn't even know what *it* was and he knew it mattered.

Ellery slipped a folder out from underneath her arm.

"Two days ago I started getting alarms about hits on your names."

He had no idea what that meant. "Okay."

"Computer searches. Ordinary, with little attempt to hide the researching." Ellery looked from Tasha to Josiah. "Not just on one of us. Someone is searching the entire team, so it can't be a coincidence. Someone had to get all of our names," Ellery said.

Tasha sighed at him. "Searching our real names."

The import of that sank in and something inside his brain exploded. *"What?"*

The news didn't make sense. A long-time CIA agent who helped set up the Alliance—Jake Pearce—had turned on them and thrown in with Benton, choosing piles of blood money over honor and decency. The Alliance had paid Jake back, leaving his remains buried in a rock pile in Pakistan. Only Benton escaped that firefight with any knowledge of the true identities of the Alliance members.

That was the point. He *knew* who they were already. Jake made it clear he had passed on top-secret intel about the entire team. So, Benton wouldn't need to hunt them down through routine computer searches. He possessed their names and could act.

No one else should have that intel. There were firewalls and protections in place. Rotating IPs and signals bouncing all over the world. Josiah didn't understand most of it, but he'd understood the people who knew him before, in his former life, would be protected by his anonymity.

He'd signed up with the Alliance based on certain assurances. When the United States and the United Kingdom decided to pool resources and form the team, they pulled in people from the CIA, MI6, and the U.S. military, and a few from places, organizations, and operations he'd never even heard of. Pure black-ops, black-box, off-the-books shit.

Josiah had entered the Alliance through the back door. His cover had always been as the clean-cut son of the UK's ambassador to Italy. Someone who obtained his position in the diplomatic service likely as a result of his impressive family ties. That allowed him to disappear for long periods of time, and no one ever questioned where he'd gone. Most assumed he worked in an office out of the country somewhere, and well-placed correspondence now and then supported that theory.

But he'd never sat at a desk in his life. He worked undercover, honing his skills and his shot until Tasha tagged him for a spot not only in the Alliance, but running one of its two teams. He hadn't looked back since.

Ellery held that file in a death grip. "I have a program that looks for certain search strings. Random words that link to the histories of the Alliance members. Code names for CIA and MI6 operations. Military operations for some of you. Relative names. Your birth names. Street names. All of it."

He took it all back. She was far more than spooky and amazingly competent. She was brilliant. But still, she was one person. Even with all the resources available to her, she couldn't possibly cull through all of that information. "That must be a massive amount of data."

She smiled. "I review it all day, every day."

For once he was relieved to be wrong. "Damn."

"That's why she is the Alliance's most valuable resource." Tasha took a step back, peeking around the hedge. She gestured to someone.

Mike came around the corner. "Which makes me wonder why she's out in the open and not hidden away in a locked room somewhere."

Tasha's eyebrow lifted. "I can protect her."

Josiah didn't argue. The Alliance had been Tasha's idea. She claimed that she'd run into random CIA agents on her operations one too many times so that she had no choice but to find a joint solution to international problems. "No doubts here."

"I'm sure as hell not arguing." Mike whistled. "Man, what is up with your family?"

Josiah wasn't sure what Mike was referring to, the fake politeness, the icy reserve, or the obvious disdain for their son. A feeling Josiah had dealt with for years since his father didn't even attempt to hide it. "I'm sure families in . . . Nebraska? Was that where you're from?"

Mike shrugged. "I'm from one of those square states. The name doesn't matter."

A country boy with a military background and an ability to sneak up and shoot anything at any time without flinching. That's how Josiah saw Mike, that and as his right-hand man. American or no, Josiah trusted Mike to handle every situation and had never been disappointed. "Well, I'm sure there are difficult families in your square state as well."

"It's the rich people, passive-aggressive thing I'm talking about." Mike stared at Ellery, the only other American standing there at the moment, before looking back to Josiah. "No wonder you threw in with us and left this country."

"Excuse me?" Tasha's eyebrow lifted as she responded, drawing out the word in her unmistakably British accent.

"I'm just saying there are a lot of people acting all nice and fine to your face over here, speaking in that refined hoity-toity way while they secretly hope you fall out a window." Mike held up a hand to her in what looked like mock surrender. "No offense."

A smile edged the corner of Tasha's mouth. "You're not wrong."

While Josiah enjoyed the U.S./UK rivalry on the team, now was not the time. "The computer searches?"

"It's elementary stuff in that the person didn't do much to hide her identity. She employed the usual safeguards, but not anything that would get by someone who was looking for a breach." Ellery handed Josiah the file. "I was able to trace her right back to her Paris apartment."

Josiah flipped through the pages with Mike right at his shoulder, following along. The name jumped out at Josiah first. Didn't tweak any memories for him. "Sutton Dahl. What do we know about her?"

"American in her late twenties. She's supposed to

be there on vacation." Ellery ticked off the biographical information as if she had it all memorized, which, knowing her, she likely did.

Josiah knew her well enough to know there was more to hear. "But?"

"She's a private investigator from Maryland," Ellery explained. "This is her first time overseas. She's alone and not spending much on her credit cards. No dinners out. No extravagant expenses. No sightseeing that I can tell."

Tasha exhaled. "We wonder if she's on an assignment of some sort. One that points back to us."

"Pretty." Mike lifted one of the pages and glanced at the woman's photo. Then he frowned at Josiah's glare. "What? She is."

Mike wasn't exaggerating. The more Josiah looked, the more tempting it was to flip back to the photo on that first page. This Sutton had a bit of an all-American look to her. Big blue eyes and long wavy hair, not quite red and not quite blond. Probably a bit of both.

"She's connected to Benton somehow?" Young, smart, and pretty. Could be the perfect type for someone like Benton, though who knew, because Benton led a reclusive lifestyle. Never seen, generally unknown. Which meant Josiah had no idea what the guy's preferences were or who, if anyone, he'd want around him.

Tasha shook her head. "There's nothing in her file or movements over the years to suggest that. She appears hardworking and dedicated. Normal. There aren't any holes or red flags. The reports from law firms and companies who used her services are all glowing."

Of course Ellery and Tasha tracked that down. Probably pretended to be someone looking for a reference. "What type of investigative work does she do?"

The smile on Ellery's face said something good was coming. "Mostly divorce."

Mike said what Josiah was thinking. "What the fuck?"

"But she has our names, which suggests a tie to Benton or someone like Benton or someone working with him." Josiah couldn't come up with another explanation for this Sutton woman possessing top-secret information she shouldn't have. Maybe she stumbled over it as part of a case she was working on, but that seemed like a reach. The Alliance's information would not be on some cheating spouse's computer.

"She could be a true believer, the female version of Benton who gave up her old life and is in Paris on a job." Ellery shook her head. "I don't know yet."

Mike whistled. "That's a scary thought. Benton with more stamina and smarts? Damn."

"The question is where and how Ms. Dahl got the information she's searching." Tasha eased her way back toward the opening of the maze and glanced around before returning her attention to the group. "And what she hopes to find."

"I'll go find out." Silence followed Josiah's volunteering. The way they kept glancing at one another had him grinding his back teeth together. "Stop with the staring. I'm fine."

"Yeah, you sound it," Mike said in a voice loaded with sarcasm.

Josiah ignored the tone and turned back to his boss. "I'm guessing we're in lockdown protocol."

Tasha did not hesitate. "I put that in place five minutes after your uncle died."

"He was murdered. No need to pretty it up. He wasn't hit by a bus." No, he was blown apart. An image that would never leave Josiah's brain. The only way he could get through the day and keep moving was to block the memory and concentrate on revenge.

Tasha's mouth fell into a thin line. "I am aware of the circumstances."

Lockdown meant team members in safe houses and minimal staff back at the Warehouse. The team would be spread out nearby and searching for leads while waiting for the call to move in. Some might be guarding the members' loved ones along with whatever reinforcements Tasha had brought in, using whatever excuses she used. The woman could work miracles.

Josiah guessed that Tasha's live-in boyfriend, Ward Bennett, one of the day-to-day managers of the Alliance and a former CIA agent, hovered close. Mike worked on Delta team but Josiah knew the rest of his men were on the ground, providing support. He'd get the specifics later. Right now, Josiah wanted to move before Sutton Dahl got spooked or wise to her computer search mistake or whatever and bolted.

"I'm the most logical one to go. Benton took his shot at me and was successful, so he'll move on to someone else." And Josiah vowed to be waiting. No one else in the Alliance was going to have to attend a funeral. Not on Josiah's watch.

"You plan to break into this woman's house and question her?" Ellery asked.

"I will do whatever it takes to get answers." Josiah didn't go into detail because he didn't have to. They got it.

Ellery winced. "It's possible this woman's computer search and your uncle's death are unrelated."

No way did Josiah buy that. "I think we all know that's not true."

"Fine." Tasha let out a long, loud breath. "Go, take Mike, and no bloodshed."

She'd never said that last part before and Josiah didn't like it now. "No way I can promise that."

"That was an order, Josiah."

He wasn't joking. He wasn't trying to test the breadth of her command either. He stated a simple reality. "This operation is well off the books. This is personal. We are at war with this evil motherfucker Benton. That means I will do whatever it takes to shake the intel out of Sutton Dahl. Whatever she has, however I have to do it, I'll get it."

Tasha moved in closer as her voice dipped lower. "You can't kill her. Not unless we know more."

He sure as hell knew he could. If Sutton Dahl said the wrong thing or withheld information, if she knew about his uncle's death or was some sort of demented Benton cheerleader, he'd pull the trigger. No questions asked.

The list of reasons to hurt this person, woman or not, was not hard for him to mentally construct. "We'll see."

Ellery's eyes narrowed. "And if she's innocent?"

That was exactly Josiah's point. "If she's mixed up with Benton she is not innocent."

4

SUTTON TAPPED her fingernails against the side of her wineglass and stared at her laptop from across the room. Since her entire short-term rental consisted of an open area where the couch folded into a bed and the kitchen area led to a tiny bath, she could read every word without her glasses. Nothing extravagant. Exactly the type of place one would expect to be able to rent weekly for cash and no questions.

Day two of searching and she wasn't one inch closer to figuring out what the random words and names in that file meant. She'd run computer searches. Called in a favor and had a friend at the office do some poking around on a few federal databases Sutton couldn't access in France without raising suspicion.

She'd also checked the cameras she planted in Bane's office during her visit, looking for clues. He and his sidekick, the guy she knew only as Frederick—and she knew that only because she overheard Bane use the name one day while she peeked out her peephole— went in and out, but nothing unusual.

Curiosity ate at her. So did the fear she'd messed up

and left something in Bane's office. Maybe she triggered an alarm. More and more she worried he had cameras watching her while she moved around in there. But if that were true, he should have made a move and confronted her by now. She'd been in her fake office, and between her presence there and the cameras and motion sensors she had set up, she knew no one snuck in.

Maybe the file she found in the safe didn't mean anything. She'd hoped it would provide a lead that would let her catch Bane in the act of something. So far, no.

Her eyes, still itchy and sore from the contacts she wore all day and hated, failed and her vision blurred. She wanted to blame the red wine but the room's punishing heat caused the dryness. The fall breeze had chilled her as she walked from the Metro. The fourth floor apartment over the tea shop, with the heat register she couldn't control, warmed her right back up. The shorts and oversized long-sleeved tee helped to keep her from breaking into a sweat as she sat there. So did being in bare feet on her hardwood floor.

She blew out a long breath. "Okay, one more time."

Her mom had taught her that. Be smart but be relentless.

With the glass still in her hand, Sutton headed for the desk sitting in front of the one window in the small apartment. A few hours of researching and analyzing, then she'd try reading one of the twenty magazines stacked up on the floor next to her makeshift bed.

She had taken two steps when a weird scratching sound caught her attention. She squinted, moving in closer to the window. The bang behind her had her spinning around. The glass fell from her hand and crashed against the floor, peppering her bare legs and toes with tiny sharp pieces.

She didn't feel any of it. The sight of an armed man dressed in black, storming in with weapon ready, had her body locked in place. Air trapped in her lungs and fear clogged her throat as she fought to scream.

He came right for her. No hesitation. No conversation. Gun up, vest on, face covered.

She tried to pivot and uneven shards of glass bit into her feet. She ignored the pain as she dove for the lamp. She'd get one good whack in before—

"One move and you die," he said in a deep voice that carried a harsh whip of anger. "Talk or scream and you die."

She struggled to listen to the list of promised threats included in his order but the panicked rush of blood through her ears blocked out some of it. She got the gist—do not cause trouble or she'd bleed out.

"Okay, okay." She tried placating but her voice bobbled and the shaking in her muscles made it hard to stay still. "Please don't shoot."

Some men liked the victim act. She could play that as she shifted closer to her knife. Since the fear whipping around inside her was very real, the act would not be a reach.

With her hands up she lifted one foot, then the other, trying to brush the glass away. Fear flooded her and her breathing came out in pants, but she forced her heartbeat to slow. Getting sucked into the darkness now could mean her death.

The longer she stood there the more confident she felt. She was trained. Danger came with her job. If Bane had created this round, that only meant she was getting close to the truth.

All of her mother's warnings came rushing back. All those years working on the hostage recovery team had made Mom paranoid, or what Sutton thought of as paranoid until *right that moment*.

Sutton mentally sorted through the memories for the right self-defense strategy. *Fight, scream, and don't let them take you. Make a scene. Draw attention.* The tiny space hampered all those options. She needed to be able to run. To bolt and not look back. The mask—whatever covered this guy's face—suggested that talking her way out of this nightmare might not be an option.

The knife gave her the biggest chance. Unfortunately it sat in her pants pocket. The same pants hanging on the knob to the bathroom door. Not very convenient.

"You don't have to . . ." Her gaze shot past the guy in front of her to the second one standing at the apartment's entry. He shut and locked the door, trapping all three of them inside.

Her heartbeat took off again, wild and frantic. Adrenaline and terror mixed inside her and threatened to buckle her knees. These two—whoever they were—had the wrong place, the wrong person. Or maybe Bane sent them. That possibility kept floating through her head. It matched with that gnawing sensation at the back of her brain that she'd messed something up while digging around his office.

"Sutton Dahl." The man in front of her lowered the gun and slipped off his mask.

She wanted nothing more than to put it back on and insist she'd never seen his face. That she couldn't identify him. She looked down, so that she saw only a flash of reddish-brown hair. Then it struck her. He'd said her name. In a British accent with a slightly off pronunciation of her last name, but he said it.

For some reason that took some of the debilitating panic away. Her head popped back up. "How do you know who I am?"

"Sit on the bed." The smooth British accent contrasted with the fury simmering in those dark brown eyes.

She fell back on the victim act. Let it cover her while she tried to work all this out in her head. "I can't . . . I don't . . ."

"If you think I won't kill you because you're a woman, you are absolutely mistaken." He gestured toward the bed. "Now, move."

She regretted unfolding the couch. Regretted a lot of things in that moment, including her decision not to find a gun once she got to Paris. Amazing how holding a weapon evened out the battlefield.

She studied her attacker, the one closer to her. The scruff over his chin and around his mouth. The broad shoulders and muscled chest peeking out from under the black protective vest. He struck her as rough and harsh and filled with fury.

This guy could hurt her and looked ten seconds away from trying.

Well, if he was going to kill her, he'd have to look into her eyes as he did it. "Who are you?"

"Not important."

"Look, I don't have anything. The entire apartment is two hundred square feet." She held out a hand. "Search whatever you want."

Maybe he could decipher that damn list for her while he was at it. If he looked at it or touched it, she'd have her answer about whether they worked for Bane. If the guy went for her wallet, he'd be surprised by how little was in it, but at least then she'd know the game and could try to devise a strategy to disarm them.

"You've been busy." The second attacker took off his mask and rubbed a hand through his blondish-brown hair as he spoke. This one had the blue-eyed, All-American look with the accent to match.

Her gaze traveled between them. They loomed over her. There was nothing petite about her. She stood five-seven, not tall but not short either. Like most everything else about her she was average. Normal. Except for the part where she could shoot better than most men back in the PI office. A fact none of them liked to dwell on, so she talked about the skill a lot.

"Sutton." The British one barked out her name.

She winced at the sound. "What?"

He holstered his gun but kept a hand close to it. "You've been investigating."

The pieces came together in her head. Yeah, this definitely was about Bane and that stupid list. She'd never seen these two on her surveillance, because she would remember guys who looked like that walking into the office next to hers. But her investigation in Paris was limited to only one thing, and that brought them right back to Bane.

The Brit, clearly the one in charge, frowned at her. "Tell me about the information you've been searching."

Her fingers dug into the blankets on the bed she'd made up only an hour before. She twisted fistfuls of material in her palms as she tried to think about the right thing to say. "What information?"

The Brit shook his head. "That's not going to work."

She wasn't all that inclined to play a game of show-and-tell with only her doing the telling. "Who are you?"

"This is the last time I'm going to ask you, Sutton." The Brit's hand slipped to his weapon.

She watched those fingers, long and strong, curl around the handle. After the initial shock of the home invasion, her brain cells ran at full power now. "If you shoot me I can't answer your questions."

"I am not joking here, Sutton."

The familiarity. The way her name rolled off his tongue. Her nerves stretched to snapping. "I got that from the gun and commando outfits."

The American's mouth twitched but he kept frowning. "Who gave you the intel?"

"No one." The Brit took a step toward her and she held up her hands in surrender. "I'm doing some work on a file. That's all."

He nodded. "Be more specific."

"I think I was pretty clear."

"Try again."

The details didn't matter. Arguing semantics with guns waving nearby crossed over from scary to surreal. "Did Bane send you?"

"No." Curt and to the point like everything else the Brit said.

But that answer didn't really help her. "Then who—"

"Benton."

Not the answer she expected. She'd showed her hand and they talked nonsense. "What is that?"

She glanced at the American but something about the Brit had her attention slipping back to him. He was dangerous, possibly a little twisted, certainly ticked off. Not a great combination. Still, she had trouble looking away.

"Benton is the person who knows the information you were searching. One of the only people who know," he said with a bit less heat than before.

She'd clearly stepped in something she didn't understand. Leave it to Bane to pull some con that had military or pseudo military running to find him. Either that or these two had the wrong place, but she didn't really believe in coincidences. Clearly knew she'd been searching, but it sounded as if they wanted him, not her.

These two didn't seem ready to spill any information or listen to reason, so she told a version of what she knew. Maybe it would get them talking. The point was these two knew she had the file, so she feared that meant Bane knew as well. "The information came from a file I got during an investigation. That file belongs to Ryan Bane, the owner of Clayton Pharmaceuticals."

"Describe him."

Smooth British accent or not, the way he issued orders made her head pound. "Why do you—"

"Sutton." The Brit squatted down in front of her, bringing them face to face. "My patience has expired."

"I missed the part where you had patience," she said under her breath.

His eyebrow lifted as a deadly stillness fell over him. "Excuse me?"

The American reached into a pocket on his vest and pulled out a folded piece of paper. "Is this him?"

She leaned in and studied the artist's sketch. Not a photograph and not totally familiar. The facial features looked right but the scars were gone. That struck her as a pretty big descriptive thing to miss. "Sort of. Not really."

The Brit exhaled. "Which is it?"

"He has scars from a fire and . . ." The men looked at each other and the American nodded. An interesting reaction and one she tucked away to analyze later. If she had a *later.* "What did I say?"

"Benton," the American said as he walked over to her window. He hugged the side of the frame and shifted the curtain to look outside.

The comment didn't make any more sense coming from the American than it had from the Brit. "I still don't know what that means."

"You're working with an international terrorist." The Brit stood up straight again. Didn't back up or give her even an inch to breathe.

His stubbornness touched off hers until she skipped over most of his words. "I am not working with Bane." She tried to stand up and almost rammed into him before falling down hard against the mattress again. "The guy is human waste, which is probably why you're here. Either that or *you* work for him."

"He's a psychopathic fucker." The Brit delivered the assessment without so much as raising his voice. Stated it as a fact.

She totally agreed but decided to keep that information to herself. She still had no idea what was happening. But terrorist? That comment floated back to her now. The only conclusion she had reached was that these two did not seem all that inclined to hurt her. They cared about the information in that file and this Benton guy, who might be Bane, which circled her right back to not knowing what the hell was happening. A frustrating sensation she didn't love and rarely accepted in her work life.

She usually dug around and asked questions. Didn't let things drop or questions go unanswered. A voice inside her head screamed at her to hold off on that for now. Not tick these guys off.

Maybe she'd had too much wine.

"Why is it so hot in here?" The American rubbed a hand across the back of his neck. "Did you play with the heat to throw us off?"

The ridiculousness of the moment hit her and she almost laughed. "I don't even understand the question."

"Sutton." The Brit snapped his fingers in front of her face. "Focus."

Before she could think it through, she knocked his hand away. "Don't do that."

He glared at her. "I can go back to threatening you."

"It's hard to listen to anything you have to say with a gun right there on your hip."

"Fine." He took his hand off the gun. "Happy?"

He had to be kidding. "Would you be in my position?"

The tightness around his mouth eased. "Fair enough."

A new sensation hit her. Not fear. Not even frustration. With the fury gone from the Brit's face and the edge easing out of his tone, she saw something else. A quiet desperation. He might have a gun and think nothing of shoving his way inside her apartment, but the energy bouncing off him didn't shout killer. He talked tough but he needed her . . . for something. That gave her the edge. Let her take the time to watch him. To assess.

Two short beeps cut through the room. Then the Brit touched a finger to his ear.

In a night full of abnormal actions the move barely registered, but she did see it. She certainly heard the noise, like an alarm. "What was that?"

"Do not move." The Brit issued the order as he took a step closer to his buddy. "Well?"

The American kept staring out the window. "Company."

She was about to ask about that cryptic answer when the Brit pinned her with his gaze. "Where is this file now?"

"Why?"

He swore under his breath. "Let's try this. How exactly did you get it?"

The intensity in his voice started a violent shake racing through her. She wanted to move back on the bed, make a run for the door . . . something. The knife she spied in his hand kept her frozen to the spot. She had no idea where it even came from.

His stress touched off hers. She swallowed back the new ball of anxiety crawling up her throat. "From Bane."

The Brit's eyes narrowed. "He gave it to you."

"Not exactly." Not at all.

"Damn it." The Brit continued to swear, making up some inventive combinations.

For some reason seeing this guy veer out of control, even for a second, sent a whole new wave of fear crashing through her. "What is it?"

"You shouldn't have it, should you? You took it."

She wished he hadn't worked that out so quickly. "Technically."

"But he knows you grabbed it, and now he's coming for it."

"That's a leap." She feared the Brit got this right, too.

"Benton doesn't leave vital information lying around. I don't know if you're working for him or investigating him, or just stumbled over the file. But you got it and he knows, which makes you a target."

The comment pricked at her. If true, that meant all those worries that she'd messed up in that office proved right. "That's possible, except for the working for him part. I'd never do that."

"Right." The clipped tone came back. "And now you've led him to us."

In her mind, the exact opposite happened. Or some version that ended with gunfire at her door and her unarmed and unable to fight back as she'd been trained. "What are you talking about? I still don't know who you even are."

The Brit frowned at her. "Get up."

That suddenly seemed like the worst idea in the world. She leaned back, trying to shift her weight and make it harder for either of them to snatch her off the bed. "No."

"Sutton, you are expendable."

"Time's up." The American made a weird hand signal. "We need to move."

She had no idea what was going on but something had these two kicking into action. They went from questioning and walking around, while scanning every inch of her apartment, to mobilizing. She didn't even know for what.

Before she could ask a question, a dot of red light bounced along the wall and landed on the Brit's chest. "Move!"

"Get down," he shouted over hers as he grabbed her arm and pulled her with him to the floor.

Her body hit the hardwood and a thumping pain started in her hip. Her head would have bounced but the Brit put his hand in her hair, guarding her, as he rolled her under him. A scream trapped in her throat as her window exploded into tiny pieces and rained down around her. Glass covered the floor and the Brit. She could feel his muscles tense as he wrapped his arms around her and shielded her from the bulk of the blast.

When the world stopped spinning and her breathing jumpstarted, she looked around the room. Her lamp had crashed to the floor and the American sat crouched under the windowsill. The man above her didn't move. She clenched her fingers against his arms, digging her fingernails through a thin layer of material to hit flesh.

He lifted up and stared down at her. "Are you hurt?"

The way he frowned with those eyebrows all scrunched up almost had her brushing her fingers over his forehead to smooth the lines. Just before she touched him, she let her hand fall back to the floor. "Stunned."

"That's probably good since you're lying on a bed of glass."

She found his whisper oddly soothing. "It's all over you." She brushed a few of the bigger pieces off his shoulder.

The American cleared his throat. "I'm fine, by the way."

Sutton ignored the joking. Ignored the weight anchoring her to the floor and the way the Brit watched

her. He'd saved her from something. Now she wanted
to know what.

"Can you explain what just happened?" She'd seen
enough action movies to have an idea but she hoped she
read the scene wrong. Last thing she needed was some
random third party firing through her window.

"A warning."

"Right. Got it." The American touched his ear, then
nodded, as if he were holding a silent conversation with
someone she couldn't see. "We have a second wave
coming. We got the sniper who was sitting in the building across the street, but we have more storming up the
stairs."

"Of course." The British accent came back full force
as he turned to her. "You have a choice to make. Come
with me and live or stay here and become a statistic."

"I don't know you." But the heat and doubt had less-
ened. Not disappeared, but if someone was going to fire
a gun at her or her apartment, she wanted to fire back.
These two had weapons and she needed one. Right now
that meant the Brit looked like the best option.

He nodded and jumped to his feet. "I'll take that as
a yes."

The impressive response had her gaze traveling
up and down his body. The guy could move. But that
didn't mean she was ready to go anywhere with him.
"What's the plan?"

The Brit glanced at the window. The window not
attached to a balcony or fire escape.

Dread filled her. "You can't be serious. We're four
floors off the ground."

Just the thought of going out on a ledge had her heaving. She wasn't wearing her contacts and scanned the room but couldn't find her glasses. Then there was the issue of her very real fear of heights.

"Technically, we'll be five since we need to keep going up."

The man needed to work on his comforting skills. "That's your argument?"

The American swore under his breath. "Smooth, dude."

"We're going up to get out. My partner will handle this floor," the Brit said, ignoring the chaos in the room and inside her.

"I'll cover you." The American took out a second gun as he peeked out of the corner of the window and into the dark night.

They acted as if this plan made sense. She started to wonder if all that diving from bullets and hitting the ground shook something loose in their heads. Rattled one too many brain cells or something.

She glared at both of them. "Come up with a better plan."

"Ten seconds," the American said without looking at her.

"One thing." The Brit glanced at her feet. "I'd find shoes. Or a jumper."

As if she had any idea what that meant. "Jumper?"

"Brit speak for sweater." The American grinned as he added to the impromptu wardrobe discussion.

The Brit nodded. "And trousers."

Trousers? "Or you could leave me here."

"We'll take care of your injuries later."

She forgot about the glass and the cuts until right that second. Now she felt like one giant throbbing ache. "How about we do that now?"

He lifted her, putting her feet on top of his and off the debris scattered all over the floor. "See? There's no need to panic."

She had a big band of nerves zapping inside her. She'd rather face a gun than a certain fall to her death. "Too late."

He treated her to a wide smile. "The good news is I'm not going to let anyone else kill you tonight."

She knew better than to be lured in by the sudden show of chivalry and a sexy grin. "And the bad news?"

"I still might."

5

Good thing he brought the harness. The thin rope held Himalayan climbers. Today it would have to hold him. Him and her, the "her" Josiah still believed might be a plant working for Benton. Someone with full awareness of Benton's plans. And Josiah was about to hand over his only harness to her, swing out a window, and trust her not to cut the rope beneath him.

Since he had about fifteen seconds to make the life-or-death decision, he ignored the risks. Just like he always did. If she tried to throw him off, she'd be the one landing in the street. Simple as that. Survival was a bloodthirsty game and he'd teach her that the hard way, if needed.

He watched as she tugged an oversized sweatshirt over her shirt and grabbed a pair of sneakers. When she made a second run for the closet, he stopped her. "Enough."

"I need pants."

"Not if finding them means you're going to die in them." Before she could argue, he slipped the straps over her shoulders and tightened the harness around her waist before clipping it in place. In the next second he had the rope connected and his arm wrapped around her. He waited for the all-clear signal from Mike to step out on the thin ledge.

"This is—"

Josiah swung them outside before she could lodge the rest of her new complaint. For a supposed captive she sure did argue a lot. He'd watched her face as determination replaced terror. Hot, he had to admit. And looking at her face kept him from focusing on the rest of her. The photos in the file didn't come close to capturing her energy. Up close he could name the color of her hair—strawberry blond.

The cool chill of the night punched against him as he held on. He ignored the street noise below and the street lights highlighting the building's gothic façade. "Keep those arms around my waist and don't let go."

Instead of fighting him or answering, she nearly strangled him in a full-body clench. Her legs wrapped around his hips and she tucked her head under his chin. Not an inch of air separated their bodies. He was pretty sure she had her eyes closed and thought he heard her praying.

Not really one to offer up reassurances, he tried anyway. "You're fine."

"I am not fine."

The words vibrated against his neck as her hold tightened. He didn't even know that was possible. She'd clamped down on him with every muscle. Much more of this and they'd be stuck hanging there. "I need my arms."

"Fine."

But she didn't adjust her grip. Didn't seem to care that he basically held both of their body weights as they dangled sixty feet or so above the ground. "I'm going to climb up, hand over hand, so you need to—"

She glanced up before balancing her face against his chest again. "Not possible."

Her faith in his abilities didn't exactly fill him with pride. "Trust me."

"I already am."

That sounded better. "Sutton, I need you to calm down. Breathe."

"Right." She gulped in two large breaths. "Shouldn't we be moving?"

He should have stuck Mike with this assignment. Would have except there was something about Sutton that made him want to hang close. "We're waiting for the elevator."

Her head shot up again. This time she pinned him with an angry glare. "Don't talk to me like that. You come into my house waving a gun. People shoot at me. You grab me and climb up a wall."

Her anger switched his focus. While she concentrated on hating him—something she appeared to excel at—he started climbing. Pulled them up and out of potential danger in long draws as he used his feet to walk up the side of the building. Not the easiest task but he'd experienced much worse. At least this time he had a rope. He'd done this trick with bare hands and no safety more than once.

"Are you listening to me?" she asked.

He really wasn't. She'd been talking and he'd been scanning the area while listening for sounds of gunfire. He heard the sounds of a struggle and figured Mike was handling the second wave just fine.

"Almost there." Not really but he hoped it might placate her.

"What?" Her gaze dropped and she swallowed. "I'm not looking." She made a choking noise. "Why did I look?"

"We're not that high." There, he could be comforting, or whatever she called it.

"You've lost your mind."

Or not . . . "Any chance you could lower your voice?"

"I should be screaming for help and for my life."

He walked them up the side, in the shadows. Past a window and the older couple sitting side by side on the small couch reading newspapers. Josiah waited until they cleared hearing range to whisper. "I thought you were a PI."

She stiffened for a second. "So?"

"Shouldn't stuff like this be second nature to you?" He knew her skills didn't rival his, but she had some.

He'd seen her gun license and read through the recommendations about her work. People described her as tough and practical. Very focused. He guessed she wouldn't shut down due to panic. Hell, he'd watched back inside as she morphed from scared to sarcastic in a flash. Made him think he'd have to be careful about believing anything she said or did. Not that he wouldn't be anyway.

"I must have skipped the falling-to-your-death class

in training." The hold she used on him suggested this fear, at least, came from a very real place.

He tried soothing her even though he sensed this fell into the lost cause category. "But you know you're safer with me than in your flat."

"I never said that."

But he felt it. She'd relaxed into him. The soft curves of her body melted into his. He tried not to notice the lean legs or press of her chest against his. The scent of flowers that wound around her and the long soft hair. All irrelevant. Distractions only. He needed to bring her in, not feel her up. No matter how much she broke his concentration.

Whatever her fears and doubts, real or faked, she clung to him. And she didn't try to knock him off balance. She won points for that. If Benton had sent her, she held back, not quite ready to launch her attack just yet. But Josiah would keep his guard up.

His muscles burned by the time he reached the upper ledge of the roof. He hooked one arm around the lip as he checked for shooters hiding there. "Here we are."

She still hadn't looked down. "I think I'm going to be sick."

That would really make this day perfect. "I'd prefer if you didn't."

Not willing to listen to one more argument, he used the arm supporting her legs to push her up. With a hand on her ass, he held her in place while she wrestled to get her arms up on the ledge. One more gentle shove and she went over, falling to safety.

"There you go." He vaulted over after her, not giving her a chance to drop him over the side.

His feet hit the roof and his gaze went wondering. Instead of standing, Sutton lay on her side. There, on the dark roof with her pale legs curled to her chest, she didn't move.

He crouched down, half concerned and half ready for battle. "Sutton, everything really is going to be fine."

"I know you think that's comforting, but it's not." She sat up and pushed her long hair out of her face. "Not coming from the guy who just engaged in a gun battle in my apartment."

"I never fired my weapon." Seemed like an obvious point to him.

Danger knocked and they ran, a response that grated against his last nerve. If people shot at him, he shot back and aimed to kill or at least cause enough pain to end the fight with a win in his favor. Racing out of danger struck him as an invitation for more danger. But the order had come down from Tasha that Sutton was to be protected at all costs until she could be questioned.

Informal rendition. *Get her somewhere safe, then extract the information.* Neutral-sounding words for the acts he sometimes carried out to gain the needed intelligence. Looking at her now, with her arms wrapped around her raised knees and her face drained of any color, his previous rock-hard belief in her complicity in Benton's plans wavered.

She eyed him up. "You can be somewhat obtuse."

He'd been called worse. His own father barely spoke to him, and that was before his uncle's death. "Possibly."

"If you let me go, I'll say it was a random shooting and leave you and the American out of it."

"And then what?" he asked because he had no idea if she understood the danger she'd launched herself into by taking Benton's file.

"You and the American go on with your lives, and I go on with mine."

After everything—the shot, the climb—she couldn't still believe tomorrow morning would come and life would resume as normal. Josiah decided right then he'd never understand women. "Wait, who?"

"In my head you're the Brit. Your friend is the American." She looked around but no one else stood on the roof with them.

That was the plan. They separated and reinforcements moved in. Even now Mike would have battled attackers and be waiting somewhere for a signal to meet up again. The whapping sound of the helicopter blades should cut through the night at any moment. These things, whether they be regular plans or contingency plans or emergency plans, all had been practiced and rehearsed. The Alliance didn't like surprises but every member could handle a crisis.

He looked at his crisis-of-the-moment and made a judgment call. "Josiah."

Her forehead wrinkled as she frowned at him. "What?"

"You can call me Josiah." He reached down to help her up.

She pushed his hand away. "I don't want to know your name."

Only she would find an olive branch offensive. Once again he thought he'd said something to calm her down when all he really did was wind her up. The cycle kept repeating and he was ready to break the habit. "You're beyond difficult."

"Right back at ya."

But the backbone, the underlying sense that she'd try to take him out if she thought she could, didn't exactly turn him off. Something about the heightened survival instinct appealed to him almost as much as the body and that face. Big eyes, upturned nose . . . freckles.

"Listen to me." This time he didn't give her a choice. He slipped a hand under her elbow and lifted her to her feet before she froze solid to the ground. The woman was going to have pneumonia by morning at this rate. "We need to keep moving."

She peeked over the side of the building but quickly backed up into him again. "We are four floors off the ground."

He had no idea how she kept getting this simple point wrong. "Five, actually."

She sighed at him. Didn't even try to hide her frustration or seem to remember he was the one in charge. "Again with the counting. Do you want me to throw up?"

He refused to talk about that possibility. "A helicopter will pick us up and—"

"I'm not going anywhere else with you." She took a step away from him. Looked like she wanted to put two buildings between them. "Not in a car, not a helicopter. Not on a bike."

For a smart lady she seemed to be missing some obvious facts. "Someone just tried to kill you in your own apartment."

She frowned at that. "I thought they were trying to kill you."

"Probably both of us, which means you don't have a choice." That was an understatement. He had Delta team members stationed in the street and nearby. Josiah stayed connected to it all through the small communication device in his ear.

She crossed her arms in front of her, closing off. Probably trying to keep warm. "I will scream my head off."

"It won't stop me. Nothing is going to stop me from getting the man I want." She needed to understand that. They all did.

For the team this was about international security. The world needed Benton shredded and the pieces buried. With Benton's newest round of threats they all had something—someone—to lose. People they cared about who now lived under a cloud, just waiting for a bomb to be strapped to them. Josiah had already lost.

He'd stood just days ago and watched the one man who'd encouraged him to be more than his name be blown apart. For only the second time in his life, Josiah stood helpless, and this time he didn't have the excuse

of being young or untrained. He'd carved a career out
of being in control and eliminating threats. All a reaction to being a beat too late to help his mother. But it
had happened again.

This was personal. The Alliance wanted to take out
Benton to save the world from his wrath. Josiah needed
the guy dead to wipe out the twisted memory of his
uncle's face right at the end. Of the dragging loss that
Josiah tried push out of his head so he could keep func-
tioning. Of his most recent failure to protect someone
he loved.

"Tell me what's really going on."

Josiah answered the question she asked rather than
the one spinning in his head. "Bane, if he's your boss
or an assignment or whatever. He's not who you think
he is."

"The terrorist thing?" She shifted her weight from
foot to foot.

Even in the dark, from a short distance, he could see
the goose bumps on her legs. She had to be freezing.
He shouldn't care, but he did. "You sound skeptical but
I should be the one questioning you."

"How do you figure that?"

Laying out his doubts and all the evidence that
pointed to her being a coconspirator didn't make sense.
If she truly was innocent, none of it would make sense
to her. And if she wasn't innocent . . . he didn't want to
think about that possibility. But either way, one thing
remained true. "Right now, I'm your best chance at
living until morning."

She bounced up and down a little on the balls of her feet. Blew on her hands. Even tucked them under her armpits. "I've been protecting myself for a long time now and have never needed bodyguards and machine guns."

The last comment grabbed his attention away from all the moving and the way her hips swayed and those short shorts rode up her thighs. "This isn't a machine gun."

"Oh my God." She shot him a you've-got-to-be-kidding scowl as her hands dropped to her sides. "Is that the point?"

"Apparently not." She didn't like details or deal in facts. Fine, he got it, but she wasn't exactly the easiest woman to read. Her emotions seemed to bounce all over the place. "For the record, you were more docile downstairs."

"I was stunned."

He guessed she'd been acting and biding her time. A smart move, if so. "You're not now?"

"I also thought I might be able to go along with you and safely get out of whatever this is." She blew out a long, exaggerated breath. "But now . . ."

"What?"

"You're not going to let me go, are you?" Her shoulders fell as she asked.

Josiah didn't see a reason to lie, so he didn't. "No. Not until I know if you're a good actress or really innocent."

"I'm angry and want to throw you off this roof." But

she didn't let go of his hands. "That makes you smile? And you think Bane, or this Benton, is the psychopath."

This time Josiah backed away. "He's pure fucking evil."

"*He's* not the one who threatened me with a gun."

Being compared to that Benton asshole sent Josiah's temper flaring. The heat rose inside him and his usual firm grip on his control slipped. "Only a matter of time since you took his file. Honestly, that was a big mistake."

"No kidding." Her head tilted to the side and that long hair fell off her shoulder. "What do you want from me?"

"For now, cooperation." But that was just the start of the list. He needed answers. Lots of them.

"I can't go with you." She shook her head.

"You'd rather die?" He didn't bother to mention that the death could be by his hands. If she didn't work with them, they would have to assume she still worked for Benton. Josiah vowed no one associated with that guy was going to walk away.

"I have work to do and no guarantee that if I go off with you I'll come back. Remember the part where I don't know you?"

She had an active imagination, but she wasn't exactly wrong. The Alliance could store people in places they'd never be found again. That's the ending that faced her if she held out or backed Benton. "I don't know you either, so it's up to you."

"I'm not a victim."

"I never said you were." This time he held her hand,

not her wrist, when he touched her. He rubbed her cold
skin with his palms. "Look, Sutton. I do not want to
hurt you. If you are who you say you are and just stumbled over this file, if you cooperate and give us what we
need, we'll keep you safe."

"We?"

"I'm not alone."

She snorted. "Of course not."

"Mike and I are part of a group." Josiah stopped
there. Talking about the Alliance and the work tasked
to it couldn't happen. They worked underground. Most
of the people in MI6 and the CIA didn't know about
the Alliance's existence. Some of those who did re-
sented the Alliance's ability to operate outside of the
law. Josiah couldn't blame them. Not being bound by
the same structure and rules gave the Alliance a lot of
room to get a job done, which explained why they'd
been so successful.

Now it was Benton's turn.

"Mike is the American?" she asked.

The telltale sound of the helicopter blades moved on
to Josiah's radar. The helicopter came into view. Instead of coming in, it circled per protocol, scouting the
area first. "Yes." He pointed in the general direction of
the sound. "And our ride is here."

6

SUTTON MENTALLY ran through her options. Jumping off the roof was not one of them, unfortunately. That left following Josiah . . . for now. If she could find a way out or a way to break loose from him, she would. Until then she intended to stick close to the guy with the gun since other guys with guns continued to run around the building after them.

She shifted her weight, trying to warm up against the cold night wind. "Fine."

"What question are you answering?"

The sexy accent didn't make his sarcasm any less annoying. "I'll go with you."

"You didn't have a choice." Before she could shoot a response back at him, he took her hand and started walking. "This way."

The walking turned into a jog that they made while crouched low and picking up speed. Her ankle came down hard on a seam in the roof lining and she lost her footing. Her ankle overturned. With her balance shot, she started to fall. Numb and suffering from what she suspected was some sort of adrenaline afterburn, she couldn't adjust in time. Her body took flight. She would have hit the hard ground but his arms slipped around her. He tugged her up close with his chest pressed against hers.

He frowned down at her with a look that happened often enough in the short time they'd known each other that it bordered on a habit. "Are you okay?"

"Not even close." Breathless and strangely dizzy. She wanted to chalk the combination up to the terror of the night, but the way her heart took off on a frantic race had her thinking she'd just plain lost her mind.

He nodded. "Right."

"That's an interesting response." It didn't connect to anything she said, which seemed to be another habit of his.

He held her away from him and steadied her. The rip of Velcro cut through the night as he slipped his protective vest off. Then his black shirt, to reveal a second short-sleeved and very skintight version underneath. The impromptu striptease ended with him holding the vest and shirt out to her.

She looked down at the items in his hand. "What's happening here?"

"I don't have extra trousers." Tucking the vest under his arm, he held up the shirt. His fingers moved quickly as he tied it around her waist.

"Are you eighty? Say pants." But all she could think about was the surge of warmth moving through her. The material hung down. Thin and not nearly long enough to cover much, but the chill that had been wrapping around her eased.

His body heat still clung to the shirt. The way it fell

down, it blocked some of the cool air nipping at her. Her teeth stopped chattering and she didn't even know when they'd started.

"Put this on." He threaded her hands through the armholes of the vest as he talked.

She glanced up at him as he fastened the straps and secured her in it. "What about you?"

"I'll use you as a human shield." He winked at her, then took her hand and started moving again. "I'm mostly kidding."

His choices confused her. He'd accused her of things, some of which she didn't even understand. Now he morphed into protector mode and talked about giving her pants . . . She didn't get him at all.

They moved to the opposite end of the roof and stopped. The side of the building led to a sheer drop. A good six feet separated the building from the one next to it. It might as well have been twenty . . . or a thousand. Just looking down gave her vertigo. The world flipped upside down and her stomach turned with it.

"Now what?" She dreaded the answer.

"We need to get to that building." He pointed to the next roof.

Nope. "Have fun without me."

"Not an option." He slid a hand under her arm and pulled her closer to the mid-thigh wall keeping them from tumbling over and into the slim alley below. Even lifted a foot as if he intended to balance on the ledge.

The man had lost his mind. She shirked her way out

of his hold. "The helicopter can land over here. Next to us. Close enough but not so close that I get whacked with a helicopter blade."

"This one isn't stable enough." He pointed again, as if she didn't get it the first time. "That one is."

One roof looked like the next to her. Both black with random fans and boxes sticking up. A gravelly texture and low light. Of course he'd probably researched the specifics on structure weight and size and all that. She didn't care. No way could she jump across that divide. Her knees knocked together hard enough to trip her up just thinking about it. Some sort of Spider-Man impression was out of the question.

"I can't—"

"Down!" His eyes widened as he put a hand on her head and shoved her toward his feet.

She dropped as loud bangs rang out above her and Josiah stepped over her back to stand in front of her. Right between her and the gunfire. She lifted her head and spied the gun strapped to his thigh. Not the type to curl into a ball, she ducked and fired. Made her body as small as possible as she tried not to be a target and felt his body jerk against hers.

The noise cleared and a new sound filled her ears. A thwapping. And footsteps. With her hands on Josiah's calves, she peeked around and saw Mike racing across the roof toward them.

He jumped over a body lying facedown, stopping only to scoop up the gun by the still man's hand. "Looks like I missed one."

"Good thing I didn't," Josiah said before looking down at her. "You shot from between my legs."

"Not at you." That seemed like an important distinction for her to make.

He reached down and took the gun. "I think I'm impressed."

Mike laughed. "The phrase you're looking for is turned on."

She decided to ignore that until her brain started working at top speed again. Despite her job, hunting people and information, she actually didn't engage in gun battles every day. Maybe that's why her legs turned to soup.

Determined not to complain, she leaned against Josiah's legs then his body as she struggled to stand up again. He didn't seem to care or mind being used as a wall. Once she got to her feet, he wrapped an arm around her waist and pulled her in tight.

The gesture contrasted with the killing talk. They acted as if being shot at happened every day. Like it was normal. She wanted to crawl away and forget this night, but she rode it out. These guys could be liars, but someone kept shooting and didn't seem to care if she got caught in the crossfire. Josiah watched out for her. That counted for something.

He winked at her. "Nice moves."

She squeezed in tighter to his side. "Any chance we could come up with a Plan B, preferably one that involves something on the ground?"

"That's what this is. Our alternative . . ." He nodded toward the steep drop. "Time to jump."

The cheese and crackers she'd eaten for dinner curdled in her stomach. "Or we could take the emergency stairs and go back downstairs."

"Too many bodies to step over." After a quick glance at the canyon between the buildings, Mike concentrated on the door that emptied out onto the roof. "You go first."

One second she held on to Josiah in a death grip. The next he opened her fists and moved away, leaving her clutching nothing but air. Then he jumped. Stepped right onto the ledge and took off. Made it look easy, like one long step instead of a death-defying maneuver.

Forget curdling. Her stomach flipped over.

Hands landed heavy on her shoulders. "Your turn."

Oh sweet Lord. Now she had two of them making this ridiculous argument. "This is a terrible idea."

"Well, ma'am, we specialize in terrible ideas." Mike pulled her up next to him, then lifted her onto the ledge.

The tread of her sneaker slipped. "Wait . . . what?"

"Off you go." Mike shoved her, half threw her.

She squealed and closed her eyes. Didn't feel anything under her foot. Then an arm hooked around her waist and her eyes popped open again. Josiah hung half over the opening and snagged her out of mid-air.

"There." Josiah had the nerve to smile at her as he lifted her over the wall on his side and finally down to the relative safety of the roof. "Not so hard."

She had no idea what had just happened. "Remember how I said I was going to be sick?"

His mouth flattened into a thin line. "This still isn't a great time."

The guy really needed a class in *How to Keep the Kidnapped Woman Calm*. He failed miserably almost every time he opened his mouth. "It doesn't really work that way."

"Do you get motion sickness?"

For a mercenary or commando or whatever he was, his conversation topics sure did bounce around. "What are you talking about?"

"That." He pointed to lights moving through the air and coming straight at them.

"I don't—" The sound of the helicopter drowned out her words. The thwapping grew louder and the wind kicked up. The landing skids danced above the ground, then bounced before settling flat. Lights brightened the space around them and cast the area outside of a close-in circle deeper into shadows.

"Our ride is here." Mike shouted the comment as he walked past them, ducking under the blades and going to the pilot's door.

"This nightmare keeps getting worse," she mumbled to herself.

But Josiah heard. Of course he did. She knew by the smile.

He leaned in and talked right into her ear. "And it's hours until morning."

"Lucky me."

They flew without talking, sticking to protocol. Josiah stayed alert and kept watch while they got where they needed to go. In this case, a landing strip at Le Bourget Airport, about seven miles outside Paris.

Not the strangest or hardest extraction of his career, but wanting to hold on to his target was new. He tended not to hug rebel fighters or terrorists. He made an exception for Sutton. Also grabbed a blanket out of the storage area behind his seat and draped it over her legs. Then he added a glare for Mike to get him to stop smirking.

Josiah saw being decent as a way to lure her in, to get her to trust him. That would make it easier on all of them. Good strategy and nothing more.

They landed in a secluded area and waited there as the engine wound down. Harlan Ross, a man who had dedicated his life to public service, sat in the cockpit. After taking care of the helicopter, he took off his headphones and turned around to face Josiah and Sutton in the backseat.

Harlan now acted as coadministrator of day-to-day operations of the Alliance along with his American counterpart, Ward Bennett. But Josiah knew not to be fooled by the Oxford-educated proper accent. Harlan came to the Alliance from the Special Reconnaissance Regiment, a division of the British Army with roots in operations in Northern Ireland. He might sound smooth, but under all that propriety lurked a nasty temper and a crack shot.

He glanced at Mike in the seat next to him, then to Josiah. "I'm almost afraid to ask how the operation went."

"Another Brit," she mumbled under her breath.

Between the wide eyes and the way she kept rubbing her hands together Josiah was half surprised she wasn't screaming. "She didn't jump out the window, so that's something."

She held up a finger. "Yet."

"Ms. Dahl, we—"

Sutton didn't wait for Harlan to finish. "You all know who I am."

Being the type to lead with manners even if he held a knife in his hand, Harlan nodded. "Of course. What you do, who you are. Everything."

"Does it matter at all that I'm not in Paris to hunt down terrorists, or whatever it is you guys are doing?" She shifted in her seat to face Josiah but the seat belt didn't let her get very far.

He decided not to lie to her. "No."

"Very comforting." She broke eye contact on a sigh and stared out the open door beside her.

There was that word again. Josiah was growing to hate it. "You may need to accept that tact and charm are not in my skill set."

She rested her head against the seat back and rolled it to the side to stare at him again. "Yeah, well. Try harder."

When she lifted up and looked past him, he followed her gaze. A group of men stood around a truck a good two hundred feet away. They worked on a tire, taking turns staring at it. Josiah made a mental note to keep watch on them just in case. But his bigger task right now was to help Sutton understand her position before Mike or Harlan switched from talking to other tactics to collect the intel they needed.

He knew he should search for the right words and ease her in, but they didn't have time. The clock counting down the implosion of their private lives kept ticking. Benton would come at them and come strong. Josiah wanted the team to be ready. "As you now know, we have been tracking an international terrorist. This guy is under the radar to the point the public doesn't even know about him."

"But intelligence operations in every country do," Harlan added.

"He's violent. He kills without thinking. He collects weapons and sells them to the highest bidder. This is not a guy who's dedicated to a cause. He believes only in money and destruction."

Her gaze bounced back and forth between the men as they talked. "And you think Bane is this guy?" She shook her head. "I still can't see it. He's a weasel."

"Is that the only reason?" Mike asked.

"He's . . . forgettable. Average height, average everything, except for his scars. He's not some James Bond type. He's not ugly. Not handsome. Just . . . regular."

"For the record, Bond is a good guy," Harlan said.

"My point is that Bane blends in. It's why he's been so hard for me to track down."

"Exactly." The perfect type to move in, cause damage, then disappear. Josiah hated Benton with every cell but the guy had skills. He bided his time. Didn't spend money or do anything to draw attention.

She frowned at him. "No, not exactly."

Josiah tried again. "I know this guy, Sutton. He

doesn't go to fancy dinners. He has few close confidants, if any. He lies about who he is, moves around a lot, and nothing he says checks out if you dig deep enough under the surface."

The seat creaked as Mike took off the seat belt and turned even more to face Sutton. "He flies on private planes without registered flight plans. His residence address is a secret. We only know about the Paris office through you. We traced your online search to you, and you're now leading us to him."

"It's like you guys practiced this routine." She rubbed her forehead. "You all fill in a blank or two. It's kind of giving me a headache."

Josiah decided to ignore that comment. "We've been studying Benton for about a year."

"This guy is the scariest of threats." Josiah prettied the description up but wasn't sure why. "No conscience. He's not a believer in any cause. Not beholden to anyone other than his own whims."

Some motives made tracking easier. Josiah understood revenge and greed. He could use those to trip up any target. True believers proved harder, but Benton fell into a whole other category. The one with a big question mark on it. They didn't know why he did what he did or how it started. Hell, they didn't even know his real name.

"He sprang up out of nowhere and no one knows his real identity, but every intelligence operation in the world is trying to find some kernel of intel so they can look for him. We're the ones who actually found him and identified him. We've seen him and can identify him, and that puts us ahead of everyone else to catch him." Harlan held up a copy of the sketch they'd compiled after hunting Benton on a mission in Pakistan. "Until you, this was our only in-person description."

Back then he'd been hiding weapons and planning something awful with a chemical weapons dispersal system scientists on his payroll had created. His one mistake had been in teaming up with Jake Pearce, agent turned traitor.

"We know why we're tracking him. Why are you tracking the man you call Bane?" Josiah had a million questions for her but that seemed like the logical first step.

"This company Clayton is a front. There is no actual business behind it. Fake offices and invoices. Dummied up tax returns and bank accounts, but it's all for show," she said. "He's a killer. A very good con man, but still a con man."

For a second no one said anything as they waited for her to spill more details. Unless she'd perfected the art of lying and was a plant, they clearly all hunted the same guy. They tracked Benton, international fugitive. She followed Bane, someone she tagged for what amounted to everyday crimes that fell outside the Alliance's interests.

Gasoline fumes from the nearby garages lingered in the air. Every few minutes the roar of an engine would break the quiet as a new plane took off.

Mike finally made a strangled noise. "A killer. And what else should we know?"

She shrugged as her eye contact wandered. "It's personal."

No way could Josiah let her get away with that answer. "Not anymore."

With shaking hands she reached for the seat belt and fumbled with the strap. "Let me out of here."

That quick Josiah reached an arm across her chest and forced her back against the seat. "He has those scars because of us."

"We shot a rocket up his ass. He just happened to jump at the right time and not die." Mike hitched his thumb in Harlan's direction. "Well, he shot it. We helped."

Josiah realized he'd skipped over the introductions. He'd been too busy watching the surrounding area and preparing for her to bolt. "For clarity, Harlan is the pilot."

"Okay, but who is 'we' again?" she asked.

That was fair. In her position, he'd want to know the same thing. "Still not answering that question."

Her mouth dropped open as she stared at him. "But I'm supposed to answer yours?"

"We have the guns." Mike chuckled at his own observation. "That's how this works."

"The Bane I know is reclusive. He has to be because he's on the run. Not wanted, per se, but a criminal, and once I put the pieces together I'll be able to show that." She closed her eyes for a second, as if she were trying to call up some level of control. "There is nothing flashy about him. Nothing real either."

That fit with everything they knew and all they'd collected. Benton, whether he pretended to be Ryan Bane or someone else, knew how to play this game. Josiah might admire the restraint if Benton weren't such a dangerous asshole. "He's someone who plans to unleash holy hell on earth."

She sighed. "And it's your job to stop him?"

"We're the only ones who can," Mike said.

Her gaze went to him. "That's a bold statement."

Josiah needed her to understand the bigger picture. He couldn't sit there and go into detail about the inner workings of the Alliance. Didn't want to either. But he could make her understand the power they held. They'd brought down dictators and stopped terrorist attacks. They were Benton's worse nightmare.

"We have stopped him a few times." He decided that didn't sound strong enough. "Only us. No one else has even come close."

"Which is why we need to find him now." Harlan sounded every bit the reassuring father. He was older than the other team members on the ground. In his early forties, he let the younger men lead the attacks, but no one developed strategies as well as he did. "He's promised to do some pretty nasty things."

"Against you guys?" she asked.

Harlan made a face as he shot a quick glance in Josiah's direction. "I wouldn't—"

"Yes." The hell with secrecy when it came to that point. Benton aimed straight for them and they all had to be on guard. That included Sutton for however long she stayed. And if his initial concerns turned out to be true and this was the best acting job ever, she needed to know that her plan would not work.

She stopped rubbing her hands together and stared at him. "Who did he take from you?"

Josiah was not ready to go there. Didn't think he ever would be. He still hadn't recovered from watching his mother's car explode the decade before. He'd planned his entire adult life and career over stopping people like the ones who'd accomplished that. "Why do you think Benton got to me?"

Her gaze traveled over his face as her frown deepened. "I can see it in your eyes."

"Poetic," Mike said, sounding less sarcastic than usual.

But she didn't take her eyes off Josiah. "I recognize loss."

He broke eye contact first. Glanced away and back to that truck. Watched the men crowd inside and head for one of the garages lining the strip. For some reason facing her seemed like a mistake in that moment. She acted as if she could see right into him and it spooked him.

He was about to come up with some response when Harlan started talking. "Then help us prevent more loss."

"On one condition." All the fear and confusion had left her voice. Now it boomed through the small enclosed space.

The confidence had Josiah looking at her again. "Frankly, you're not in a position to make demands."

"That's the only way you're going to find out what I know."

No one could be that naïve. "Not to debate the point, but there are other ways."

"You mean torture?" She pulled back a bit, putting a little more room between them. "That's not funny."

"I wasn't really kidding." But he was ready to curse Harlan and Mike. They sat there, listening in, and in Mike's case, grinning like a fool. They didn't rush in or take over. They let him handle this, as if truth telling and veiled threats were his specialty areas.

She waved off the comment. "I'm going to ignore that and pretend you're the good guys."

"We're close enough." As close as anyone could get. No one in this business had clean hands, and Josiah didn't kid himself into thinking he did.

"If he is as dangerous as you say—"

Mike nodded. "Worse."

Her eyes narrowed as she watched Josiah. "Then your job, your number one job, is to keep me safe until I can find out what I need to know."

Good speech but Josiah knew she still didn't get it. "Benton or Bane, whatever you call him, will find you. Thanks to that file you found, I assume while snooping for this personal assignment of yours that you refuse to talk about, you are a loose end. So long as you're alive, he will need to dispose of you."

Mike scoffed. "That's a nice way of putting it."

Her gaze shot to him again. "Then I guess you better aim that rocket a little better this time and actually kill him."

Silence greeted her comment. Harlan was the first to break it. "You heard the woman."

That time Mike laughed. "I'm starting to like her."

Josiah didn't say anything because he wasn't quite sure what he wanted to say. She tended to jump around, leaving him to figure out how to catch up. He figured sooner or later she'd get to the point.

She didn't disappoint. She stared right at him. "I hope you are, too, because you're stuck with me for now."

The tension crashing into him stopped and the weird twisting inside him eased. Rather than risk saying the wrong thing, Josiah repeated her earlier comment back to her. "Lucky me."

7

BENTON PICKED Ronda, Spain, by accident. Ever since the incident in Pakistan, he craved warmth. He also needed an area one associated with tourists. Hiding in plain sight would defy expectations. Throw the Alliance off as they searched in vain. A place free from dictators but where powerful people, the right influence, and a measure of loyalty, if only temporary, could be bought.

After years in Morocco and too many months living first in a glorified shack, then a cave carved out of a mountainside in Pakistan, the villa with its open archways and cool breezes suited him. Sitting high on the steep hill that separated the old city from newer developments, Benton could feel the rich history of the region. Its medieval roots. The centuries of conquering and fighting. The days of invasions and executions. The blood of the land seeped into his bones.

A city perched on a scaling rock wall. A landscape that created a dramatic fortress. This was the perfect place to stage his siege.

Frederick Heinz cleared his throat before walking out onto the veranda. "They have Ms. Dahl."

Of course they did. Send fifty men after the Alliance
and they still somehow escaped with the woman. So
predictable. The mix of chivalry and rescuer instincts
eventually would lead to their downfall but for right
now they proved an annoyance.

Benton appreciated the training on an objective
level but the group had become a fucking nuisance.
Always showing up where they should not be. First
they grabbed the toxin and that brilliant scientist kid
before he could exploit either. Then the attack on his
supply chain in Pakistan and, worse, the killing of Jake
Pearce, a man Benton had come to depend on for veri-
fiable information. Retired CIA with serious intel and
connections Benton needed to expand his operations to
every corner of the world. Pearce had fed him information and warned of intelligence resources tracking his
movements. Helped Benton stay under the radar.

But the cancellation of the Dark Web auction for that
toxin had started it all. The loss cost him credibility.
One thing Benton depended on was his reputation. He
counted on being able to manipulate details and events
to his benefit. The Alliance popping up at the least welcome times threatened that, which was why his attention had switched to the group. He'd toy with them,
causing enough pain to wound them, then deliver the
killing blow.

And it looked like the final days of the Alliance
would start with one woman. Sutton.

"She clearly figured out something about the file.
That's the only explanation for the Alliance to come

running to find her." He'd seen her that night, sneaking into his office. She never registered until then. But she set off his motion sensor, and then the hidden cameras clicked on. He watched the whole thing unfold on video through his phone.

She'd gotten into his safe and found the file. At first he thought she might be a new Alliance agent, one sent in to search his known property, but he couldn't figure out how they'd found him. He'd covered his tracks so well.

A little investigation into Sutton Dahl gave him the answer. She was a loose end he should have tied up years ago. But, really, who knew the daughter of a throwaway cop would grow up to cause so much trouble.

Benton had debated wiping her out of existence while standing with her in the hallway that night. He'd grown to appreciate his choice not to act. Leaving her alive ended up bringing the Alliance to his doorstep sooner than intended, but he could make allowances. Make it work for him.

Having witnessed the Alliance team's never-ending and quite annoying need to play hero, Benton knew he could use Ms. Dahl. She'd unknowingly act as bait, then die with the rest of them. But not yet.

"We could have shot the helicopter and taken out at least three of the team plus the woman." Frederick stood at attention in the doorway as he always did. Trained by the Bundesnachrichtendienst, or BND, Germany's intelligence service, he possessed the obedience-to-command gene. One of the many characteristics Benton liked about his right-hand man. That and his background, which had proved invaluable.

When Frederick's enthusiasm on the job for catching human traffickers had morphed into what his file described as an "unnatural excitement" for eliminating them, his superiors moved him to a less visible spot. Working behind the scenes fueled his rage and boredom. He developed underground contacts and caught the attention of black-ops types, which was where Benton found him two years ago. Pulled him out of a backroom job that didn't suit his talents and dropped him in the middle of the action. To the extent Benton trusted anyone, and he didn't, Frederick came closest.

But that didn't mean he filled Frederick in on every step of an operation. "Too soon."

Frederick folded his hands in front of him. "I understand, but while your focus is on the Alliance, our contacts are getting nervous."

Dangerous men in search of very dangerous toys. "They should concentrate on being grateful for what I have supplied to them already."

"People are looking to you to—"

"What?" Benton snapped back.

Frederick visibly swallowed. "The chemical weapons. You promised an undetectable dispersal system that would work in large metropolitan areas."

Benton tried to tighten his hand into a fist but the burn scars tugged against his flesh and forced him to loosen his grip. "I am aware."

"The rebel group in Yemen wants to test it. The

central government is destabilized and the U.S. has withdrawn its embassy personnel. That leaves U.S. special forces still on the ground, and the rebels want to launch an attack in a very visible way." Frederick handed over a piece of paper. "Send a significant message to the U.S."

Benton crumpled the paper in his good hand without reading it. Coded demands didn't rile him. He didn't care what anyone in Yemen wanted. What anyone anywhere wanted. He didn't take sides in conflicts and political bartering. He'd willingly furnish weapons of mass destruction to both sides of a war, if there was money in it. His end goal had not changed one bit since he started: destroy and profit.

"Waiting to supply the weapons will drive up the price." Benton spelled out a rudimentary explanation of market theory, or his version. "Scarce resources lead to higher demand. That's how my business works."

"These people are not particularly concerned with financial theory." Frederick's accent had him emphasizing each word in a staccato burst.

"They should not be concerned with anything." They could either wait and be satisfied with his placating gift of surface-to-air missiles, or he could unleash the toxin on them first as a test case. Seemed simple enough to him.

"The whispers I'm hearing have to do with your attention being split," Frederick said.

Benton's nerves reached the snapping point. No one questioned him. Not anymore. He'd tried to play fair, follow the rules. That life brought a bloodbath to his door. Now he fought without emotion and eliminated all dissent.

He eyed his assistant. The man who possessed a bulky muscular build and was an expert shot. That did not make him invincible. He needed to remember his place in the organization . . . at the bottom. "Is that your theory, Frederick?"

"No, sir."

"Then what do you say to those accusations?"

"I support you." Frederick nodded. "Always."

Benton guessed Frederick's comments came more from not knowing the full plan than an actual failure of loyalty, but the question in his eyes made Benton want to pluck them right out. "I would hate to hear a different answer from one of our so-called contacts."

"Of course."

"This side business is a service to every group that comes crawling to us, asking for assistance. Destroying the Alliance assures the ongoing survival of rebel troops and freedom fighters everywhere." Benton learned that while lying in that medical tent, having the burnt flesh stripped off him. As he'd regained his voice he strengthened his resolve. Every Alliance member would die. "Remind our whining clients of that."

For the first time, Frederick moved. He shifted his weight. Even looked down for a second. "They want proof."

The words sent a flash of white-hot anger spiking through Benton. He struggled to maintain his tone because the fire had made it impossible for him to yell without straining his throat. Just one more reason Harlan, Josiah, and Mike would feel the most pain. They had fired the rocket that caused this. Now they'd feel the fire.

"These are dangerous people," Frederick said.

"So am I." Benton walked past Frederick and back into the villa's great room. Sofas sat clustered around a fireplace on one end. He headed for the bar at the other end. "Where is Josiah now?"

Frederick poured Benton his usual drink, whiskey neat, and handed him the crystal glass. "Outside of Paris. We lost contact."

Benton tightened his grip on the cool glass. "How?"

"We tracked them to the airport, then they evaded. They're experts at that sort of thing."

The simple comment almost cost Frederick his life. Benton had a gun on him at all times. He never did anything without protection and had honed his skills until he could shoot better than most highly trained military personnel. And he didn't show any weakness. Unlike most of the Alliance members, he killed without regret.

The fact Frederick did not seem to comprehend the reason for involving Sutton in this operation without it being spoon-fed to him proved to be a significant disappointment. She led him to them. But Benton reined in his fury, funneling it instead into his hatred for the Alliance. They thought they'd won this round, but he had an alternative strategy. He always did. "I thought I was paying for expertise."

"That's how good the Alliance team is."

The words sliced into Benton. The last thing he needed was for his man to become their cheerleader. "It's time to draw them out with a new personal target." He tipped the glass back and downed the shot before slamming it on the bar with a loud clank. "Who is closest?"

Frederick's gaze went from the bar to Benton's face. "The boy."

Perfect. "Grab him."

Sutton liked to think of herself as smart and resourceful, but she had no idea where they were. They'd traded a helicopter for a car and now had arrived in what looked like a field. She'd been blindfolded with her arms tied behind her and her body tucked down on the floor of the backseat. She'd thought about complaining until she realized Josiah likely would shove her in the trunk in retribution.

Then the circling started. They winded their way around. Turned and swerved, sending her body flying from one side of the small space to the other. She felt every turn. When the car finally stopped she almost crashed through the window and kissed the ground.

Her nerves screamed for her to do just that as a strong hand lifted her up and helped her out. Her legs shook but held her. She could hear the wind whistle through trees and the steady thump of what sounded like a door banging open and closed in the distance.

Fingers brushed against her skin, then the blindfold

was gone. She opened her eyes and stared into a palm. Panic rose up from her stomach but quickly subsided when she realized Josiah was shielding her eyes, giving her time to adjust before he dropped it again.

The sun had come up and morning had arrived. She glanced around, taking in the rolling hills and bright green lawns. They stood on a driveway consisting of what looked like beige sand and pebbles. She caught the scent of something, dried herbs maybe, and saw a small shed with a door that inched open and banged shut every time the wind caught it.

Josiah swept his hand over the landscape. "Here we are."

She followed the arc of his arm. Took in the grove of trees and the fence outlining the property. What looked like a farmhouse made of stone. "Where exactly?"

"We'll discuss that later."

She would have bet all her money, which admittedly was not much, that he'd say that. "You really need to find a new response."

He put a hand under her elbow and steered her toward the house. "Noted."

Mike met them at the door. He stood in the opening with a big smile and an even bigger gun strapped to his side. Without a word, he stood back and let his body language signal for them to come inside.

She didn't see Harlan or anyone else. Just these two and her. A creak had her spinning around. Mike closed the big wooden front door, trapping them inside, but not before scanning the distance. Then he turned

around to face her. They both did. Seemed to be a staring problem with this team . . . or whatever they were.
She couldn't really keep track of all the ways they
didn't say who they really were.

The verbal sparring, the running, the lack of sleep.
It all combined to give her a pounding headache. She
didn't have the energy or the will to go another round
with Josiah.

"What happens now?" She hoped the response
would include the words "shower" and "food."

Mike let out a hmpf sound, then took off for the
doorway to her left. "I'll be in the kitchen, checking
on the status."

Status of what? "That sounds ominous."

When no one answered she let her eyes wander over
the sparsely decorated room. She stood in a room with
a big stone fireplace and overstuffed chairs sitting in
front of it. Two doors on the opposite side of the living
area led somewhere. She guessed bedrooms. The
place was small and cozy but bright from the sunshine
streaming through the windows.

Josiah stepped in front of her. "You need to answer
questions."

"I don't know anything about the man you call
Benton, unless he really is Bane, which I still doubt."
The last of her energy reserves gave out. Every muscle
turned to liquid and all she wanted was to curl up in
one of those chairs and drift off to sleep. Not a smart
choice for a captive, but she didn't sense Josiah wanted
to harm her.

He talked tough and could frown a person into submission, but if they wanted her dead they would have
shot her and left her behind in the apartment. Or that's
what she kept telling herself.

"That's not the right way to play this, Sutton." He
shifted his weight until he seemed to grow and take up
more space. Those shoulders looked broader. And with
his hands on his hips he blocked her view of most of
the room.

"It's the only answer I have." Unlucky for him, she
was done being intimidated.

Yes, he could shoot her, strangle her, do a whole list
of horrible things to her. She got that. She'd also begun
to suspect that this team, or whatever it was, didn't con-
sist of mercenaries or trained killers. They were fighting a battle; she just thought they were fighting with the
wrong information.

"I hope, for your sake, that's not true." His gaze shot
past her. "That was a quick check-in."

Mike didn't hide his entrance. There was nothing
stealthy about the way his boots clunked against the
hardwood floor as he walked. "We have a problem."

Josiah glanced at her. Apparently he thought she
could read his mind because she didn't know what the
look meant. Since he didn't let her out of his sight, she
doubted he wanted her outside, roaming the property.

"Yes?" she asked, knowing they wouldn't answer.

"You need to . . ." He looked around.

Mike shook his head. "There's no easy solution, is
there?"

They had to be kidding. "If you go outside to talk or into another room I'll try to listen." She tapped a finger to her forehead. "A PI, remember? So you may as well say it in front of me."

Mike angled his body so his shoulder moved in front of her and he talked directly to Josiah. "Benton is making a move."

Josiah touched his ear, then shook his head. He slipped a small silver disc out of his front pocket and held it. "How do we know?"

"Ellery intercepted chatter." Mike's voice dropped even lower. "The target is Iselwood."

"Motherfucker." Even with the accent, the anger in Josiah's voice was unmistakable. His hand tightened into a ball.

She watched him pace. Long strides as he rubbed his hands together. For some reason his agitation touched off hers. "I don't understand. Are those people or things?"

Josiah stopped and his head shot up. "Iselwood is a private school."

He glared at her and she knew they'd circled back and he come down firmly in the she-can't-be-trusted camp. Again. Rather than risk saying the wrong thing, she tried to stay neutral. Even as waves of anxiety crashed through her. "Okay."

"We have to go," Mike said.

"Right." Josiah shoved that disc into his ear then pulled something out of his pocket and held it in his hand. "We'll tie Sutton to—"

"Nothing." Now she saw the strips. Zip ties. "Absolutely not."

She backed up. She'd back the whole way up to Baltimore if she had to. There was no way she'd agree to be tied up here while they ran off to do whatever had them both talking in clipped tones. These two liked to shoot. They attracted danger. With her luck something would happen to them and she'd die out here alone.

And the idea of being separated from Josiah, after all those hours of wanting to be rid of him, hit her like a kick to the gut. She'd told him he was stuck with her and she wasn't kidding.

"I can break a zip tie." She could if they tied her a certain way. She'd actually practiced getting out of the bindings. She pretended she needed the skill for work, but she'd really just been curious.

"You can't come along," Mike said.

But even he didn't sound sure of the logistics of leaving her alone. Sutton saw the opening and dove for it. If Benton really was Bane and they were going hunting, so was she. No way would she be left behind. "That's your only option here. I have skills. I can use a gun."

Josiah shook his head. "No."

"I can help, and leaving me here could be a problem for you." She looked from one unreasonable man to the other. "This is an easy choice. You're saying we want the same guy. Good. Let's go stop him."

Josiah touched her arm. Didn't grab or manhandle. Just a gentle hold. "This is a potential kidnapping."

She tried to keep the frustration out of her voice.

"Then I'll have something in common with the person being attacked since I'm still in the middle of my kidnapping."

"Benton is launching an attack on an innocent." Josiah's hand dropped to his side. "You haven't been hurt. Benton won't show that sort of restraint."

"And you keep saying I'm a loose end for this guy, so why risk leaving me here without you."

He frowned at her. "No one knows where you are."

"I could escape." She actually had no intention of doing that. Not until she saw this through.

These guys had power and resources. If she found the right evidence against Bane, they might be the ones to take him down. She didn't care who got credit so long as someone took Bane out, regardless of whatever name he was using these days.

"Not from how I intend to tie you up." The zip ties dangled from Josiah's fingers.

He had an answer for everything. On the rank of annoying character traits, that one suddenly zoomed to the top of her list. "What if I am working with Benton? Are you just going to leave me here without a guard?"

Both men froze. They glanced at each other. She was pretty sure Mike reached for his gun. She was about to call them off with a "just kidding" when Josiah's eyes narrowed.

"You are playing a dangerous game." Anger vibrated in Josiah's voice. He took a step toward her.

Mike held up a hand. "We don't have time for a debate. We're talking about a kid."

The comment sunk in, making her chest ache. "Who?"

Mike's eyebrow lifted. "Does that matter?"

"No." It didn't. The idea of a kid being yanked into the middle of danger made her even more clear about what needed to happen. She looked at Josiah. "Is this your child?"

"No."

Relief knocked her breathless. The tension bouncing around the mood wasn't about a father's worries. But the child belonged to someone they knew. She could feel it. Some parent was about to be thrown into a nightmare.

"Boy or girl?" Neither of them answered her, but she didn't let that stop her. "Fine, pretend a boy. Do you even know him?"

Mike shook his head. "Never met him."

They could not be this clueless. "Then it's settled."

Josiah watched her with an unreadable gaze. Mike didn't stay silent. "Sounds like you skipped a step in your argument."

"According to you I'm not safe alone anyway, and maybe even can't be trusted. Honestly, you are all over the place on who and what you think I am." She focused all of her attention on Josiah. The way he carried himself, the confidence. He was in charge. He had the final say, which meant she needed him to agree. "But I can help here. I don't know how old this child is, but he might be more willing to come to me, a woman, than some male carrying a gun."

Instead of launching into another lecture about how she couldn't be trusted, Josiah waited. After a few beats of quiet, he started talking. "A life is at stake. More than one since this is a school."

The thought of kids and gunfire made her want to heave. So many innocents and so much danger. She had to concentrate to keep from breaking down in a flurry of panic.

"Your file says you can shoot," Mike said.

Josiah immediately turned on him. "What the hell?"

Time to educate him that he wasn't the only proficient one in the room. "I'm the daughter of a badass policewoman. A single mother who raised her daughter not to be a victim. Add in my hours on the gun range, gun license, and job, and I'd think you'd have some level of comfort with me being able to hit a grown man."

"Have you ever shot a person before?" Josiah asked in a flat tone.

Not the question she expected, but a fair one. Unfortunately she had an answer that might bring Josiah some relief. "Yes."

She waited for him to argue.

He tucked the zip ties back into his pocket. "Welcome to the rescue team."

8

THEY'D SPENT all day practicing how they'd move in until Sutton practically begged for mercy. Even made her prove her shooting abilities, which she passed without trouble. Josiah had to admit there was nothing amateur about her skills on that level. Now they waited a safe distance away through the trees, just out of surveillance range, for the "go" signal.

They depended on Ellery to work her magic from miles away. Josiah and Mike were hooked into her and other members of the Alliance team who were listening in through a communication system. The small discs in their ears allowed them to hear and talk, though Josiah knew there would be little time for chatter.

Tasha could direct them around inside as Ellery handled the safety protocols. But even Ellery's powers were limited when it came to Iselwood, the private boarding school consisting of rolling hills, centuries-old stone buildings, and armed guards. Which made this, like almost every other Alliance operation, a potential death mission.

Josiah watched Sutton stand at the front of the car

and slip on her protective vest. She wore black pants and a black shirt, courtesy of the clothing stored at the farmhouse. The place wasn't one of the Alliance's usual safe houses. They'd dumped all those locations to eliminate any risk that Benton had discovered them. Tasha secured the farmhouse, bought it . . . who the hell knew. She somehow worked her magic and had it stocked and waiting when they got off the helicopter.

"This is for you." He opened his hand to reveal a silver disc.

Sutton poked at it as she frowned. "An earpiece?"

"The comm."

She turned her frown on him. "Is that a British thing?"

He slipped it into her ear, careful not to pinch her. Didn't rush the process. Not after she put her hand over his to guide him. "We communicate through these."

"You and this team you keep talking about but I never see, except for Mike and the one appearance of Harlan."

The comment set off a warning bell in his head, but he ignored it. "You'll be able to hear what Mike and I say, and whatever else we want you to hear."

"But not everything, right?"

Ellery could manage the comm in that way, blocking access and opening up lines. Josiah depended on her to maintain that control. "Right."

Sutton said the right things and her file looked clean. Her story about chasing another guy who just happened to be the same guy every intelligence organization in the world sought had a ring of truth to it. But the just-happened-to part kept him skeptical and questioning. He had no plans to let down his guard until he had the opportunity to walk her through every single question he needed answered. Even then . . .

Sutton sighed at him. "Please say you'll tell me before someone sneaks up and puts a gun to my head."

"Probably."

She rolled her eyes. "You're hysterical."

"I like to think so." He tapped on the disc in her ear. "Ellery is going to walk you through a sound check and fill you in on some directional cues you need."

She made a face. "I didn't even understand that sentence."

"You're going to be fine."

"So you keep saying."

He walked away then because that look on her face, the mix of reluctant trust and worry, tore at him. He shouldn't care what was happening in her head. Shouldn't be thinking about how he was going to protect her and make this mission work with limited resources. Shouldn't be looking. Period.

After a quick check to make sure the disc had Sutton occupied, he joined Mike at the stash of weapons and electronics equipment hidden in a compartment in the trunk. Talking to Mike would help . . . or piss Josiah off. One of those.

Josiah slipped a knife out of the case and slid it into the guard hooked to his belt and within reaching range under his vest. "You realize this could be the trap, right?"

"Benton can't get into the school, so he has us walk

her in so she can snatch the kid and wipe us out." Mike wiggled his eyebrows as he whispered, "Yeah, I've thought about that."

That scenario had run through Josiah's head, too. Benton would not think twice about using her as a decoy. Josiah couldn't figure out why she'd agree to that, but people often did shit that made him wonder about humanity.

"But you believe we should bring her." Josiah still debated handcuffing her to the metal ring in the backseat and knocking her out.

"Her as a Benton minion doesn't feel right to me. I mean, she has a gun, so shoot us now. Or she could have radioed to bring Benton running to our safe house today."

"Thoughts like that may keep me up at night."

"I think she's clean." Mike kept loading up on weapons. "Besides that, we may need the manpower and clean shooting ability. We're operating with limited hands here."

"And she can provide all of that?"

"Ask her. She can probably lecture you about it." Mike slipped extra ammunition into the deep utility pocket on the side of his pants leg.

"I continue to delude myself that we're in charge." Though it was starting to feel like Sutton might have too much say when she shouldn't have any.

"That's adorable, by the way." Mike glanced in Sutton's general direction. "But seriously, you need to understand something."

Whenever Mike slipped into that serious tone, Josiah knew something pretty shitty was coming. "This should be good."

"You're not going to like it."

Yeah, very bad. "I'm listening."

"She's pretty."

As if Josiah hadn't figured that out. The woman was so fucking hot that his concentration blinked out when he stared at her for more than five seconds. He'd never let an impressive pair of legs or amazing body kick him off stride. He focused. Did what had to be done. He'd do the same with Sutton, but something about her kept dragging his attention away from necessary things to stupid stuff, like the color of her hair.

The way she breathed through the terror and didn't let the fear clamp down on her. Her refusal to shrivel and hide from him. The fierceness that grew stronger as the hours passed. She didn't come out kicking or shooting. She acted like a woman caught in the wrong place at the wrong time, and that made him feel for her.

Not that he planned to admit any of that. He barely admitted it in his own head. "Your point?"

"You've noticed her."

"I'm not blind." Josiah had noticed. Any guy with half an interest in women would notice.

Mike peeked around the trunk lid to where Sutton stood before dropping his voice to a whisper that barely registered. "If she makes one wrong move I will kill her. Head shot and done. No questions and no chance for explanations, regardless of what she looks like or how into her you are."

The words ripped through Josiah but he knew they were right. "I'll beat you to it."

"That's just it, Josiah. It's got to be me." Mike rested a hand on the lip of the trunk and leaned in. "You'll hesitate."

That was a fucking insult. He'd never whiffed on an operation. "Are you forgetting who runs Delta team?"

"I'm not questioning your commitment or your leadership."

"Are you sure?"

Mike wiped his forehead against his arm. "I'm not blind either. I've seen you watching her."

Josiah refused to believe that was true. "Which is my job."

"The way you held her on the roof. The touching." Mike shook his head. "Since when do you do that shit?"

"I've slept with women on assignments, then had to kill them. You know I don't buy into the argument that only men can be bad. I've known some pretty fucking lethal women and taken them out." Not actions he boasted about, but necessary moves to protect the public.

"Yeah, I bet you didn't look at them the way you look at her." Mike pushed away from him and stood up straight. "Just laying it out there, boss. She so much as twitches in a way I don't like, she's going down."

Josiah's stomach went hollow. "Agreed."

"Happy we're on the same page."

Sutton came around the side of the car and stopped right in front of Josiah. "Are others meeting us?"

Mike smiled at her. "Like who?"

"We're going to set off alarms and corral people as they come out and grab this kid . . ." Her gaze bounced from Mike to Josiah. "Or not."

Mike shook his head. "Not."

"Definitely not," Josiah said at the same time.

She finished fastening her protective vest. "Maybe I need a second vest. Do they make these in full-body armor?"

They'd gone over the particulars all day. Her part anyway. Josiah skipped over what he and Mike would be doing. But she'd been quizzed and repeated every detail back. So Josiah didn't quite understand the nervousness now. "We sneak past the alarms, grab the kid, and get out. Simple."

"Well, I get that." She put her hand over her ear and whispered, "But this place is huge. Are we sure this Ellery person I've never met but can hear in my head can beat this alarm system?"

"She can hear you right now, by that way," Mike said in a dry tone.

Josiah jumped right to the point. "The kids who go here are children of very powerful people. They're sent here because it's a lockdown facility. Retinal scanners, security card access at every door. We may have forgotten to tell you that these kids have trackers on them."

Some of the color drained from her face. "Are we sure this is really just a school? It sounds like a weird sort of military training ground. I mean, come on. Trackers?"

"Small and less than the size of a breath mint, implanted under the skin." Mike used his fingers to demonstrate just how small he meant.

Her mouth dropped open. "Who are these kids' parents? Like prime ministers and such?"

Josiah didn't sugarcoat it. "No, the real power brokers."

"Forget it. I don't want to know." She waved her hand in front of her. "How is Benton getting in?"

Mike shrugged. "You tell us."

Her hands dropped to her sides as her shoulders drooped. "You can watch me the whole time and you won't find anything."

Little did she know. "Sutton, you need to assume someone is always watching you."

"Is that your way of warning me you'll shoot first if I do something wrong?"

This time Josiah didn't hesitate. "Yes."

9

An hour later night had fallen and the temperature dropped. A chill filled the air, but Sutton didn't know if the weather or fear of what could happen next had her teeth tapping together. She wanted to bounce around, walk, do something to force more blood into her legs but she stayed still as ordered. This was not her usual night on the job, but she appreciated the level of danger and did not play games.

There, at a side gate by the landscaping staff's garage, they bided their time as Ellery, the woman Sutton knew only by voice, did whatever she did on her end to unlock the entrance. Sutton continued to pretend it made sense that she stood in front of a steel door in the middle of a wall around school property. A school that felt more like a prison.

Josiah had inserted a card into the reader but the light stayed red. Since neither of the men panicked, Sutton decided not to either. She could hear the clicking of a keyboard over the comm. The speed astounded her. Every part of what they were doing right now—crouching, hiding, waiting, grabbing some kid she didn't know—piqued her interest.

She spent her days collecting evidence for legal cases. The ridiculousness of that work compared to this struck her as she hunkered down in the grass. She would have started laughing, but she feared if she did she'd never stop.

"I'm still surprised you didn't tie me to the steering wheel." Once more Sutton looked around, took in the equivalent of a castle wall and remembered the guards stationed at the main gate, and wondered what kind of families that sent their kids here.

Josiah's attention never strayed from that light. "I still might if I find out this is a setup."

Again with this argument. Other than hand him Benton's head on a stick, she didn't know what she'd have to do to win Josiah over. "You have serious trust issues."

"I grab you and all of a sudden Benton goes after one of ours who's located close by." He stole a quick glance at her. "I'm not big on coincidence."

She still didn't understand where this kid fit in, but she didn't bother to ask. He'd evade anyway. "Is this where you threaten to kill me?"

"If you're looking for regret about killing killers, you have the wrong guys."

The light switched to green and Mike filed in first. Following the instructions they'd drummed into her head, she went in second. Stayed between them and didn't make a sound as they skimmed the inside of the wall. Security lights bathed the green lawn in a soft glow, making the buildings looming behind in the darkness look even more menacing.

Dodging around buildings and evading the lights, they moved around the side of the property and kept going until they drew even with the end of the first building. She glanced back and spied a group of guards gathered by the main gate. The shift change. Somehow Josiah knew what happened inside these walls and when. Without the change, guards would line the wall and walk the grounds. This was their one chance to get in unnoticed.

The walk switched to a jog. She's known it was coming but still cursed her recent lack of exercise. She walked everywhere, but that didn't mean she'd be able to run any distance without heaving. Good thing they only needed to slip around two buildings.

They made a beeline across the back of the first without trouble. They got to the end when Mike came to a halt. He held up his fist and they all stopped. That hand signal she remembered. There were others and they all blended, but this warned of an emergency stop.

"Heat signatures." The whisper came over the comm as clear as if Ellery were standing with them.

"Copy." Josiah's response barely registered above a sigh.

Sutton wished she could be half as calm. Her heartbeat soared as the thumping slammed against her chest. Air punched her lungs and had her on the verge of panting. Adrenaline. All of it readying her for the job ahead, or so she convinced herself.

Josiah slipped around her. Actually passed close enough to rub his body over hers and poke his gun into her side. She understood. They waited just outside the circle of the security light. If he moved too far away from the building he could be seen.

Mike held up two fingers and Josiah nodded. Not that anyone but her could see the agreement. She wanted to point that out but knew not to move. Not to breathe, if possible. Then she heard them. Two male voices speaking in a language she didn't know.

Mike lifted his head off the wall, then put it back down again. From the sound of the voices, she knew they were close and moving in. In another few minutes these unwanted visitors would run straight into Mike and then the rest of them. The makeshift hiding place behind the wall would be blown. She feared alarms would start ringing after that.

Josiah turned back to her and leaned in until his body crushed hers into the wall and his mouth settled on her ear. "Do not move."

He backed up and held up a finger as if to say he meant business. Not that she needed the demonstration. She'd still rather take her chances with Josiah than with two men guarding a scary school. She was about to tell Josiah that when he took off in the opposite direction, heading back where they came before disappearing into the darkness.

Shaken, with her brain cells misfiring, she turned around to find Mike staring at her. He winked. His attention went to his watch. After a few seconds he held up three fingers and performed a countdown. She didn't know what she was supposed to do at one, but she'd try to at least move.

The sound grew closer. The shadows came first, then the men turned the corner. One almost ran into Mike and jerked at the sight of him. He opened his mouth to yell or say something, but a beat too late. As he reached for his gun, Mike landed a shot. Rammed the heel of his hand into the other man's throat until he grabbed his neck and coughed. Then came a second shot to the stomach that doubled the guard over.

The whole thing happened in a flash. Bodies blurring in front of her as they moved. Sutton watched it all as she stood with her back plastered against the cold stone wall.

The other one reached for a radio but Josiah came up behind him and wrapped an arm around his throat. With his neck in Josiah's elbow, the guy flailed. His boots pounded the ground and his ankle dug into the grass, making divots. The choking sound grew louder as Josiah squeezed harder.

Maybe five seconds later the thrashing stopped. The guy slid boneless to the ground. By the time her gaze flew back to Mike, he stood over the guy he hit. Both guards lay facedown and unmoving.

Her gaze traveled over the men as she realized they'd simply been doing their jobs. "Are they dead?"

"Out cold," Mike said as he stepped back and looked around the buildings.

"Which means we need to move fast." Josiah looked at his watch. "Our time just got cut in half."

Sutton waited for Ellery or someone on the line to call this off, but the order never came. Instead Mike dropped down on one knee and zip tied the unconscious men's hands behind their backs and put something over their mouths. She was too busy being relieved they were alive to ask why they needed this extra step.

"The next building." Josiah took the lead this time.

They made it to the dormitory, or house, or whatever really rich people called it, without running into more men. As planned, they skipped the front and back doors because of the extra security protection of the retinal scanners there. They went to the assigned door but there was no handle. This qualified as a way out but not a way in. Not that Sutton could see.

But Josiah didn't panic or get upset. He nodded to Mike, who went fishing for something in the utility pocket of his pants. He pulled out a small packet and knelt in front of the door.

Sutton watched but she didn't know what she was seeing. Despite all the discussions and planning, she couldn't make this rescue make sense in her head. Their secrecy didn't allow for many questions. But she waited there, ready to put her life on the line for a kid she didn't even know, she thought they could cough up some information. "Why didn't this kid's parents just have the school release the kid to us?"

"We don't know who works for Benton or where his people are." Josiah kept checking the area. "If we tipped the wrong person off, the kid would be dead. Maybe many kids."

She still didn't understand how the pieces fit together. They had to have friends inside the school. Powerful people who could help out. "But the parents work with you."

"His father is on my team." As if he read her mind, Josiah answered the question on her mind. "We used his knowledge of the school and our verified contacts to help Ellery break the security system."

Even hearing that bit of information filled her with hope. Josiah didn't view this as a routine operation. This meant something. She didn't even know she cared about that until right now. "That makes sense."

"And the kid's name is Danny. If he balks about going with you, say Kingsfield."

"Why?"

"It's his arranged safe word." Josiah shrugged. "You'd have to ask his dad what it means."

Before she could say anything to that, the door clicked open and Mike looked up at Josiah. "We're in."

A wall of warmth hit her as soon as she stepped inside. Not too hot and not too cool. Perfect, just as she expected from a place like this. A place that must cost tens of thousands, maybe more, to send a kid here each year.

They had two floors and miles of hallways to maneuver but the quiet gave her hope. She'd half expected alarms to go off and the police to come crashing in. But nothing. They got to the stairwell and swiped the security card. The light immediately switched to green.

Josiah typed in a code and they opened the door. Up they went. Repeated the same procedure to get onto the floor they needed. A click, and Josiah eased the door open a crack. They knew the guard schedules. While the men outside might switch shifts, the guards inside the buildings had settled in hours ago. Guards roamed the halls, checking the building floor by floor every few minutes. They could run into one at any time.

She closed her eyes and hoped for a little luck. Just enough to save this kid.

They slipped into the hall one by one. Part of her wanted to stay in the stairwell but a guard could come at any time. And she'd been the one insisting she might be needed. She pledged to follow through with that.

They were able to skip the retinal scanners by coming in the door without a handle or any recognizable access, but they needed a handprint to get into the room. Josiah had told her not to worry about it, but now . . .

"Can you do this?" She asked the question as she stood by his side staring at the locked door.

He was about to answer when something thumped not inside the room but out. He nodded toward Mike. "Check it out."

"Right." Mike took off down the hall, fast and smooth and not making a sound.

She had no idea what kind of training produced that skill, but it impressed her. She hoped Josiah had a few hidden talents as well. "Are you going to—"

"Quiet." He slipped something out of a pocket on his vest. Unrolled what looked like a glove, but was clear. He flattened it against his hand until it almost disappeared into his palm.

The seconds played like a scene out of a spy movie. "You stole someone's palm print?"

"His father's, and it wasn't stealing since we have it

on file and he knows I'm using it." Josiah touched his ear. "Ellery?"

A soft whisper came over the comm. "You're good."

Sutton knew the timing had something to do with all entries and exits being logged at some central computer. Ellery's job was to prevent that so that the guards didn't notice and come running.

Josiah touched his hand to the pad and the light turned green. After a click, he opened the door. Sutton peeked around him. The room was large, with a bed and sitting room. Not like any dorm she'd ever been in. She saw a lump on the bed. A pile of blankets and dark hair on a pillow.

"Is that him?" She took a step forward and a series of rapid bangs rang out. Not in the room, not even in the building.

Josiah jogged to the window and looked out. He turned and faced her as he touched his ear. "Code red."

The words sent fear spiraling through her. The bangs grew louder and she realized what they were. Gunfire. Her thoughts went to Mike and then took off on a wild ride. Horrible scenarios ran through her head.

The previously dim hallway lights flicked on high as an alarm screamed. A little boy with ruffled black hair sat up, at first confused, then with eyes glazed with panic. He grabbed the covers and shoved his body back against the wall.

She wanted to soothe him. Chaos ruled as voices and footsteps sounded in the hall and all around them. People shouted. A voice called out instructions over a loudspeaker. Someone knocked on doors and read out names. Floodlights clicked on outside. It looked like a military camp had sprung to life, but she focused only on Danny.

She bent down and saw his dark eyes. Asian with a round face. She guessed his age to be about seven. She held out a hand to him. "I won't hurt you."

He shook his head as he cowered.

Steps thundered in the hall. It sounded like a herd. Heavy footsteps and slamming. A shot followed by screaming. Josiah pushed off from the window and passed her on the way to the hall.

"What are you doing?" she asked.

"Providing cover. Making sure no one gets in here. I'll be standing right there. If I have to go into the hallway, I won't go far." He turned to Danny for a second. "Kingsfield."

The boy's eyes widened, then he nodded. He let the sheet and blanket drop as he scooted to the edge of the bed closest to her. "I'm ready."

With that kind of smooth response to danger this kid could be on Josiah's team. "You stay with me, okay?"

Danny nodded as he dragged a box from under his bed and pulled out a sweatshirt and sneakers. "We can go now."

The kid had a go bag for emergencies like this? "Wait, you keep that—"

He kept on nodding. "Dad taught me."

Of course he did. Still, she wanted to hug the kid for being so brave. So calm. "Come here."

Before he could grab on to her hand the door slammed open. Two men burst in, both dressed in black and holding weapons. One kicked the gun right out of her hand. The memory of the scene in her apartment played in her head. But this felt different. Neither of these two looked or acted like Josiah. The bigger one scowled as his finger moved to the trigger.

She grabbed Danny and shoved him behind her. "No."

The big one approached. He aimed the gun at her as he stared with dead eyes. "Both of you come with me."

Hate pulsed off him. If he felt any guilt about threatening a woman and small child, he hid it well.

No, these two weren't with Mike and Josiah. They wouldn't rescue and protect. They were the type to throw her out of a car or off a roof to get her out of the way. She sensed it to her bones.

He took another step and nearly stumbled when Danny wrapped his arms around her waist and pulled her tight against him. The touch, that trust, fueled her.

She reached behind her, desperate to grab anything. Her fingers touched the lamp on Danny's desk and she wrapped her fingers around the base. A yank and she pulled it off the top and swung. Aimed for the head but connected with his shoulder. He winced as he ducked but she struck him. His arm wavered and she reached for the knife sticking out of the pocket of his vest.

With weapons in both hands, she wound up again. The other attacker caught her hand just in time. Twisted until she dropped the lamp. One shove and he knocked her down, tumbling her onto the bed. Danny tumbled with her. She bounced and rolled over, put Danny behind her, half underneath her, as she held that knife in front of her.

"The boy." The noninjured one didn't look impressed. "Now."

"No one touches him."

"Listen to the lady." Josiah's voice burst through the room and over the rumbling of noise outside and in the hallway.

Both men turned but didn't get far. Josiah fired two shots in rapid succession, dropping both men where they stood. The violence rumbled through her. She saw blood and bodies. Her first instinct was for Danny and she used her body to shield him from as much of the horror as possible.

Her second was to demand answers. She looked up at Josiah. "Where were you?"

"Killing two guys in the hall and creating a path."

After another shot just outside the door, Mike moved into the room. "Well now."

Sutton followed his gaze to the knife. She clenched it, digging ridges into her palms, but she didn't care. "And that was without my glasses."

Mike's eyes bulged. "You wear glasses?"

"With or without them, you did great." Josiah slipped his gun into the holster and reached over. Peeling each finger, he loosened her grip and took the knife. Bending down, he grabbed her gun and handed it to her. "Here."

"The kid okay?" Mike asked.

She started to see why Josiah got so frustrated with her questions. Now wasn't the time for chitchat. They had to move before more men arrived, and there always seemed to be more men. "Can we get out?"

"We think Benton's men are fighting the guards."

That sounded like a promise of death and more bullets. "How do we—"

"While they're busy taking care of each other and the other kids are running through their practiced escape drill, we sneak away." Josiah held a hand out to her. "Ready?"

She shook her head as she picked up Danny. The weight nearly knocked her over, but she locked her muscles. With his head tucked under her chin, she let Josiah help her up. She looked up at the men who had once scared her and now made her feel safer. "Now I'm ready."

Mike nodded. "Impressive."

Through all the noise around them and the panic that threatened to take her over, she focused on Josiah. His face, the confident way he stood there, grounded her. "I told you I could help."

"I should have listened." He held his hand out to her again.

This time she took it.

10

THEY HANDED Danny off at the prearranged spot to guards chosen by his dad and sanctioned by the Alliance. The kid was shaken but fine. Josiah could say the same about Sutton. She didn't buckle, didn't turn on them. But her protection of the kid, the way she held off trained commandos with a knife, would stay with him for a long time. Those moves went beyond training as a PI.

When they got to the temporary mobile operations center, Josiah took Sutton's blindfold off. They walked into the windowless warehouse building with its chipping green walls and concrete floor. Except for the impressive array of technical equipment, all the monitors, and the state-of-the-art security, it could pass as any run-down building in any run-down city anywhere.

Lucas Garner, Bravo team's explosives expert, who could also shoot the tab off a soda can from a distance at which most people couldn't even see the tab, leaned with a thigh on the table and watched as Ellery typed. He watched her a lot, so seeing him hover over her now was not a surprise. Neither was the fact he had volunteered to act as her bodyguard until they caught or killed Benton.

He spied them and stood up. "Nice job out there."

Ellery got up, too. "Ms. Dahl, welcome."

"Please call me Sutton."

For some reason Sutton stopped walking halfway across the room, so Josiah put a hand low on her back and guided her toward the row of desks and computers. "This is Ellery and Lucas."

A smile, genuine and far too inviting, spread over Sutton's mouth. "You were the voice in my head."

Ellery winced. "I know it's disconcerting to have someone speak through those little speakers."

"I actually found it comforting."

She just never let up with that. Josiah didn't know what she expected but he'd grown to dread her saying that phrase. "There's that word again."

Mike joined them with a water bottle in his hand and another one that he passed to Sutton. "Yeah, they have inside jokes already. It's cute, right?"

Not to Josiah. Not when all of them were staring at him now. "I'm still holding my gun."

"Did you really do that without glasses?" Ellery asked Sutton.

She nodded. "I only use them when I'm tired."

Josiah remembered her mentioning something about glasses. "Wait, that was real?"

"Sure. Is Danny okay?" Sutton asked, directing her comments to Ellery and clearly ignoring the men in the room.

Lucas answered anyway. "He's fine. He'll be re-united with his father in a few hours."

"You're not the dad?"

Lucas laughed. "Did the not-Japanese thing give it away?"

"I didn't want to assume."

The conversation bordered on painful. Josiah debated turning the topic completely but decided she deserved more than that. She'd put her life on the line without question. The least he could do was fill in some of the blanks.

"Danny's father's name is Gabe." Hiroshi, but Josiah didn't add that part. He didn't see the need to provide last names, none of which were real anyway. "Mike, Gabe, and a guy named Parker are all on Delta team with me."

Her eyes took on a new intensity and her body language switched from slumped shoulders and tired to high alert. "That's the name of your organization?"

His black-ops instincts kicked in. The change in her demeanor had him wanting to test her. "It's the Alliance."

"When did Josiah get so chatty?" Lucas asked.

But Josiah didn't break eye contact with her. "She's in this now."

She actually smiled. "Thank you."

"Besides that, if she really is working for Benton she already knows who all of us are and the name of the group." Seemed logical to him. He could drop hints, maybe plant a false lead or two, and see where it all led.

If this all amounted to some big play by Benton to get a person deep inside the Alliance again, Josiah would be ready.

It was possible she truly did travel to Paris hunting a guy she thought was named Bane. The paper and digital trail of her life sure made the explanation seem real. Someone had gone to a lot of trouble. If she had, then he would look like a gigantic asshole. But if it came down to his ego or his team's safety, he didn't care how he looked.

"You ruined it." Her mouth flattened into a thin line. "Is it that you can only be the nice guy for short periods of time?"

Ellery crossed her arms in front of her. "Are we missing something?"

"Josiah still thinks I'm working for this Benton guy."

Mike took a long swig of water, then refastened the cap on the bottle. "You did have his file on us."

"I'm pretty sure I mentioned I took that."

"Any IDs on the guys we took out?" Mike used his bottle to point to the largest screen with a feed of the cleanup at the school. When no one answered, he glanced at Josiah. "What, that conversation wasn't going anywhere. We needed to move on. You know I'm right."

Ellery turned around and went back to typing. "No identification. I'm running facial recognition."

A necessary waste of time. They had to check but Josiah knew that road wouldn't lead anywhere. "My guess will be mercenaries for hire even though that doesn't add up."

"Because?" Lucas asked.

"Benton doesn't trust anyone. He is not going to give orders to men he potentially can't control. Men who could turn on him if someone—namely one of us—offered more money." That's the piece that never fit. Benton had a never-ending supply of hired guns. Someone somewhere should have turned on him. To their knowledge, and Ellery had dug and checked, no one had.

Sutton nibbled on her thumbnail as she watched the movements on the screen. "Frederick."

"What?" Mike asked.

"Bane has a sidekick named Frederick. I think the last name is Heinz, but my digging might be wrong on that. There are about a billion guys with that name in the world." Sutton's gaze traveled around the room before landing on Josiah again. "But whatever the last name, he's Bane . . . Benton's right-hand man."

Josiah took every word apart in his head and analyzed them. He'd never heard this name. Never seen a sidekick. Getting the details now, from her, started those alarm bells ringing in his head again.

The roller-coaster ride of trusting her and not trusting her really pissed him off. And he blamed her. "You forgot to mention this guy until now?"

"You didn't ask."

The words lit a match to his anger. "Wrong answer."

"Okay, wait." Mike held up both hands. "To be fair, it's not like you guys had a lot of time to sit down and have a get-to-know-you chat."

"Since when are you the voice of reason?" Josiah didn't want that now. He needed to have this out and get it settled. Fight it to the death, if necessary. With three highly trained operatives in the room, they should be able to coax the truth out of her one way or the other.

Mike shrugged. "I'm trying something new."

"Run the name along with Bane's." Josiah nodded at Ellery before turning back to Sutton. He almost hated to face her. To see the wariness in those eyes and know he put it there, real or imagined. "Tell us what you know."

"In his thirties, maybe. Tall and bald. A big guy with a German accent. He travels with your Benton, if that's him, and I'm thinking yes, at all times."

No way. "We didn't run into anyone like that in the caves in Pakistan." They found Benton there, hiding chemical weapons and readying to ignite the region in a battle to end all battles. Jake Pearce had been his sidekick. He lied to them and played the role of traitor and ate a bullet in return.

Sutton frowned at them. "Did you say Pakistan?"

"Our last date with Benton." Mike pitched his water bottle into the trashcan by Ellery's side.

Lucas nodded. "Good times."

"You're going to give information for us to compile a drawing of this Frederick guy," Josiah said. They'd start there, then he could hand it all to Ellery to work out while he assessed the trustworthiness of the intel Sutton provided. "Then we are going to walk through the information you have on Bane and every single conversation you've ever had with him or Frederick."

"The Bane part is a lot."

He was officially tired of hearing her denials and excuses. "You'd be smart not to leave any of the important parts out." He reached for her, to show her to the interrogation room in the back.

She stepped out of his grasp. "Stop threatening me."

"They have communication issues," Mike said to Lucas and Ellery.

Josiah ignored the sarcasm and kept staring at Sutton, willing her to understand the seriousness of this issue. "We're also going to talk about everything you saw and all you know, no matter how minor or unimportant you think it was."

She blew out a long breath. "This is going to be a long night."

He kept at it. Blocked out the other people in the room and the look of disapproval on Ellery's face, as well as the concern on Lucas's. Spelled it all out to Sutton. "And then you're going to go over it again and again until Ellery can find something we can use to track this motherfucker down."

"Can I shower first?"

A totally reasonable response after everything that happened and the early morning hour. Still, a fevered fury had him in its grasp and wouldn't let go. His voice grew louder. "No."

Sutton threw her hands up in the air. "What do I have to do to prove myself?"

"You can't."

Her face flushed and her jaw locked. "What the hell is wrong with you?"

The fury had all piled up—the near-miss in Pakistan, his uncle, almost losing Danny tonight—and now spilled over. Rage that had nothing to do with her lapped at him. He wanted to vent and yell and punch a wall. Instead, he aimed it all at her. "We have a maniac gunning for every member of this team and you are our only link to him. I'm still not even sure which side you're on."

"How can you say that after what happened with Danny?" The question came out on shocked breaths.

"Because Benton will do anything, use anyone." Mike tried to talk. Ellery said something. Josiah pushed it all out and kept going after Sutton. Part of him wanted her to break. If she was bad, if she didn't deserve to be trusted, he wanted to know now. Maybe that would help him not care about what happened to her. "He will lie and cheat and kill. He would have blown up that school and every child in it tonight if he thought that would get him what he wanted."

"Which is? Oh, wait. You think I already know." Her rage matched his now. She talked with her hands, gesturing and pointing as tension pulled her expression tight. "I don't know anything about this Benton. The man I knew has pretended to be a lot of people but I never found that name. And when you talk about trust . . ."

"What?" He shouted the question at her.

"How do I know you're not the bad guys in all of this?"

She wanted proof? Fucking fine. He stepped past her toward the desk. "I'll show you."

Lucas stepped in front of him. "Josiah."

"Don't do what I think you're going to do," Mike grumbled from behind him.

Josiah shoved them all away, physically and mentally as he hovered over Ellery. "Cue it."

She lifted her hands off the keyboard. "This isn't a good idea."

"Fine, I'll do it." He reached around her and hit the button. He knew which screen had the video ready and how they all worked to make sure he never saw it playing.

Mike grabbed his arm. "Calm the fuck down."

But Josiah was too far gone. He stood by the screen and pointed his finger at the horrible scene unfolding. The scene he saw every time he closed his eyes. "That is Benton's idea of a good time. Whatever petty bullshit you're chasing him about, this is bigger. I guarantee it."

The dialogue replayed.

About forty and scarred with burns. He said his name is—

The words cut off at the loud boom.

Sutton jumped and her hands went to her mouth. "Oh my God."

Josiah felt sick inside. "Exactly. Now maybe you have a clue."

Her eyes widened. "That is sick. So sick."

She stood there, frozen in place, and repeated the phrase over and over. Her body actually rocked back and forth. If she relished his pain or the death, she was conducting a master class in how to act out the opposite. Her body curled in and her face paled. She was the picture of despair.

Much of the punch left him but the need to torture himself, to pay penance, remained. "Want to see it again?"

"Goddamn it, that's enough." Mike reached around him and punched a button that made the picture freeze.

Numbness settled in Josiah's bones. "Want us to play it again so you can be sure you want to talk?"

Sutton closed her eyes and shook her head. "Turn it off."

He couldn't stop. The world crashed in on him and he lashed out at her. "Does that look like something you want to be a part of?"

She dropped her hands and glared at him. "I said turn it off."

"Listen to her, Josiah." Tasha's smooth voice boomed through the room as she walked in. "At the very least, you need to listen to me. Do it now."

She kept walking until she stood in front of Sutton with her hand out. "My name is Tasha."

"She's the boss," Mike said, filling what might be the most important piece of information for Sutton.

"Yes, I am." Tasha pinned Josiah in her sights as she said it.

At first Sutton just stared at the outstretched hand, but then she shook it. Pain still lingered in her eyes, but a healthy dose of confusion played there, too. "You're also British."

"Half the team is." Tasha glanced at the screen

and then back to Sutton. "And, no, I won't fire Josiah, though it is tempting at this moment."

He wasn't in the mood for a scolding. "She needed to see the truth."

Even Ellery turned on him. "There might have been a more tactful way to handle it."

"I apologize if you were traumatized." Tasha guided Sutton to the nearest chair.

Not that she was in the mood to be placated or coddled. She kept right on glaring at Josiah. "For which part? The kidnapping, being shot at, almost getting killed at the school. That tape."

Mike stood next to Josiah and whispered under his breath. "Clearly you are not a people person."

He had been before this job. Before all the death. Before her. Josiah didn't know what the hell he'd become now.

"She should see the rest of the tape." He held up his hands when it looked as if Mike wanted to launch an attack. "For ID purposes."

Tasha sighed in a way that said she was done with all the nonsense. "On that I agree."

Ellery started it up again. The camera scanned the destructive aftermath of the explosion in the room. Josiah saw those legs and the blood spilled on the floor and looked away. He'd had enough Benton for one day.

The name is Benton, but then I think you know that.

Ellery turned it off, but Tasha shook her head. "Let it play."

I started with Josiah but you'll all get a turn.

This time Tasha hit the button and stopped the tape. "Is that the man you know as Bane? Is it his voice?"

Sutton just stared at the monitor. She seemed lost in thought. Maybe just lost.

Guilt tugged at Josiah. "Sutton? Do you recognize him?"

She nodded, slow at first, but kept going. "It's his voice . . . his hand. Bane and Benton are absolutely the same person."

Josiah started to go to her but Tasha stopped him with a simple flick of her hand. He thought about disobeying. Actually wanted to ignore her, tell Tasha this wasn't her business, but that would be an overstep. Josiah couldn't go there, not with his emotions all churned up and regret pounding in on him. So he stayed still and thought about what he should say to her, if he could even find the right words to explain the doubts.

"Why don't we take a break?" Tasha cleared her throat, which was her way of telling people to clear the room. "Ellery, maybe you can show Sutton where she'll be staying for a few days. Let her shower."

"Babysit her," Mike said.

"Don't help." But Tasha focused on Mike now. She pointed at him, then at the doorway behind him. "You and Lucas start digging into this Frederick guy and go through everything Ellery collected on Bane and this fake company Clayton Pharmaceuticals, and that office. I want a preliminary report in thirty minutes."

With a nod, Lucas and Mike took off. "Yes, ma'am."

Ellery ushered Sutton in the direction of the bathroom. "It's this way."

She got halfway there before turning around to face Josiah again. "You're right about one thing. You suck at comforting."

11

JOSIAH DREADED the next five minutes. He sat down hard in the chair Ellery had just abandoned and stared at the closed door she just slammed shut.

With the fire inside him back at a low heat, the reality of what just happened hit him. He'd forced Sutton to watch his uncle get blown apart. He couldn't get through five seconds of it without wanting to drop to the floor, and he'd played it for her.

He'd seen her eyes. Wide with horror and unshed tears. The way she rocked back on her heels and then went blank. Just shut down.

No doubt about it. Somewhere along the line he'd turned into a fucking asshole.

Tasha rolled up a chair and sat next to him. Rested her elbow on the table and watched him. Waited a good thirty seconds before saying anything. "It's not your usual style to attack women."

Every word sliced through him because he knew what came next. "That's an overstatement. I didn't—"

"Stop. This is me you're talking to. I hand-picked you for this team." Tasha sat up straighter in her chair. "Showing her that video? That was pretty cold-blooded."

"She's supposed to be a PI."

"That doesn't make her heartless."

"That's what you do with hostiles. Shake them." Josiah sat forward in his chair with his elbows resting on his knees. But that position didn't feel comfortable either.

"Is she a hostile?" Tasha's head tilted to the side. "Do we know that?"

He sat back again. Kept moving because he couldn't sit still. "I can't tell yet."

"After reviewing all we have on her and listening to the audio and reviewing the available video of the school incident, I'm convinced she didn't know about the existence of Benton."

Most of the time he thought so, too, but he slid back and forth. With Benton nothing was clear and Sutton just added a wildcard to the mix. "I know that's what she says."

"What has you hesitating about believing in her?"

He stretched his legs in front of him and leaned back. "Good fucking question."

"So answer it."

Truth was he couldn't figure out a way to shut off the operative side of his brain. He'd been racing forward in this career, trying to exorcise every demon and pay for every sin. He could never go fast enough or far enough to wipe it all away.

But her fight, that spirit, enticed him. Made him

think of sunshine and light when he spent most of his life in shadows. Maybe that's why he fought so hard, grabbed on to any crumb that suggested she wasn't as innocent as she seemed to be in this mess. Then he could be right and leave his life unchanged. If he hurt her, pushed her away, proved her wrong, he could write her off and slink back into the darkness.

Josiah couldn't say any of that out loud. He already had to undergo mental health checks and physical checks for this job. They all did on Tasha's orders. He'd bet as soon as this operation ended she would insist on time off and some counseling over his uncle.

She cared, and that meant a lot to the team. They all knew she had their backs and would pick up a rocket launcher to save any one of them. But he didn't want to feel anything. That's the part she didn't get. She was in love and in charge. She had Ward and her life made sense. He had a history that included responsibility for his mother's death. Just one more sin piled on top of a stack of others.

And now he had to add Sutton to the mix. "Why her?"

"I don't follow."

He wasn't even sure what he meant when he said it, but one point did pick at him. "She works in Baltimore. Benton is an international arms dealer. He bargains with lives and toxins and rocket launchers. How does she end up chasing him?"

"We need to ask her."

Josiah could almost see Tasha thinking through the possibilities. She was in charge for a reason. She not only started the Alliance, she ran it with precision, keeping the suits and intelligence agencies who would try to impose restrictions away from the members. As former MI6, she also got strategy. That's why Josiah wanted her opinion. If she could soothe his doubts, maybe he'd stop unloading on Sutton.

"It's possible the man she knows is tied to a much simpler case than the ones we've dealt with around Benton. The point is, she could have names and facts that will lead us to the real guy, and she might willingly share those." Tasha smiled. "There are innocent people out there, you know."

He knew that was true in theory. In practice, he didn't come across true innocents all that often. "Benton has everyone from dictators to Chechen rebels on speed dial. Hiring her makes no sense and he is a guy who has a reason for everything he does. He doesn't make mistakes like letting an important file get into someone else's hands. And why not take her out since then?"

Tasha exhaled and groaned while doing it. "We need to pull her background apart. I mean, we've already checked her out. We did that before you and Mike went in back in Paris, but we're missing something."

"Either she is not who she seems to be or there's something connecting the two of them in some way. She used the word 'personal' so I'm thinking what she's working on is not your usual case. Either way, we need to know." No matter which scenario they picked, Sutton would be used and discarded. That's how this game worked. He'd never tired of the game before, but the idea of her being churned up in it made him hate it now. "This is a priority, Tasha."

She rolled her eyes. "Yeah, this isn't my first day on the job."

Josiah changed the subject. "Where's Ward?"

"Now there's another problem." Tasha shot him a big smile. "Running point back at the Warehouse and pissing about it every two seconds."

Ward had been injured on the job right before the forming of the Alliance and now had trouble with the muscles in his hand. But he rarely let that limitation stop him from being in the thick of battle. Josiah half expected him to fly in and start issuing orders. He'd do just about anything to protect Tasha and tweak Harlan. Those two shared administrative duties for the team and battled almost every day.

Josiah never thought he'd miss the fights but he did right now. "Yeah, I can't imagine he likes the idea of you out on the firing line without him."

"That's the point, Josiah. Everywhere is the firing line. Benton gained intel about us and our pasts from Jake Pearce."

"We should have killed that guy long before we did." Josiah thought about all those conversations with Pearce. When Alliance started they'd traded war stories, talked about personal stuff. He'd been one of them, or so they all thought of Pearce. The only good thing about the guy was the fact they killed him in Pakistan. They might have missed with Benton but they got Pearce.

"No kidding. But my point is we might not know Benton but he knows a hell of a lot about us. That's why he needed Jake. To collect information," Tasha said.

And with that lifeline broken, Benton would have to get the information from somewhere else, which brought them right back to the questions about Sutton. "And now he's going to use what he knows."

"So Ward is shifting safe houses and moving the team around. Trying to protect the people closest to all of us in as quiet a way as possible, without breaking cover."

"If Benton could get into that school . . ." No one should have gotten in there. Gabe almost went mad with rage over the idea of his son being in danger. Even now he had Danny stashed somewhere safe and stayed there with him.

Tasha leaned forward. "Be careful."

This was new. The boss didn't express doubt. She and Ward operated in tandem, pumping them all up and letting them know they took for granted their high expectations would be met. Josiah didn't like this change. "Always."

"I'm serious. You need to stick close to Sutton."

That's what he'd been doing. Sticking and getting more confused and disoriented by the second. "And?"

"Are you blind?"

Josiah refused to have this conversation for the second time today. Once with Mike was weird enough. "I've guarded pretty women before."

"I was talking about the fact she's fit and resource-ful, and that you needed to be careful you didn't lose her trail." Tasha's eyebrow lifted. "What were you talking about?"

"Nothing."

"That better be the answer."

Problem was Josiah didn't know what to think anymore.

It took one blindingly hot shower, a pair of Ellery's thick socks, and a blanket wrapped around a sweatshirt for Sutton to warm up. She sat on the edge of a bed in a room with concrete block walls. No rug, one pillow. She'd lived through worse. That wasn't the point. This issue that had her stomach flipping came with seeing so much death.

And Josiah. The whole get-close-then-repel thing he did made her dizzy. One second he'd touched her or put a hand around her or did something to rescue her. The next he accused her of awful crimes. Keeping up with the flip-flops had her wanting to hide in this room forever.

She looked at him and saw this larger-than-life guy who could command. Who appeared fearless. The brown hair with subtle red highlights. The intense way he stared at her. The way his gaze wandered over her when he thought she wasn't looking. He was all wrong for her and yet she couldn't stop wanting him.

She'd never been the rescuer type. She didn't have a need to fix or heal guys, but under all Josiah's strength pain lingered. He'd known loss. It thrummed off him and that bound them in some weird unspoken way.

After one quick knock the door opened. She'd sat

there assuming Ellery had locked it, but no. In walked Josiah, freshly showered with damp hair and faded jeans. Some of his cocky assurance seemed to be missing but his presence still demanded attention.

She tried to call up the will to fight but couldn't get there. Didn't even have the energy to stand up. "Please tell me we're not sharing a room."

He sat down next to her. Close enough for their thighs to touch. "We are."

"Terrific." She rubbed her hands together. Brushed her thumb over the opposite palm. The move usually calmed her, but not today.

"Sutton." He put his hand over hers. "Look at me."

She let her fingers rest there, tangled in his, and glanced up at him. "What?"

"That was harsh but I needed you to see the kind of man we're dealing with here."

She wondered if he meant Benton or him. "You wanted to punish me."

For a few seconds he caressed her fingers with his. The touches, so light and gentle, stole her breath. She knew she should pull back and wallow in her anger, but seeing him now, struggling to find the right words and unable to hide behind his gun, she felt a closeness. A kinship.

She squeezed his hand, trying to coax him to talk. And because she loved touching him. Those strong hands with long, lean fingers. The calluses on his palms. The firm grip. Every part of him from those shoulders to the pronounced chin to the way his fingers easily circled her wrist without ever pressing too hard, all of it made up the man she found so compelling.

She could look at him, watch him, for hours, but right now she wanted him to talk. "Josiah?"

He exhaled. "Maybe a little."

"For what exactly?"

He shifted until he almost faced her and cradled one of her hands in both of his. "I'm not really sure."

Other women might take offense but she appreciated the honesty. She still didn't fully understand this group or what they did, be the truth hit her. With a sudden clarity she knew she needed him to know her. "I followed him everywhere and this time it led to Paris."

Josiah frowned. "What?"

"I grew up outside of Baltimore, went to college in DC, and then took a job back in Baltimore. Basically lived my life within a forty-mile radius. But I had to venture out because I made a promise."

"To?"

She thought about her mom and those long and lonely days after she died. The pain had walloped her. Despair and hatred mixed. She knew the rationales for her death were all wrong. Everyone kept talking about the freak attack and her being killed in the line of duty. Sutton remembered those days another way. All those private meetings at the kitchen table. Her mom's paranoia on overdrive. Then she walked into an ambush and never walked out.

Seven years ago and she'd been fighting to gather the evidence to get someone to listen ever since. "My mom spent her whole life in one state. She raised me alone, pushed herself. Worked her way up to earn this spot on this impressive team."

"You're speaking in the past tense."

Just thinking about her mom and the sacrifice made Sutton's heart ache. The pain in her chest had faded over the years but not gone away. She doubted it ever would. "She worked in hostage recovery. About seven years ago a job went wrong."

"She was killed in the line of duty?"

Sutton swallowed back the lump of sadness. "That's what the police report says."

"I'm sorry." His hand went to her neck then slipped into her hair.

The gentle massage had her leaning into him. The temptation to sit there and let him ease away the sadness pulled at her. At first she tried to get someone with power to believe her and reopen her mom's case. No one wanted to listen to a grieving twenty-year-old. So she'd waited, gained power of her own. Built her skills. Learned how to investigate and track leads. Gathered evidence. Tucked the churning need for revenge away as she learned.

"What do you think happened?" Josiah's voice, complete with the soothing accent and deep tone broke through the quiet room.

She had to fight off the flinch as she sat up. "What?"

"The report says one thing. You clearly believe another."

She didn't share easily, and this topic remained on

the off-limits list. The few times she'd tried to tell a friend or boyfriend over the years, the response hinged on some form of the it's-time-to-move-on speech, and she shut back down again. She stewed and planned.

But being so close, smelling the scent of the outdoors on his clothes, hearing the gentle coaxing in his voice, had her opening up for the first time in a long time. "After she died I wanted to avenge her. She dedicated her life to me and to her job and to keeping food on the table and providing all she could to me on her own. I made this vow that I would find the people who killed her."

"Did you know who they were? Do you now?"

So many questions. The way he asked, all concerned, felt right. The way all of this played out, with people hovering nearby and his team seeking information, made her wary.

"I know who the authorities said did it." Street violence gone wrong. Not an abnormal occurrence in that area of Baltimore, but too convenient for Sutton's comfort.

He frowned at her, which seemed to be a habit for him by now. "You're talking in riddles."

"You're not the only one with secrets to protect." Truth was she still didn't really know where Josiah fit into all of this. The school and that horrible tape, it all pointed to Bane being the mastermind Benton, the horrible guy Josiah claimed him to be.

Sutton could accept that on one level. Welcomed it even, because Bane being Benton meant others were tracking him down. That someone else saw him for the vile creature he was—dangerous and deceitful. But she'd gotten this close to the man she'd hunted for so long, and spilling every last piece of the puzzle without any sort of assurance, while her emotions were in freefall and clouded by her attraction to Josiah, struck her as stupid.

When the adrenaline rush wore off and he got the information he needed and dumped her off somewhere, she'd kick herself for being naïve. She couldn't let that happen. Holding back meant they needed her with them. If that closeness in turn kept her close to her prey, so be it. Josiah had the resources and the weapons and the strength. She planned to use that to her advantage.

"And this all relates to Bane somehow?" he asked.

A careful question instead of an interrogation. She admired his skills. "I am after him because he used to be someone else and disappeared. He took on other aliases. There are a trail of scams and bodies that can be linked to him. According to you, his crimes go well past what I just mentioned."

His fingers slipped through her hair in a soft caress. "I don't know about that. Murder sounds pretty big."

"There's an understatement." An air of comfort wrapped around her. That might not be his style but he brought it out now. "Are you always so eloquent?"

"Are you asking what lines I regularly use on women?" He smiled as he joked.

Amusement lit up his face, making him even more

appealing. The harsh lines of tension around his eyes eased and some of the stiffness in his shoulders fell away. "Do you date a lot of women on the job?"

"That kind of thing gets in the way of the shooting."

She didn't know if that was real or a joke or if he needed to tell her something before it was too late. "That sort of thing would be a problem if you were married."

"Very true." He shook his head. "A single life makes more sense."

The words kicked off an unwanted ball of excitement and had it bouncing around inside her. She tried to tamp down on the feeling, focus on him being a loner and reclusive and all the things she hated about that side of Bane. But truth was Josiah didn't share any traits with the man she hunted.

One thought led to another. She suddenly wanted to be very clear. The words tumbled out. "So you're . . ."

"Single?" His fingers tightened against the back of her neck then let go. "Very much so. This job is extra tough on married guys."

"I still don't understand what your job is." She regretted the words as soon as they were out. She wasn't looking for a fight. The exact opposite, actually. Sitting there with him, soaking in his presence, provided the comfort she'd been craving from him, even as she walked the careful line between telling all and telling enough to keep him intrigued.

"The Alliance is an undercover black-ops team." He hesitated for a second then continued. "We're made up of retired and former members of intelligence communities, like MI6 and the CIA."

No wonder she felt as if she'd been whipped around and dropped into an action movie. When he talked about it before, even briefly, she assumed he was waving her off with a touch of embellishment to make his position seem bigger than it was. The typical if-I-told-you-I'd-have-to-kill-you nonsense some guys used to puff up their importance.

On him, the comment worked. "You're serious?"

"We neutralize threats and sometimes break into the apartments of American women working in Paris, then throw them from one rooftop to the other." He sounded serious but ended by winking at her.

Just talking about it spiked her fear of heights. She doubted she'd be able to get even as high as a stepladder ever again. "I still haven't forgiven you for that."

"I caught you, didn't I?"

Since she wanted to look forward and not back, she ignored that. "Did Tasha give you the okay to tell me more about your team?"

"No, but I figured if you really are working with Benton you already know that much."

"Again with that." The air went right out of her and she let go of his hand. "You're exhausting."

"That might also explain why I'm single."

She waited for a new round of questions. He'd lured her into this state of being relaxed, then verbally whacked her. It's what she would do. Get to know her subject, establish a connection of sorts, then ease in. An interrogation had to be next.

Well, if he was going to ask a bunch of questions, so was she. "Who was the man?"

Josiah shook his head as confusion washed over him. "What?"

"In the video."

Without warning, he stood up and walked the small space between the end of the bed and the small table by the wall. "It doesn't matter."

Right before his expression went blank she saw something else. A flash of pain and a brief moment when he closed his eyes, as if to block her words. She'd asked as a way of fitting all the parts together in her head and to slow down the rapid-firing questioning she sensed came next. But his reaction switched her focus off her to him.

Everything inside her shouted and begged for self-preservation, but she went to him. Stopped right behind him. Lifted her hands to touch his back, then let them drop to her sides again before making contact. "I'm pretty sure it does."

The muscles across his shoulders tensed. She saw them bunch under his thin T-shirt.

"My uncle."

She touched him them. Had to. The memory of the horror flashed in her mind and her palms went to his biceps. Out of instinct, she rested her cheek against the space between his shoulder blades. "Josiah, I'm so sorry."

"He wasn't some distant relative. He meant something to me. This game Benton has devised is designed to hurt. My uncle's killing was a message to me and the rest of the team. Benton is coming after each one of us." Josiah touched a hand to hers, then dragged her arm around his waist. "This is personal."

She held on as if letting go would sink her. "I keep thinking I'll wake up and this will be some weird wine-induced dream."

His weight shifted, slight but perceptible, until he leaned into her. "If so, wake me up, too."

"Are you really British?" The question popped into her mind out of nowhere.

He turned around. "After everything that's happened and all the unanswered questions between us, that's the one you want to ask?"

"No." She had a hundred of them but figured that one wouldn't send him spinning. Wouldn't ruin the moment, which he'd proven he was quite capable of doing.

But that made her a hypocrite. She took risks every day at work and convinced others to step into that void with her, all while blocking out what she needed on a personal level. For once she let that side of her win and peeled back the shield she placed around her for protection. She let someone in—Josiah—even if only a little. That choice led her here. She didn't know if that was good or bad, but the sudden need to seize the moment gripped her.

She slid her palms up his torso and across his chest. Let her fingers dance across his collarbone and brush against the dip at the base of his neck.

He shook his head but didn't let go of her. "Sutton."

"I know. You don't trust me. You might even hate me." She dropped her forehead against his chin and balanced it there. "Still, that tape. I don't shake easily and that . . . it made me sick. And sitting here instead of following my instincts and watching over Bane leaves me with this desperation inside that keeps trying to claw its way out."

Those strong arms wrapped around her. Loosely at first, then a palm slipped to her lower back and pulled her in close. "Hey, it's going to be fine."

"You keep saying it and it's not believable."

His fingers slipped under her chin and he raised her head. That gaze searched hers before landing on her mouth. "Believe this."

They met in the middle. He leaned, then she did. Warm lips brushed over hers, light at first. Back and forth, barely touching, almost like flirting. The fluttering inside her went wild and her brain filled with images of him naked with a hand slapped against the wall as he pushed inside her.

Fantasy mixed with reality until he kissed her, really kissed her. Hot and deep, full of wanting and need. His hands traveled over her back and down to her ass. Those long legs shifted and he brought her to stand between them. Pressed his body hard against hers as a groan rumbled in his chest.

The kiss went on. His mouth crossed over hers. The heat simmered until she wanted to strip off his T-shirt. Throw off hers. Right as her fingers slipped down to his belt, he backed up.

His forehead rested against hers as he held her hands away from his body. "Yeah, that can't happen."

Disappointment slammed into her as her body switched from hot to cool at a rapid pace. She offered everything and he . . . Maybe she would never understand men. But she was starting to get how this one operated. "Because you still think I might be working with Benton?"

He lifted her hand and kissed the back. "Because you are a temptation I can't afford."

Her heart did a little flip. "What if I want you to give in?"

"Then I fear I'm doomed to disappoint you." He glanced at the bed, then back at her with regret shining in his eyes. "Get some rest."

And then he was gone.

12

BENTON WATCHED the video a second time. Leaned in close to the screen and followed each darkened figure in the grainy feed. He knew from experience the best way to learn about his target was to follow every movement and analyze every choice. He had to anticipate every strategy, and the more he saw the easier that became.

Josiah and Mike did not disappoint. Sutton turned out to be more resourceful than expected. Benton did not appreciate that surprise. The last thing he needed was for her to break out and go off on some tangent. Once he figured out who she was and that she'd had the nerve to follow him and somehow managed to stumble across him when no one else had put those pieces together, he'd added her to his plot to destroy the Alliance.

She would pay for the company she kept. For her continued nosiness and failure to appreciate he could have killed her at any time during the seven years.

Once he'd settled that in his mind, her job was to change the dynamic but within expected parameters. Mainly to throw Josiah off, make his attention wander so that his eventual fall would be that much harder. Benton sensed the waver in Josiah's concentration. It looked as if he didn't know what to make of Sutton. Benton needed Josiah's feelings to trump his thirst for revenge. That would make the blow so much sweeter.

But all of that depended on Sutton being who Benton thought she would be. Focused on her revenge, out of her league, rushing to catch up. Led by emotion in a way that would trip up every step. So far, no. She gave herself away by sneaking into his office and assuming he hadn't prepared for that sort of possibility. He needed her to continue to be that sloppy.

Frederick entered the second-story office of the villa with a file in his hand and without fanfare, per usual. Instead of looking around the office or engaging in insipid conversation, he walked in a direct line to the massive L-shaped desk.

He placed it on the corner. "I obtained all the reports and interviews on the incident at Iselwood."

Of course he did. That was his job. Benton paid top dollar for Frederick's loyalty. Anything less than perfection would not be tolerated.

Benton glanced at the file but didn't bother to open it. He preferred oral accounts. Leaning back in his chair, he enjoyed the warmth of the sun streaming in his window and the heat bouncing off the tiles. "What is the official story?"

"Last night was a training and emergency exercise. The official word is school officials worried the children were getting too complacent and came up with a new drill." Frederick sounded as if he had the report memorized and was reading from it.

"An interesting choice, though it's likely easier than explaining the extreme security violation to the parents." Benton gazed at the video monitor again. "Though I'm sure the dead bodies scattered all over the property provided some difficulty."

"They dumped their kids in a school and rarely fly them home. I'm not convinced these people care all that much about their offspring and what's happening at their school."

A touchy subject for Frederick. Benton knew his background. About his father and the demanding training schedule he used on his children to make them tougher. The skills benefited Benton. So did the rage simmering just below Frederick's surface.

"You don't understand how the very rich and powerful operate." Benton did. He'd studied them for years. Learned their secrets and their weaknesses. Took advantage of every greedy, self-serving move they made.

"I guess not."

"Children are toys. One more piece of property to haul out and impress the business associates. They don't become valuable until they're old enough to be bargained away in marriage or become prodigies who can create more wealth."

Frederick clenched his teeth together then nodded. "The school insists no one was hurt and all the children are fine."

"Well, we know that's untrue." Benton rested his useless hand on the armrest. Too long without any support and his shoulder ached. The pain made him want to set Josiah on fire but he'd burn the emotions out of him first. "How many bodies do we have?"

"Four. I've taken care of the disposal arrangements but we have the problem of the boy."

The comment brought Benton's attention back to the problem at hand and off the planned revenge. "What problem?"

"The Alliance removed him before we could—"

"Enough." The kid didn't matter. Benton had no qualms about using children and that's all this was. A means to an end. "His acquisition would have been an interesting benefit. Watching Gabe squirm and beg for his son's life may have been worth something, but the school threat was never really about Daniel Hiroshi."

Confusion spread across Frederick's face. "I don't understand."

"I want someone closer to the group. Someone they're truly invested in." A relative here. A boyfriend there. That was about toying with them. Whipping them into a panic and nothing more. He had bigger plans. One that hit the Alliance on a more fundamental level.

"Okay."

But Frederick still didn't get it. For some reason that amused Benton. "Getting close to the group was the issue. Now we have."

"So, you're not disappointed about the boy?" Frederick hesitated between each word.

"I am not thrilled with our men being killed. I'd prefer the losses to be on the Alliance's side, not ours." And the idea of seeing Mike in a body bag moved up on his list. "But I got what I needed."

Frederick's gaze flicked to the monitor and the video feed running on an endless loop. "You have them on tape."

He still didn't get it. That annoyed Benton because it amounted to a waste of his time. "The car, the direction of their escape. The surveillance photos showing their movements. I now possess all of it."

"You mean they didn't lose the tail this time? You know where they went, unlike after the airport?"

Only because he had found a solution to the human failing issue. Even Benton admired his own brilliance on that score. "It's much harder to lose a drone flying above you that you don't even know is there."

Frederick's eyes widened. "You have control of a drone?"

"I can control most things." People would be wise to start learning that fact.

"Okay." Frederick still sounded stunned. "Now what?"

The next phase of the plan. The one where the Alliance realized he could get to them at any time. Sneak in while they watched and steal what they cared about.

That meant it was time for another bomb.

Benton thought about the step to come and smiled. "We grab a woman. Only this time we don't need a group of men to accomplish the task."

"How many then?"

"Just one." Benton smiled. "You'll do fine."

Josiah looked at the stairwell door for the tenth time in five minutes. He made it through the night without wandering up there and opening the door and checking on Sutton while she slept. But he'd been tempted.

That kiss. Holy fuck. Eyes opened or closed he could call up the taste of her and how right she felt under his hands. He'd overstepped, put the operation on hold and forgotten his line of questions so he could take something for himself. Now he had to figure out how to pull back.

Harlan cleared his throat, managing to sound both haughty and disappointed at the same time. "Are you listening to me?"

"Not really." Josiah looked at the row on monitors on Ellery's desk and her empty chair. They slept in shifts and Lucas had been up all night on watch and intel-collecting duty with Tasha. It was Ellery's turn to man the comm. Part of him wondered if she'd slipped in to say good morning to Lucas. God knew those two seemed inevitable as a couple.

Harlan moved in front of Josiah, blocking his view of the screens. "We have everyone's closest connections under watch but we still need Mike's contacts."

The conversation Josiah dreaded had arrived. They had all turned in a list of people to be protected until the Benton mess ended. Mike's included exactly one name. "You tell him."

"Josiah."

"Right. His raging case of denial." They knew Mike had been hiding and evading. Josiah had known almost from the beginning and told Tasha and a few others after Jake Pearce sat in a jail in Islamabad and hinted at knowing Mike's dark secrets.

"It's time and now he has no choice." Harlan folded his arms across his chest. "There will be repercussions due to his failure to disclose and we'll have to investigate his ability to beat the polygraph, but—"

"Anyone with a little bit of training can do that." Josiah learned those tricks long before he threw in with the Alliance.

He and Ford Decker, the head of Bravo team, ran the men through exercises to ensure every one of them could beat the machine, could withstand torture for long periods of time, and could kill on command. The work wasn't pretty but it was necessary. Not that they'd shared the particulars of those extracurricular with management, but then he and Ford weren't exactly rules followers.

"It's probably best that you keep that theory to yourself," Harlan said. "I'd hate to have people around here view you as a security risk."

The guy had a habit of threatening while acting as if he were being helpful. That trait of Harlan's annoyed the piss out of Josiah. "You can be a dick."

"And yet you answer to me."

Josiah wasn't really in the mood for a chain of command lecture or a personal talk with Mike, but he'd do the latter. "I'll handle it."

"Good. Do that and then we can figure out how to

crack Sutton." Harlan wore a satisfied look as he stood up again and walked over to the conference room table. Without breaking his perfect posture, he studied the intel that came in overnight.

Josiah knew he should join him but the upstairs kept calling to him. He turned to go up when Ellery rushed into the room. She knocked into him on the way to her desk and mumbled something. She kept patting her hand over the stacks of paper and tablets, as if searching for something.

He'd never seen her flustered or out of control. She'd slipped into both. "What are you doing?" he asked.

She spun around. Her gaze bounced between him and Harlan. "We have a missing tablet."

Harlan froze. "Excuse me?"

That didn't make any sense. Josiah didn't throw around words like "impossible" on this job, but losing a vital piece of information in a locked facility came close to impossible. "What's on the tablet?"

"Most of my files. The tracking we've collected on Benton."

That didn't sound catastrophic. The benefit of a tablet was being able to pass it around. They'd all taken a look at the collected data, added what they could in the way of analysis. "Lucas was on watch duty last night."

"I just woke him up and he doesn't have it. I'm sure it was here earlier." She crouched down, checking under the table through the mass of cables. "He's on the way down to help me look. I'm going to check the video feed from the room since I left it."

There was no way . . . Josiah's gaze jerked back to that upstairs door. He knew in that second exactly where the vital information had gone. "Motherfucker."

Ellery frowned. "What is it?"

"Sutton," he answered as he took off at a run.

Taking two steps at a time, he made it to the second floor in record time. He didn't stop when he hit the landing and arrived at her closed door. One hand on the knob and he shoved it open with enough force to make it bounce against the inside wall. He caught it before it knocked into her. Then he slammed it shut behind him.

He didn't need to ask about the tablet because it was right there, in plain sight on the mattress in front of her. Rage poured through him. Every cell filled with his need to shake her. To pick up the tablet and whip it against the wall.

"You should have locked the door." His voice trembled with anger as he spoke and he didn't do anything to rein it back in.

"What are you—"

"This." In one step he was beside the bed. Grabbing it by the edge, he shook it in the air, right in front of her face.

She drew back, pushing her body closer to the wall. "I can explain."

"Oh, you will. While strapped to a chair during an interrogation." He couldn't control the heat rolling through him or the stabbing pain in his gut. Fury like he'd never known thumped inside him in time with his heartbeat.

She'd lied from the beginning and he'd fucking bought it. Sure, he put up a token fight, but he kissed her. Hell, he still wanted to kiss her.

Sutton stared at him with haunted eyes. "You are blowing this out of proportion."

The act could be guilt or part of her plan. He couldn't tell anymore. "And you are going to regret this."

He walked out then. Had to for fear he'd lose it. Even now as his footsteps pounded on the stairs he wanted to go back up and let her tell him her excuse. Maybe Benton threatened her family or someone she cared about. Josiah could understand that. Could fix that.

He stopped on the bottom step and stared at the door that led out to the main floor. Instead of going through he leaned against the wall. The door almost slammed into his side when it opened without warning a second later. He jumped back as Mike slid to a halt in front of him.

Mike let the door swing shut again. "You okay?"

"What?" The question hit Josiah wrong. He'd expected something else, not concern. Friend or not, he hated that anyone felt sorry for him. "Yeah, I got the tablet."

Mike looked down at his feet and swore. "I was hoping you were wrong. Fuck, I bought her act and hear she was waiting for a chance to slip that out and take a look."

He didn't need to explain. Josiah got what he was saying. "When she looks at you . . ." The eyes, that sad expression. "She's believable."

"But you didn't get sucked in."

Josiah ignored the hint of sarcasm in Mike's voice and tried to answer. "I've been careful."

"Come on." Mike slapped a palm against the closed door. "You can't be that deluded."

Somewhere along the line he'd lost control of his team. Gabe and Parker were scattered, protecting others. Mike tested him at every turn. Sutton lied and he bought it. Hell, maybe he shouldn't be in charge.

"We work together. We know each other. We hang out together. Fight together." Mike wasn't one for emotional outpourings, but delivered one now. "The one thing you're not is neutral. Not when it comes to her."

"No, not neutral. I'm pissed." And in that moment it wasn't a lie. Her newest betrayal wiped out the memories of the kiss. If he'd given in and taken her to bed she probably would have tried to kill him. Tried and failed.

"You were in her room for a long time last night."

The comment snapped Josiah's attention back to Mike. "You're fucking checking up on me?"

Mike shrugged. "Tasha's orders."

Of course. That's what that little talk was about yesterday. She assessed his mood and made a plan. He admired her no-nonsense way of keeping them all on task and safe, but he hated the invasion of privacy. "Goddamn her."

"She's worried and, frankly, it looks like she wasn't exactly wrong to be."

"Nothing happened." But almost. He'd been so close to the line. Thought all morning that tonight he might cross it. He made a bet with himself that if Sutton had shown any interest in him staying with her tonight, he would. "We're done talking about my personal life."

"You sure?" Amusement moved into Mike's tone. "It's kind of fun watching you get all twitchy."

Josiah knew with blinding clarity that now was the time to step up and act like the team leader. "Let's talk about yours."

Mike dropped his hand from the door and stood up, all traces of humor gone. "There's nothing to say."

"Everyone else provided a list of people potentially in harm's way thanks to Benton's newest round of bullshit."

Mike's face went blank. Nothing about his body language or expression gave away what was happening in his head. "You have my dad."

"That's not the guy I'm talking about." When Mike just continued to stare, Josiah gave in and pulled it out of him. "Jesus, Mike. How about you drop the act and admit you're gay?"

"I've never denied it." But his expression slipped, just for a second. His eyes widened a fraction, then he went back to blank. Even widened his stance and folded his hands together in front of him in some sort of odd battle pose.

"That's not really true." He'd never disclosed it, which was close to the same thing and Josiah knew it. He was pretty sure Mike did, too.

"How is my love life relevant to anything?"

Besides the obvious, that a secret could be used

by hostiles to break Mike, there was the hiding issue. Josiah had reached his end with people keeping things from him. "When you're not on assignment, you're living with a guy. A guy who has not undergone a proper security check."

Josiah had seen the photos in the file Mike didn't know he kept and read about the guy's background. He was out. Mike didn't pretend to date women or stay cloistered in his house. He and this guy named Drew lived a life together. Undercover on Mike's part and careful, but anyone analyzing Mike's movements and savvy enough to find his residence—which should be no one, but Benton had skills—would realize they were a couple. Yet Mike never advised anyone in the Alliance.

"I vetted him." Mike leaned against the door. "He's not a threat."

"But you're still a threat to him. You think I wanted my family drama dragged out for the team to dissect? Sometimes you don't get a choice." Some of Mike's stoic look faltered and Josiah knew he understood the seriousness of this topic. Point made. Time to move on. "What does he think you do?"

"Personal security. It explains all the time away and being on call."

"Where is he now?"

"Home. I've been checking in."

Not good enough, and from the tension tugging on the corners of Mike's mouth, Josiah guessed Mike had been quietly wading through a river of worry. "We need to get him somewhere safe." Josiah dropped the piece of information that concerned him the most. "Because, and I can't stress this enough, Benton knows about Drew."

"No fucking way." Mike kept shaking his head. "I've been careful."

Josiah refused to argue about this because he knew he was right. "Every second you deny and evade and whatever the hell else this is, the bigger danger you're putting this guy in." Despite his frustration with Mike's secrecy, Josiah felt bad for the guy. None of this could be easy. "I'm assuming he means something to you."

Mike nodded. "Everything."

Well, shit. "Then his name goes on the list."

"Fine."

Josiah went to leave but stopped before he opened the door. "You know, I don't give a shit about who you love or fuck or whatever, but the fact you tried to hide this pisses me off. You put me in a position of knowing and tracking you."

"I know there are rules about disclosing close contacts and I skirted them."

That's not what he meant at all. "Screw the rules."

Mike winced. "How long have you known?"

"From the beginning. The entire administrative staff knows."

Shaking his head, Mike started walking around the small space. Talking to himself. "That's fucking great."

Josiah didn't want to make it worse, but it was too late to hold back now. "Ellery runs checks all the time. As Delta leader I have to run checks. I don't like it, but I do it."

"You didn't say anything."

"I figured one day you'd trust me enough to tell me."
Josiah hated that the day never came and he'd been the
one to push the issue. It took an emergency to get Mike
to open up, as he should have done long before now.

"It's not really about that."

"Mike, come on."

"Trust doesn't come easy." Mike opened his mouth
and closed it. It looked as if he was searching for the
right words. "With my past . . . it's taken a while to
fit in with the team. But I do, and I do trust you." He
smiled. "Not to be an ass but you're not exactly great
at it either."

No way was he going to be thrown off or sucked into
this conversation. Josiah had played enough games for
one day. "I'm not the one hiding my feelings."

Mike glanced up the steps. "Go tell that to the
woman you have locked upstairs."

Something froze inside Josiah. He didn't like the
parallel. Didn't really like the team talking about his
personal life . . . Okay, yeah, maybe he could understand Mike holding back on that score. Still didn't
mean he liked the conversation one damn bit. "That's
different."

Mike opened the door. "You keep telling yourself
that."

13

Sutton seriously considered kicking Josiah in the balls. A half hour after accusing her of whatever he accused her of this time he stopped at the end of her bed, still fuming. All that confidence and ego slamming into her as he put his fists on his hips and stared her down.

She was done. With the name calling and the threats, the back-and-forth with his feelings, and the kissing. Yeah, that last one was *so* done. And here she thought . . . It didn't matter. Fantasies about touching him, being with him, died a vicious death.

His newest round of fury strangled that right out of her.

"I'm giving you a chance to come clean." The words said in quick staccato beats came out like a demand.

She was done with that, too. "Go to hell."

She folded her legs in front of her, crossing one over the other, and stared at the gray blanket underneath her. The stitches blurred together as she sat there. Tiny rows with little holes. She poked her finger through one as she counted down the seconds until he stormed out again. The guy deserved a medal for the most dramatic storming around in a minute.

The mattress dipped as he leaned in and placed a palm against the bed. "You don't get to be angry, Sutton. You're the one stealing computers."

According to him she had all sorts of criminal skills. Pretty soon he'd convince himself she could build a gun out of bed parts and haul that away, too. Make her sleep on the floor. "That's not what happened."

"Did you get a message out to Benton?"

She'd always hated Bane. Didn't matter what name he used. He'd masterminded her mother's murder. Sutton would bet on that. But now she despised him for something else. He'd taken her life and spun it around. Turned it inside out. She had no idea how she was ever going to get back to the States and her old job.

"Sutton!"

She winced as his yell bounced off the walls in the confined cell of a room. "I have no idea where he is."

"Sure." Josiah practically spit the word out as he stood back up.

She unfolded her legs and slid to the end of the bed. "Maybe instead of accusing me, you could ask me."

"Ask what? Give me the question that will get you to start telling the truth."

She was about to tell him where he could stick his question when the door opened. This time he hadn't locked it and in walked Harlan.

He pointed at Josiah. "I need to see you."

Josiah didn't even spare his superior a glance. "Not now."

"I'm not asking. I'm telling." The anger in Harlan's tone matched Josiah's.

She was starting to like this Harlan guy. She peeked around Josiah at him. "You're a pilot."

Harlan's eyes narrowed a fraction but his proper British accent never faltered. "We all can fly, but yes."

"Of course. Heaven forbid there be something you guys can't do." For some reason their excessive expertise at everything pissed her off right now. With all those skills at least one of them should involve listening. Or at the very least being able to reason out that she was telling the truth.

Harlan cleared his throat. "Did you have a question?"

"Fly me out of here."

Josiah exhaled, long and loud, as if to signal how little he thought of her comment. "That's never going to happen now that you've been caught."

"I looked at a laptop. I'm a PI and the information is right there. Was I supposed to stop investigating when you guys have only told me pieces of the story?" Never mind that she'd treated them the same way. She'd gone down to talk with Ellery and saw it there. Snuck it off the edge of the desk while she handled a call.

Sutton knew she should have waited. Maybe asked to see what they had on Benton so they could compare notes. Work the whole scene that way. If the constant churning in her gut had died down, if she could have shaken off the sense that Benton or Bane or whoever he was had something bigger planned. Something headed right their way.

She chalked this up to one time when her PI skills

overtook her common sense. But Josiah's reaction had been so over the top. So soul crushing. He refused to listen for even a second and that made her want to punch him.

"You were giving away our position. Contacting Benton," he said.

"Neither of those things happened." He'd shown her a video of this Benton blowing up a human being and still he thought . . . God, he must really think she was a piece of human garbage.

"That's what I wanted to tell you." Harlan's deep voice boomed through the room. "She's right."

Josiah stopped glaring at her and turned the harsh look on Harlan. "What?"

"She wasn't searching for Benton or even looking at the work files on the tablet." Harlan looked like he was trying to hide a smile.

Sutton suspected she knew why. What started out as intel gathering had taken a sharp left turn once she held the tablet. Her search hadn't been about work or being kidnapped or Benton or anything she wanted to talk about.

"Who was she searching?" Josiah asked.

Harlan glanced at her then back to Josiah. "We should go downstairs and talk about that."

"Fine." Josiah motioned to her. "Get up."

"No." She did not want a front seat to this humiliation. Not after the stunt he pulled. Her radar had been off. Whatever she felt for him, the attraction, would go away. She'd make it go away.

"I will throw you over my shoulder and carry you downstairs. Is that what you want?"

She was convinced the whole forgetting-about-him thing would not be too hard so long as he kept talking. He could kill a moment faster than any man she'd ever met.

Her interest in him only sprang up from her adrenaline high anyway. That had to be the right answer. "You're an asshole."

"Not the first time he's heard that," Harlan said.

"Let's go." This time Josiah took a step toward her.

She jumped up. Having Harlan talk about the real target of her searching sucked. Being carried downstairs struck her as even worse.

They walked the steps in silence. Josiah didn't touch her, which was a good choice on his part. They entered the main work area and everyone turned. Tasha hadn't turned up, but Ellery, Lucas, and Mike all stood over the tablet. Sutton knew then the next few minutes were going to veer into annoying territory.

Josiah didn't say anything until he stood on the opposite side of the conference table from the others. "Ellery, you have something for me?"

"Yes."

Josiah's eyes bulged. "Well, who was she searching?"

The moment of truth had arrived. Sutton looked at Mike's grin and then to Lucas. There was no use delaying the inevitable. They all knew. All but Josiah. She decided to speed this up. "Just tell him."

Ellery's eyebrow lifted as she stared at him. "You, Josiah."

"Maybe she's right." Harlan walked by but hesitated next to Josiah for a second. "You are an asshole."

"I don't get it. What about me?" Confusion still clouded Josiah's face. He looked around at his teammates with a frown growing deeper each second. Then he glared at her. "What, my uncle wasn't enough? Who are you going after now?"

Sutton didn't even try to call up a well of patience. She really was done. "You can't be this stupid."

Mike nodded. "Sure he can."

Ellery spun the laptop around. The split screen showed the last site she visited. The other side was a series of lines of what looked like computer code. Sutton could only guess Ellery ran some sort of diagnostics on the tablet. Sutton had never been more grateful for people with the skills in her life since the talents might save her from whatever awful interrogation Josiah wanted to subject her to.

"It looks like a general search to learn more about you." Ellery clicked on keys and different sites flicked by.

"I should have stayed upstairs," Sutton mumbled.

Ellery shot her a sympathetic smile. "Which is something a woman who's interested in you might do."

"That's not . . ." Josiah looked around, looked at everyone except Sutton. "We don't know that she—"

"This is getting embarrassing." Mike looked at Sutton. "Him, not you."

Sutton didn't quite agree with that. "For both of us, actually."

"Ellery, explain it to him. Use simple sentences since he seems to be lagging behind," Harlan suggested.

She nodded and started talking. "Nothing was compromised. She didn't stray. Didn't play with the settings or try to figure out where she is."

Lucas put his hands on the back of a chair and leaned in. "It looks innocent, man."

Josiah stumbled over his words before he finally spit out a coherent sentence. "Why steal the tablet then?"

"I didn't steal anything. I thought I was free to move around." That wasn't quite true, but Sutton felt the need to say it.

"Do you know anything about women?" Ellery asked.

Josiah swore under his breath. "Apparently not."

"You think she wanted to announce to all of us that she's interested in you?" Mike snorted. "I'd hide that."

"Shut the fuck up." Josiah stood there not moving. Barely looked like he was breathing. "Everyone."

Well, that was exactly the sucky few minutes Sutton had expected. She'd stayed quiet through most of it because, well, talking didn't seem to help when it came to dealing with Josiah. And because the others seemed to be fighting the fight for her. Not a sensation she was accustomed to, but she didn't hate having the support.

She did hate the smile on Mike's face. Too much of that would piss her off. "For the record, I am not interested in doing anything other than shooting Josiah."

Ellery nodded. "I can understand that."

Harlan pulled out a chair and sat down. "We're moving her back to the farmhouse tomorrow."

"Why?" That wasn't close to what she wanted. There she'd be isolated. At least here she could wander around on two floors, watch the monitors, and talk with a few people.

Josiah's scowl suggested he didn't like the relocation idea either. "No one told me."

"You were too busy running around about the tablet and for the last few minutes making an ass of yourself," Harlan said without missing a beat. "My point is someone needs to go with Mike and protect her. Right now I'm thinking it should be me."

Josiah butted before Harlan finished his sentence. "She doesn't go anywhere without me."

The room went still. Ellery peeked at him over the back of the laptop. Even Mike froze in place. Looked pretty entertained as well.

Lucas was the first to talk. "I wonder how she'll feel about that."

Sutton started to answer but Josiah held up a hand to stop her. "She doesn't get a say."

The man deserved that kick she'd been aching to give him. "You're right. You don't know anything about women."

A few hours later Josiah grew tired of the staring. He sat next to Ellery and studied the footage from the school and the pieces they had from other jobs tied to Benton.

He looked for anything that could aid the operation or point to Benton's newest hiding place.

Every time he looked up one of them was staring at him. Usually Ellery, sometimes Mike. Harlan even walked in twice and grunted at him. The only blessing was that Tasha had been locked in a secure room talking with other intelligence officials about the bombing and how to stop the next one.

The upstairs remained quiet. He'd sent Lucas up there twice to make sure Sutton hadn't somehow gotten out. Not that she could. But she'd refused to stay down here. Refused to answers questions about her investigation. Begged off when Harlan started digging and going over old ground again. Normally they would have pushed but Josiah decided to give her a few minutes of space. But not many. Too much time and she'd hone her anger at him into a finely pointed weapon.

Fuck that.

Josiah stood up. They all openly watched him now, so he didn't try to slip out. They wanted an announcement, fine. "I'm going upstairs."

Lucas nodded before returning to the pile of papers spread out in front of him. "About time."

"You're a bit slow but it's good to see you finally moving," Mike said.

That was about the reception Josiah expected. "Thanks for the support."

Truth was he didn't exactly relish this confrontation. He'd accused her and she'd been looking into him. Really, looking at the news about the bombing, then tracing that back to his family. If she were Benton's close associate she'd know all the information already. Maybe Ellery was right and the search was about Sutton checking on the guy she kissed. Sounded like something a smart woman would do.

He couldn't figure out how to kick his own ass, so he walked the steps and got to the door. This time he knocked. She didn't say anything until he opened the door.

"Get out." She never lifted her head or took her attention from the file in her hands.

He took a second to study her. She sat on the bed with her back balanced against the pillow and far wall. She wore dark jeans that hugged her curves. With her knees up and her bare feet flat on the bed, she looked relaxed. He sensed that was an illusion.

Ignoring her command, he came into the room and closed the door behind him. Kept going until he stood at the end of her bed. "You don't get a say."

"I will scream every time you come in here." She lowered the file to rest on her knees. The one Ellery made for her, outlining some of missions they could trace back to Benton. "How about that?"

"Mature."

"You should talk." She snorted and performed the perfect eye roll at the same time. "It's like being with the ten-year-old boy on the playground who pulls your hair to get attention."

"I have no idea what that means." But he was pretty sure it wasn't a compliment.

"Of course you don't." She stretched out her legs. "Do not even think about sitting down."

After that he had no choice but to try. He gently shifted her feet, keeping a handle on her ankles, as he sat down. "We need to—"

She pulled her legs in and tucked them underneath her. "I want to talk with Tasha."

"Why?"

"Or that Harlan guy."

This was going even worse than Josiah feared. "About what?"

"I will answer questions about my investigation. To them, not you." She stared at him without blinking. "In case you're not clear, I'm done with you."

The flatness of her voice tore at him. He rubbed a hand over his face. "Okay . . . fuck."

He had no idea what to say. His thoughts jumbled in his head. He wanted to trust her but felt better not doing so. He wanted to kiss her but knew he'd regret it. She had him spinning in circles and losing control. He despised the sensation.

"I get that you hate that we kissed." She picked up the file and dropped it on the floor.

Talk about misreading the situation. He tried to stare some sense into her. "Wrong."

"It won't happen again, but—"

"It sure as hell will." He grabbed on to her ankle and pulled her down the bed.

The move flopped her onto her back as she slid across the comforter. When he had her where he wanted her, he let go. Looming over her, he balanced his weight on his elbow. Then he kissed her, going in slow, giving her time to push him away. He expected the rejection but it never came. When his mouth hovered over hers, she held on to his shoulders and tugged him in closer.

This kiss exploded like the first. Rocked through him, leaving him ready for more. His hand slipped up and under her shirt. His palm rested on her flat stomach as his heartbeat shot into danger territory. He could feel her fingers clench and unclench against his shirt. He ached to rip it off and savor the friction of skin against skin.

Forget the people downstairs and every stupid misstep. Ignore the lingering doubts and concerns about his loyalties. He wanted her with a white-hot need that left him feeling ripped apart and raw.

He deepened the kiss, sliding his tongue over hers. The touch sent a shot of electricity spinning around them. The tension filling the room had nothing to do with fighting. It wove around them as their hands traveled and their lips roamed.

Desperate to taste her, he slid his mouth down her neck, breathing in her scent and licking her soft skin. Every part of her came alive under his hands and tongue. His erection pushed against the front of his jeans and his common sense evaporated. He wanted her with every ounce of strength inside him.

A soft sound filled the room. She sighed as her hand slipped through his hair. She lifted his head, slightly but enough for him to see into her eyes. "Are you familiar with the concept of mixed messages?"

The spell snapped but he couldn't get angry. It would take a while for his body to cool down, but he got it. His timing, as usual with her, sucked.

He dropped his head to her shoulder and placed a row of tiny kisses there. "I've been told I can be an asshole."

"Understatement." Tough talk, but the way her lips skimmed over his forehead said her anger had disappeared, or at least decreased enough for him not to get punched.

He lifted up on his elbow again and stared down at her. His fingertips brushed over her cheek and across her forehead. Just touching her soothed some of the frustration boiling inside him from this assignment. "I guess I deserve that."

"I like kissing you and want more, but I was serious. I am done."

They sure as hell didn't feel done. "You said that already."

One hand fiddled with the buttons on his shirt. The other wandered over his face to the back of his neck. "I thought repetition might help."

All of that touching made him crave more. He slid his thigh between hers. Didn't try to hide his erection or his need for her. "You or me?"

"Both."

He didn't want to ask, but . . . "Okay, done with what exactly?"

"The suspicions." She lifted her head and moved up higher on the pillows until their faces were on the same level. "If you accuse me again, we really are done. No kissing. No anything."

The words, strong and bold, cut through him. "I have a job to do."

But that's not the part he'd miss, and that's what scared the crap out of him. The idea of not following through with this and seeing where this charged attraction could go hit him like a punch.

She nodded and her hair spread across the pillow. "So do I."

"But you won't say exactly what. You dance around the facts. That needs to end. The work I do can be harsh and, frankly, pretty shitty sometimes." He couldn't deny it and didn't want her to think he'd turn into some smooth-talking Prince Charming. Those days were long behind him. He could turn it on for a job, but he didn't want to fake it with her.

"And dangerous."

"Always but that doesn't bother me." That came with the work and he accepted it from day one. "But it doesn't stop the fact I want to strip these clothes off you, wrap your legs around my waist, and fuck you until neither of us can speak."

She treated him to a sexy anytime smile. "That's subtle."

"I'm not subtle and I'm not all that nice."

She brushed her fingertips over his bottom lip. "You can be."

Something about her caught his blood on fire. He looked down at her and saw a beautiful, intelligent, determined woman who didn't cower at the sight of his gun or shout of his anger. She deserved better, but he couldn't let her go. "My duty is to this team."

"And if I get in the way I'm expendable?" When he didn't answer she frowned. "Then I guess I know where we stand."

"I wish it were that simple, but I can't keep you out of my head." Nothing about his feelings for her, his attraction to her, what he wanted to do with her, was simple. Anything but.

"You make things hard." She took his hand and put it on her chest, right between her breasts, and slid her fingers through his.

His brain misfired. "Probably."

"Here." She turned on her side and when she did, she took him with her. His front pressed against her back and his face nuzzled her hair.

"What are we doing?" Other than slowly torturing him, he wasn't sure.

She wrapped his arm tighter around her waist and held him there. "Resting."

She had to be kidding. She had to feel his erection and what she did to him.

"I doubt I'll be able to sleep much in this position." He was already sweating. Thinking about something awful would come next if he had any shot at chivalry here.

"I'm still ticked off at you," she mumbled into the pillow.

"Oh." That admission tamped down on some of his

excitement. "Will lying like this make it better?" He couldn't quite bring himself to say "cuddling" but he hoped she understood his point.

"Yes." She scooted back until nothing separated their bodies but a few pieces of flimsy clothing.

"Make you willing to open up and talk about why you're in Paris?"

"You can stop acting like I've been hiding information from you for months." She sighed in that way women did when they couldn't believe they had to spell out a point. "We've known each other less than three days and I've trusted you enough to share pieces of my life with you for the last five hours of that time."

"All true."

"But yes. I'll tell you."

He sensed this was a test, and damn it, he would pass it. Even if it killed him. "Then we'll stay here as long as you want."

14

THE BELL would not stop ringing. Sutton shifted and a heavy arm tightened around her. The memories came floating back. The fight . . . the making up. Josiah didn't exactly apologize but she assumed the cuddling was his way of trying.

With a sigh she settled back against him, then it hit her. He was awake and alert. Muscles stretched taut and glancing at his watch.

By the time the bell wound up again Sutton knew something terrible was happening. "I thought we were safe here."

Pulling an arm out from under her head, he shimmied to the end of the bed. Stopped only to glare at her. "Stay here."

Wrong. She was going with the guy with the gun, and he'd better hand one over. She wanted to know what had him snapping into operative mode and be prepared for whatever was about to hit. "What is it?"

He shook his head as he grabbed the knob and slowly opened the door an inch. He squinted as he looked out. "I'm not sure."

He opened the door wider and stepped into the short hallway. He didn't admit they'd somehow landed right back in trouble but she heard it in his curt tone. His mind was somewhere else. Planning and coming up with strategies to solve whatever problems faced them now.

"If you're looking like that I'm not staying up here alone." Despite the moodiness and constant change in position, she trusted him.

"Maybe."

"You don't have a choice this time." She dropped her voice to a whisper because it felt right. The floor had taken on an eerie quiet. None of the sounds of the ground floor seeped through, and that had her insides jumping and twitching.

He stared at her for an extra second before nodding. He looked at a space on the floor. "Shoes."

"Right." She didn't bother to untie the sneakers. Just slipped them on and then jammed her heel inside as she walked.

He held up a finger in front of her face. "You stick right to me and follow everything I say. Got it?"

"Yes." So long as her legs worked, they'd be fine.

As they moved toward the stairwell, then down the steps, she tried to force her mind to focus. They'd only been up there for a few hours. That put the time somewhere late at night. Her stomach picked that moment to growl and remind her she'd skipped dinner.

Despite Josiah's size, his feet didn't make any sound when they fell on the concrete. Those lean muscles flexed beneath his shirt and he took sure steps. She tried to control the anxiety welling inside her. All of her training clicked together in her head. She'd feel better with a gun of her own. Until she had one, she'd depend on her other skills. Kicking, screaming, biting.

At the ground floor door, Josiah repeated the exercise with the door. Whatever he saw must have satisfied him because he threw it open and walked out into the large area.

"What the hell is going on?" he asked.

Sutton glanced around the room. The space buzzed with activity. They were all there, all on alert. Images filled every screen. They kept moving and shifting and passing papers and looking at notes. All but Mike. He stood so close to one of the screens he almost brushed against it.

"Mike?" she called out.

He glanced around with eyes glazed with worry. His gaze fell on Josiah. "It's Drew."

Josiah put his gun back in its holster. "Fuck."

She didn't know who that was or what was happening. Tasha called out a series of clear orders. Every time she stopped talking Sutton would hear a click, then static. She guessed she was seeing an operation in real time. Something to do with Drew, whoever that was.

"Okay." Josiah went up to stand next to Mike. "Who do we have there?"

Mike didn't break eye contact with the screen. "Most of Bravo team."

That explained where this was happening. Likely somewhere in the U.S. Sutton had heard enough and deciphered the information enough to figure out the Alliance was made up of two teams—Bravo and Delta. Josiah ran Delta. A guy named Ford ran Bravo. The men were spread out but Ford stayed back in the U.S. That meant Ford and his men, all except Lucas, were rushing in to help this Drew.

This office had enough going on with the limited personnel on hand. The constant clicking from Ellery's typing on the keyboard played in the background. Lucas wrote notes and Tasha would nod, then relay some new command. The feed stayed dark but Sutton could make out shadows and movements. They all seemed to recognize what was happening. She wanted them to fill her in but dared not ask.

She moved up closer to Ellery's desk. Stood right behind her, hoping to pick up some bit of information.

"The chatter stopped." Tasha made that comment and Lucas winced.

Mike shifted and touched his head, then put a hand on his lower back. He was alive with anxiety. It pounded off him and covered the room like a suffocating blanket.

Sutton didn't see bombs or Benton or anything she recognized from the last horrible video. This scene looked more like the one at the school. Only this time she stayed inside and warm while other people ran around. She feared that meant the gunfire would soon start.

"Is that a house?" She didn't mean to ask the question out loud. No one really listened anyway. They all concentrated on the screens.

Harlan moved in beside her. "Alarms went off at Mike's place."

"Is Drew his brother?"

Harlan stared at Mike's back for a second. "Boyfriend."

Sutton's heart turned over. A new and very personal target. Someone for Benton to hurt while he really attacked Mike. "Oh God."

"Our people are moving in." Harlan dropped his voice low and managed to keep it even despite the steady beat of activity. "It's just a race to see if we can get to him first."

She couldn't make out faces and wouldn't recognize them if she did. "Are the men I'm looking at yours?"

"No." Harlan slipped away again, joining Lucas.

The word just sat there. It poked and jabbed at Sutton.

"What is taking so long for Ford to get in place?" Mike practically yelled the question.

She could hear the pain in his words. Frustration swamped her as she stood there. After a lifetime of staying sharp and walking into danger, or what qualified as danger to her but wouldn't even register to these guys, she felt useless. She watched a figure get close to the side of the house on the video. If the attack had her nerves snapping and the breath dragging in her lungs, she could only imagine how Mike felt. She had no idea how he was surviving this.

"Here we go." Josiah made the comment as he clapped Mike's shoulder. "They'll handle it."

Sutton had no idea what Josiah saw. She heard the conversation back and forth between Tasha and a harsh male whisper over the comm that sounded even more curt than Josiah's. Short bursts of words, some of which didn't make all that much sense. Sutton figured they talked in codes and shortcuts. She just wished she knew what had Josiah sounding a bit more relaxed even though his body stayed stiff.

"We need to—" Tasha's voice cut off when the room went dark and the screens blanked out.

All the fans and electronics cut out for a second, then wound back up again. The lights switched from white to green as the room broke into chaos. All but Mike ran around grabbing weapons and unplugging cords. Dim emergency lighting clicked on as two screens came back on but with scrambled images.

Sutton spun around in a circle, taking it all in. "What's happening?"

"Breach." Josiah called out the word as he stalked back to her.

Before she could say anything else, a fire alarm whirled to life. Loud and booming, it screeched through the building and bounced off every wall. Sutton wanted to cover her ears. She tried to yell over the din. Noise crescendoed around her. Thumps shook the walls as smoke floated through the air.

Josiah tugged on her arm, pulling her away from the screens. "Fire."

The word refused to compute in her head. "What?"

Everyone ran around, shouting directions and grabbing bags. She saw Lucas shoving something into his pockets, then checking the ammunition in his gun.

She felt something in her palm and looked down to see a gun. From there she glanced up into Josiah's eyes and the darkness looming there.

He held her gaze. "You shoot at anyone who comes near you who isn't us."

Before she could answer or say anything, he was off. He rushed up to Mike and started talking to him. Sutton couldn't hear the words over all the crashing. Smoke rolled into the room and climbed up the high walls. She stepped closer to the men, hoping to get them moving.

Mike's voice came into focus. "I'm not leaving."

He fought and pushed as he tried to keep his position in front of the screens. But Harlan pulled one last cord and all the video blinked out.

"What the hell are you doing?" Mike lunged for Harlan but Josiah got in the way.

"We have to leave now." Josiah didn't give his friend a choice. He shoved him in Harlan's direction and he took over.

Heat stung Sutton's skin. She tried to inhale and ended up coughing. Bending over, she hacked until a strong arm banded around her waist and dragged her toward the far door. She looked up, seeing them all scatter. Josiah had her and a hand on Mike. The others used other exits, including two Sutton hadn't even known were there.

Her vision blurred as the smoke grew thicker. She heard crackling and pops. She didn't know what was on fire or which direction to turn. She moved without thinking, following in Josiah's steps and ignoring the bite of his fingers on her arm as he guided her where he wanted her to go.

They ran down gray hallways lined with emergency lights. One turn to the right and an orange glow greeted them. Flames licked up the walls and spilled over the floor like water. The smell of burning electrical clogged her throat. A new fear washed through her. Forget bombs. Benton might have turned the building into one large explosion.

As soon as the worry hit her it floated away. She couldn't hold on to a thought. Her legs grew heavy and her muscles froze. She wanted to shout but her throat closed. Still, she pushed on. She refused to die in a ball of fire. Not like this. Not now.

Just when she thought she couldn't take one more step she saw a door. Josiah stepped in front of her and Mike protected her from the back. Over the broad shoulders she saw hope. That let her block the fear spinning in her belly.

She glanced back and watched the flames dance. The red seemed to rush in on them, getting closer. A wall of heat smacked into her as she stood there. Then it hit her that they'd stopped. Both Josiah and Mike pounded on the door. They shoved it, using their joint weight. Something or someone blocked their path.

As the fire inched closer the panic built inside her.

She tried to inhale and calm her nerves but the hot air burned her lungs. "We have to . . ."

She couldn't think of any other words. She grabbed on to Josiah's back and held on. For some reason that made sense to her.

"Stand back."

She heard his voice and felt her body get passed from him to Mike. Josiah aimed the gun and fired. When that didn't work, he tried again. The bang of the shots mixed with the roar of the fire.

She handed Josiah her weapon. The one he'd given her. With a gun in each hand, he fired again. Something pinged and the wall next to the door splintered. Josiah stepped back and lifted his leg. Slammed his foot right next to the knob and the door bounced open.

They looked and checked and ran through their usual drills. She waited until a piece of the ceiling crashed to the floor behind her to push the issue. Then she bolted past Mike and ran right into Josiah.

Struggling against the crashing around them, he got them outside. The cool night air hit her face. She tried to draw in a huge gulp of fresh air and ended up doubled over and coughing again. When she finally opened her eyes, she spied Josiah's sneakers and realized he stood next to her.

Her brain started to click into action again. She spun around. She hadn't seen where they were but now she did. Some sort of commercial warehouse area filled with boxy buildings hidden behind high fences. Fire engulfed the building right in front of her. The side they had just come from had caved in, and flames multiplied and flared before her eyes.

"Stay alert." Josiah issued the order as he scanned the area.

Mike stood right behind her, close enough to jump on her if commandos appeared. "Someone set it and that someone might still be here."

"Benton tried to catch us on fire." The thought kept playing on a reel in her head. He blew people up, tried to take kids, and now he set them on fire. That level of evil, that kind of disregard for life, stunned her.

"He probably found it poetic after what we did to him," Harlan said.

"We need to find the others." Josiah motioned for her to follow him.

Sutton didn't hesitate. With her mind slowly blinking back to life she could see the destruction around them. Pieces of the building lay in chunks around them, and the smell of gasoline and burning materials lay heavy in the air.

They jogged along the front of the building. Josiah put a hand out and grabbed her right before she turned the corner. He nodded for Mike to go first. He led with his gun, then held up both hands as he exhaled.

"Clear." Mike fully slipped around the side of the building and out of sight after gesturing for them to join him.

Sutton saw Tasha first. She studied something on the ground while Harlan watched the area.

"Not an accident," Tasha said as she got up and

wiped her hands on her black cargo pants. "Someone set us on fire."

"Where are Lucas and Ellery?"

As soon as Josiah asked the question a shiver ran through Sutton. They all stayed calm, but she saw them looking around and starting to move.

"This is the muster spot." Tasha glanced around then shook her head. "They've had time."

"I'll go—"

"No." Tasha shut down whatever Josiah's plan was going to be before he could spell it out. "We all go."

"Because this feels like a trap," Harlan said.

Just when Sutton thought the danger was winding down it ratcheted back up. Somehow her legs carried her as they all rushed to the next corner of the building. About halfway down the side she saw something. She turned to tell Josiah but he was already staring.

He took off running. Harlan stopped and set up, aiming his gun and watching around them. She guessed his job was to make sure Josiah didn't get shot. At least she hoped so. When Josiah got to the lump on the ground he dropped to his knees.

By the time they got there Sutton knew what happened. Lucas lay on his back with his arms stretched out to the side. She could see his gun by his hand and the blood caked on his shirt and pooling on the ground.

Josiah stripped off his shirt and pressed it to the wound near Lucas's shoulder. "Stick with me."

Lucas's eyes closed, then opened again. His chest rose and fell on rapid breaths as his eyes darted around. "You . . . need . . ."

"Come on, buddy. Put all the energy into breathing." Josiah pressed harder as Tasha joined him. She had one hand over Lucas's wound and a phone in the other.

One thought popped into Sutton's head and refused to leave. "Where's Ellery?"

They all started looking around. Mike checked the immediate grounds. Harlan pulled in closer. Sutton didn't know what else to do but stand there.

Lucas grabbed on to Tasha's arm. "He has her."

The words screeched across Sutton's brain. Benton got in there and snatched Ellery. He knew how and when to act and took her out.

"She'll be fine." But Tasha's voice sounded strained and her eyes dulled with sadness. "She's resilient and smart."

"Help . . ." Lucas said in a voice dropping to a whisper. His hand fell off Tasha's arm as he closed his eyes again.

"Don't sleep." Josiah pressed down even harder. "I need you to look at me."

One of Lucas's eyes opened. "Save her."

15

No matter how many times Josiah washed his hands he still saw the blood. The exact moment when Lucas gave in and the life started to drain away played in Josiah's mind. A million little things had kept Lucas alive. The hard pressure on the wound, how healthy he was, the clotting powder Tasha applied. Pure fucking luck.

Ellery needed all of those now. Benton had her and they had no idea where. Harlan set up the equipment they had from an emergency stash Tasha kept, working with Ward back in DC. Together they were checking satellite photos and connecting the pieces. Trying to trace the escape route so that they could track the vehicle.

So many moving parts. Josiah wanted to do something to help but he sat on the armrest of the couch right by Sutton. The woman made him proud. She'd held it together and tried to keep Mike calm as he teetered on the edge of falling apart.

So much waiting. Two hours out from the fire and they sat there waiting for news about Drew. Waiting for news about the rest of the team. Waiting for Lucas to pull through. Waiting to get the intel to rescue Ellery. Josiah was an action guy. The waiting dug at him.

Communication had been intentionally spotty in case Benton was tracing their chatter. Now Tasha had it up and running and stood in the kitchen, pacing back and forth in front of the refrigerator as she talked with whatever contacts she had.

Since he couldn't think of anything smart to say, he didn't try. Maybe Sutton was right. He sucked at comforting. Not his skill at all. Still, he wished he could speed up time or take them back for a redo. Something.

Sutton slipped the back of her hand along the side of his thigh. The soft touch, not demanding, took the edge off the fury building inside him. Instead of ignoring her attempt to reach him, Josiah took her hand. Slid his fingers through hers and held on. Didn't care who saw or what they said. In that moment, he needed to feel the warmth of her skin against his.

Tasha walked out of the kitchen. Fatigue pulled at her mouth and eyes. "I have news."

She sounded as exhausted as she looked. Josiah almost dreaded hearing this. Any other time, he'd want the information so he could process it and act on it. This one time he wanted to hide from it. From the landslide of desperation that could hit.

"Lucas is in surgery." Tasha swallowed as her voice bobbled. "The bullet missed his heart. The doctor is hopeful."

The woman had contacts everywhere from her MI6 days. People she trusted came in and took Lucas away.

Trained medical professionals had him hidden, with armed guards ready to unload if anyone unauthorized came near him. Josiah liked that plan.

Mike stepped away from the fireplace where he'd been leaning and staring into the empty grate. "And?"

"Good news. Ford and West got to Drew in time."

Mike drew in a long breath. He made a noise Josiah couldn't describe right before bending over with his hands on his knees. "Okay."

Mike kept repeating the word as he nodded. Josiah didn't blame him. If Ford had taken over Drew's protection the guy would be safe. It wasn't a surprise they got Drew to safety. Ford and West Brown could take on a trained army if they had to.

Josiah trusted Ford and appreciated the way he ran his team. Kept them ready and on edge. Insisted on extra training but set aside time for them to go out so they could build rapport. And West was a fucking machine. He had handled most of the Pakistan job and was the first to see Benton.

No one said anything until Mike got his emotions back under control. When he stood up straight again, some of the tightness had left his face and relief washed over him. He tended to hide his pain and worry and whatever else he felt behind a blank stare. Not this time.

"What did they tell Drew to get him out?" he asked.

Leave it to Mike to worry about his cover. The guy was rock solid. Josiah loved that about him.

"First, here he is." Tasha typed a few keys on her phone then turned it around for Mike to see. Josiah caught a glimpse of a photo. Looked like a man but that's all he could see. The idea of Tasha using the encryption software and then convincing West or Ford to snap a photo, all to bring Mike some relief, made Josiah smile.

Mike nodded. "Thanks."

"They said you had a job go sideways and you worried he could be in danger and asked them to watch over him." When Mike started to say something, Tasha talked right over him. "They assured Drew that you were fine. Apparently he was pretty upset at the thought of you being in danger."

"Okay." Mike stared at the photo on the phone. Held it for a few seconds, then passed it back to Tasha. "Thanks."

For Mike that was big. Josiah tried to remember if he'd ever heard Mike say that word. He was the guy who pushed forward and never complained. He didn't care what the job was, he was up for it. He joked and gave the other guys a hard time, but they knew they could count on him for anything.

"He accepted that excuse?" Sutton looked stunned by the idea. "Is he in your group or with the CIA of something?"

"He's a college professor." Mike smiled as he said it.

"What?" Sutton's mouth dropped open. "Really?"

Josiah knew all about Drew. It was Josiah's job to know, even though Mike tried to hide the relationship. But the oddly shy look on Mike's face when he talked about Drew and what the guy did for a living made the moment even funnier. So did Sutton's stunned re-action.

"That's kind of unbelievable since your vocabulary consists mostly of profanity," Harlan said.

Mike shrugged. "What can I say? I like 'em hot and smart."

"That's probably enough information on that." Tasha blew out a long breath. "And now we have Ellery."

"Anything?" Harlan asked.

Tasha shook her head but didn't say anything. Josiah got it. Something about giving voice to the concerns about Ellery's safety made it more real. If they could talk in the abstract, deal with her situation as they would with any other person they needed to extract, they could keep the distance and maybe get through this without slamming things.

"I'm assuming Lucas got shot protecting her." Sutton gave Josiah's hand one last squeeze, then let go.

Tasha nodded. "All of the blood at the scene is his, so it doesn't appear she's injured."

"That's a relief." Sutton rubbed her palms up and down her legs.

But they knew better and Mike made it clear they did. "Not really."

"I'd really like to know how this happened." Harlan started walking around the room. Tall and lean with perfect posture, he came off as the desk jockey type when he really could keep up in the field with the rest of them. His aimless wandering ended when he stopped in front of Sutton. "Any thoughts?"

She glanced up and did a double take. "Are you blaming me?"

Harlan dropped down, balancing on the balls of his feet, and stared at her. "You were on the tablet and then a few hours later we were attacked."

There was nothing threatening about the tone or the questions but Josiah had enough. He stood up and pushed Harlan away. "Back off."

They faced off now. Both stood there, locked in a battle of wills. Josiah kept his back to Sutton, putting his body between her and the rest of the room.

Harlan shrugged. "I'm just pointing out a fact."

This could not happen. Turning on each other would make them useless to Ellery. "Well, stop."

"It doesn't work that way and you know it." Harlan shook his head. "It's all too convenient."

Josiah didn't see it. He'd accused Sutton before and still felt conflicted about that, but Harlan's arguments didn't fit. Yeah, Josiah had been skeptical and shot rapid-fire questions at her. He'd also seen her face and the worry for Mike.

Fact was, Josiah had handed her the gun on their way out of the building without hesitation because deep down he knew she wouldn't turn it on him. She'd had every chance. She could have wiped out part of the team numerous times and didn't. Never planted a device or came out shooting. Benton wanted her with them for some reason, but Josiah didn't buy Harlan's reasoning.

"Ellery cleared her," Josiah said, pointing out the

strongest argument. The one not based on a gut feeling and instincts.

"Benton didn't know about that location. He couldn't. Tasha acquired it after Jake Pearce was already dead. Right?" Harlan looked at Tasha for confirmation but she stayed quiet. "This isn't about an inside man feeding Benton information." Harlan hesitated for a second. "Unless he has someone else on the inside."

Sutton stood up and inched her way around the couch, away from Harlan. "I can't believe this."

"Hold up." Mike caught her as she turned the corner. Caught her and put her behind his back and faced down Harlan. "It wasn't her."

"Both of you now?" Harlan exhaled with what sounded like a wealth of frustration.

Josiah appreciated the support. With Mike next to him they formed a protective wall in front of Sutton. Anyone who wanted to go after her would have to come through them. But Josiah didn't want it to go this way. In-fighting would destroy them, and right now they needed to be in top form.

"This, all of this, was a setup," Josiah said as he laid out his theory, the one he'd been mentally working through as they waited. The only one that made sense and answered all the questions once he realized Sutton truly wasn't a spy sent in by Benton. "He used the incident at the school to locate us, then track us. There's no other reason to take the risk at such a high-security facility."

"Unless he wanted to destroy Gabe." Harlan looked to Tasha again. "Isn't that Benton's big plan? To take us all apart."

"Nah, Josiah's right." Mike crossed his arms in front of him. "There were other ways. They could have gone right for the kid or went in like we did. But through the front gates? That's ballsy shit. Kind of stupid and Benton doesn't do stupid."

Relief nearly pummeled Josiah. He didn't realize he was holding his breath until he let it go. Knowing Mike had his back on this made it easier.

"But the kid was not the main priority of that job. Finding us was." All the pieces clicked together in Josiah's brain until he didn't know why he hadn't seen it before. "Then tonight he goes after Ellery and Drew simultaneously. Our focus was split with Drew."

"A decoy." They were the first words Tasha had spoken. She stood there, taking it all in as she always did. She listened and assessed.

Josiah wanted to sell it to her because he knew he was right and because he needed her support. He'd go around her if necessary but he'd hate it and be at a disadvantage. He needed her help. "Exactly. The plan was simple but brilliant. Have our people scrambling. Take out Lucas and put Mike on edge."

Tasha nodded. "And I had to give the scatter code."

"What does that mean?" Sutton asked.

Sensing the worst of the fight had passed, Josiah moved to the side and brought her up beside him. "We keep team members away from each other to prevent the sort of thing that happened tonight where we potentially all go down at once."

"Now I have to keep the team and assets in the U.S. We can't get Alliance reinforcements here quickly, so we're vulnerable. Or as vulnerable as these guys can be," Tasha said in a voice growing angrier with each word. "If he wanted to separate us and take care of us first, this is the right way to go. Pretty smart on Benton's part. With Pearce gone he had a problem and he fixed it."

Harlan stepped back as some of the stiffness left his shoulders, leaving only the usual amount of stiffness. "But that still leaves Ellery in danger."

"If he wanted to go after the heart of us, taking her would do it," Tasha said as she turned to Sutton. "Knowing what you know is now imperative."

"My mother dated a man named Ronald Kirn," Sutton said, then stopped.

The name meant nothing to Josiah. "Should we know him?"

"He worked as a scientist at a place called Blennen Richard."

Always a scientist. They messed up more cases. Almost made Josiah distrust the entire field.

Mike spun the nearest laptop around and started typing. His gaze moved over whatever he pulled up in front of him. "The company did serious research on all sorts of nasty chemicals. It operated as a public front but got most of its work through black-ops jobs, testing all sorts of potential weapons. It got shut down due to security issues."

The words "black ops" set off a warning bell in Josiah's head. The "security issues" part sounded pretty shitty as well. "I think I hate where this is going."

"I don't know what he did, but he spooked my mom." Sutton rubbed her hands together until her skin turned pink. "My mother knew him, how isn't clear." Sutton delivered the information in a clear voice. "I know now that she reported him to the FBI. Looks like she then helped to gather information on him while pretending to get close to him."

Mike whistled. "Ballsy."

"Tough." Like mother, like daughter, as far as Josiah could tell.

Sutton smiled. "All five-five of her. Petite and a great shot and not someone who rattled easily."

"This was a police assignment?" Josiah asked.

"No, personal. That's why it's not in her official file." Mike looked around the room but his gaze landed on her. "She, or someone in the FBI on her behalf, made her involvement almost impossible to find."

Harlan moved to stand behind Mike and watched the typing from over his shoulder. "Ronald is Benton?"

"No, Ronald is dead. Killed years ago in a raid in a private lab he'd set up. A raid that came about, in part, because of my mom's reporting." Sutton balled her hands into fists. "Upon investigating it became clear he'd been selling weaponized anthrax and some other treats. Had stockpiled a lot of money." She hesitated. "Well, in theory."

Josiah could see it all. A policewoman, curious and questioning by nature, runs into a mess in her personal life and digs deeper. Hits on something way beyond her expectations. "Meaning?"

"The money went missing right around the time his half brother, Rick, supposedly died." Sutton shot them all a lopsided smile. "I think he's your Benton, my Bane. He's had other names over the years."

Mike shrugged. "That might explain how he got into the terrorism and weapons selling business."

"Here we are racing all over the world and we find him by accident." Tasha laughed. "It's as odd as the Son of Sam being found because of a parking ticket."

"I had no idea he was a terrorist or someone people other than me were hunting."

Josiah had mentioned something about investigating a con artist. Her fervor went well beyond that. "But you think he killed your mom."

Her gaze didn't waver. "Yes."

Josiah got it now. This was personal and ingrained. A part of her she could not let go. Her drive and determination. Why she didn't just cough up the information. Trust would be as difficult and unnatural for her as it was for them. "That all could make a difference. Thanks for telling us."

"Right." Tasha opened another laptop. "Now we have somewhere to start, another avenue to explore, so we're not just sitting around waiting."

Mike nodded. "Maybe we can get to Benton before he comes for us."

"We need to take shifts. You two should get some rest." Tasha motioned for Josiah to take Sutton and go. "Mike, I want you to stick with me and search through this. Harlan, you too."

Mike stepped around the table. "Yes, ma'am."

"Sutton, Josiah—go." With a wave of her hand, Tasha dismissed them and went back to her phone. "Josiah, you can relieve Mike in a few hours, unless we're ready to go before then."

Duty tugged at him. Josiah didn't walk away from an investigation but one look at Sutton and he changed his mind. She'd pulled off a pretty big information dump. One that had to impact her on an emotional level. They needed her and for now she needed him.

Before she could balk or insist on being in on the investigation, he took her hand. Walked with her in silence toward their assigned bedroom. She followed him inside and shut the door behind her.

When he turned, she stood there looking drained and tired and ready to drop. "That was impressive."

"What?" But the spark in her eyes said she knew.

"You didn't have to give all that up."

"Yeah, I did. I want him caught." Her body listed to one side. "But right now I could sleep standing up."

That was the last thing on his mind. He backed her up against the wall. Balanced her there and hovered over her, not touching. Not yet. "You did great tonight."

She flattened her hands on his chest. Instead of pushing him away she skimmed her fingers back and forth over him. "Unloading all of that makes it real again. I feel like I could break into a million pieces at any moment."

His insides churned with need. She talked about sleeping and all he could think about was getting inside her. It took all of his willpower just to keep the mundane conversation going, but he sensed she needed to talk. "That's normal aftermath. I can't think about my uncle's last moments or I'll get derailed from the job. The mourning will come later."

"How do you handle it?" Her hand snaked up to the base of his neck. Her thumb slid over his chin.

The gentle touches drove him wild. "I usually punch things."

She smiled, so sweet and alluring. "Well, let's not do that."

"I have other ideas." All kinds of ideas that involved them getting naked and all over each other. He tried to push the thoughts back but they kept creeping into his head. If she needed time or distance for all the horrors, he'd give it to her. Somehow.

"Huh."

He couldn't read her. Not right now. "What does that mean?"

"I thought this sort of thing was a bad idea on the job."

Very true. Not smart at all, but with her the need bubbled up from a purely personal place and spilled over. Wiped out his common sense. All of his rules faded away and the last bit of control holding him back finally snapped. Completely abandoned him, leaving him ready to touch her . . . taste her.

He inhaled and let go of every good argument about why he should stay away from her. "You act as if I can resist you, which I can't."

"Interesting." She pressed a quick kiss to his lips. "Tell me about those other ideas of yours."

He leaned in and brushed his mouth over hers. Once then twice. "I'd rather show you."

"Your friends are down the hall."

He'd thought about that problem, then decided to ignore it. "It's a long hallway and we'll be quiet."

He kissed her then. Not the flirting, lingering type. No, this was about taking possession. His mouth covered hers as he pinned her hands against the wall by her head. He heard the thump of her body against the wood, felt every curve as he slid against her.

Heat overwhelmed him. She lured him in and made him crazy like no one else. He knew he should pull back and walk away. Maybe do some work and wait until she fell asleep to slip back into the room. Should but wasn't going to. Not when she looked like that, kissed like that.

He lifted his head and smiled at the sight of her swollen lips and the way she opened her mouth as if she wanted his finger inside. Felt the small puffs of air against his cheek as she fought for breath.

He wanted her so fucking much. "Sutton?"

"Yes." Her hand traveled down to his stomach.

But he needed to be honest. "I'm not stopping this time."

She started to undo his belt. "Sounds like we're finally on the same page."

16

ALL THE uncertainty and trauma of the last few days fell away when Josiah kissed her neck. His hot mouth touched bare skin, and every nerve ending sparked to life. His body rubbed against hers as a harsh groan escaped his lips. The sound vibrated through her. It was as if her body hummed in time with his.

Sensations bombarded her. Excitement whipped up inside. Sutton didn't fight the loss of control. She turned off her mind and let her body go. The list of things she should be doing had been playing in her head, overwhelming her. Threatening to suck her under. Now she only saw him. Felt him.

When he switched from kissing to tiny nibbling bites, her breath hiccupped in her chest. She tilted her head to the side to give him more room. "God yes."

She wanted to touch him, strip those clothes off him, but the feel of being held down set off something wild inside her. She never got into submission, but this . . . he didn't hurt her or order her around. He took charge and threw them both straight into the fire. And the way he slid his lower half across hers made her crazed with need.

"Josiah. Bed." That's all she could get out.

He mumbled something before licking a long line up her throat. With a tug, she came off the wall, but her feet didn't stay on the floor. He lifted her and held her there until she wrapped her arms and legs around him. There was no part of her that didn't touch him. She fit against him snug and perfect.

The room spun as he turned and walked them to the bed. The world blurred around her. She expected him to throw her on the mattress and crawl on top of her. She welcomed it. But not him. With an arm supporting her, he lowered her, slow, inch by inch, watching her the entire time. Her body bent back and his mouth went to her stomach but that gaze never left her face.

When she finally reached the mattress, she reached for him. But he had other ideas. Still wearing her jeans, all her clothes, he spread her legs and knelt between her thighs.

"I'm going to savor you." His palms traveled up her legs, starting at her knees.

The slow trail amounted to sensual torture. Her body revved up and the need churned. She'd never felt like so desperate to touch and taste.

"I can't . . . we can't . . ." She'd explode. Scream and chant his name. Bring the others running.

"I've been dreaming about this from the first time I saw you." He opened the button at the top of her jeans. "Of fucking you." The zipper made a ticking sound as he lowered it.

"Josiah, please." She didn't even know what she wanted. His hands, his mouth. The feeling of him over her, inside her. Anything. He had her mind spinning and all sense of self-preservation fleeing.

Her underwear peeked out and he opened the jeans wider. Pressed his palm over her. "This?"

The heat from his hand seeped into her. The promise of those fingers had her shifting her legs. "More."

Taking his time, not stripping her or jumping on her, he slipped his hands inside her jeans and peeled them down. Actually peeled them, letting the rough edge of the denim brush against her now sensitive skin. When he got to her ankles, she kicked the jeans off. She would have done anything to get naked and start on his clothes.

She started to jackknife into a sitting position, but he gave her a gentle push to send her sprawling again. Her hair fanned out around her, as she watched his hand start moving again. Those palms traced the line back up her legs until his finger disappeared under the elastic band of her underwear.

Air pumped through her with enough force to make her chest rise and fall in rapid succession. Those skillful fingers danced around her, learned every inch of her. Then a finger slid inside her. Not deep and not hard. A steady back and forth, in and out, that had her shoulders lifting off the bed.

"You're wet." His voice was filled with awe. "Tell me what you need."

She was ready and willing but she couldn't say the words. Every time she tried to speak she could only force out a puff of air. But she could show him. She gripped his arm and pushed his finger deeper. Raised her knees and trapped him there between her legs.

He leaned down and kissed her knees, one then the other. "Tell me."

She couldn't breathe. Her whole body shook.

"You. Everything." She opened her legs wider. Her hand went to his shirt and she tried to lift it off. She didn't want the barrier. The clothes scratched against her, making her even more excited and ready for his touches.

He leaned back on his heels and his hands left her. Need crashed through her as she struggled to sit up with muscles that had turned to jelly. The pleading died in her throat as he stripped off his shirt. Up and over his head. As it fell to the floor she studied him. The scars and cuts on a body so sleek and muscled he qualified as a weapon.

She didn't ask for explanations. Didn't want to know. This one time her brain didn't seek out information because her heart knew the pain of knowing all he'd been through would double her over. She skimmed her fingers over a pucker of skin near his collarbone. Kissed the obvious scar from a knife wound under his left nipple. He'd been attacked and lucky to survive, and now all she wanted was to hold and love him.

With aching slowness, she fell back on the bed and dragged him with her. This time he didn't hold back. His body came down, crushing her into the mattress. The weight anchored her, freed her. Her hands skimmed over his skin, loving the hard angles of his body . . . those muscles.

He shifted his legs and his erection pressed against her. There was no question he wanted her. And she was on the verge of losing her mind. She wanted to feel all of him. Her fingers dipped into the space between the waistband of his jeans and his lower back to touch the top of his underwear. She felt the band and his warm skin.

"I want you naked."

He didn't say anything. Just nodded as he lifted his lower body off her. Without waiting, she slipped her hands between them. Found the bulge behind his zipper and cupped him.

"Jesus." His head dropped to her shoulder as he groaned.

The sound spurred her on. With careful clicks, she lowered his zipper and slipped her hand inside. His erection filled her palm. He sprang to action then. No more gentle coaxing and slow flirting. He sat up and grabbed something out of his back pocket before pushing the jeans down. He moved fast with jerky movements. All finesse gone.

She could feel the need pulsing off him. His excitement ratcheted up hers. When he came back to her his hands went to work on her shirt and bra. In two seconds she lay underneath him, naked and shaking with desire.

His fingers trembled as he brushed them over her cheek. "You are so lovely."

The accent made the compliment sound even better. It rolled off his tongue. The intense stare, the way his hands moved over her. She knew he'd laid his doubts to rest or at least put them aside. Right now, right here, he wanted her. Not just a warm body. She knew that was true down to her soul.

"Josiah." She slipped her hands into his hair and pushed the strands off his face. "Now."

The corner of his mouth kicked up in a sexy smile. "Yeah, baby. Now."

Her heart flipped over. Then her body took over. She kissed him while her hands went exploring. She lifted a leg and he caught it behind the knee and balanced it against his thigh. The workings in his mind might be a mystery but not this. Her fingers wrapped around his erection, slipping from top to base. He grew under her palm. Thick and long, she wanted him inside her.

His head dipped and he took her nipple in his mouth. Sucked and licked until her back arched. She heard a low tumble and realized it came from inside her. Every part of her body pulled tight in anticipation. When he lifted up on one arm she saw the condom in his hand. Not willing to wait, she grabbed it and opened the wrapper. She would have ripped it with her teeth by this point, but it didn't come to that.

With a smile he took it out of her hand and rolled it on, letting her watch as he covered every inch of his erection. It was the most sensual thing she'd ever seen. No embarrassment or strangeness. So intimate but yet so right.

He treated her to another smile. "Now we're ready."

She so was. She wanted to shoot back a response

but he started to enter her and she gasped. Her vision blurred as he slid in, slow but determined. The inner muscles stretched and her breathing kicked up along with her heartbeat. It pounded in her throat.

When he filled her, he stopped. His forehead dropped against her. "You okay?"

On fire. Ready to explode. Ten minutes from digging her fingernails into his back. "You need to move."

He wiggled his eyebrows. "Oh, I will."

Then the pumping started. In and out in a rhythm slow at first, then fierce in its quickness. Her fingers slipped through his hair and her thighs clenched his hips. She couldn't get close enough or drag him in deep enough. She wanted all of him all over her. She could smell him. She pressed a kiss on his shoulder and tasted him.

The speed picked up even more. With each press forward, a rough sound escaped his throat, half groan, half something raw and delicious. She wanted to watch him and draw it out but her body tightened. She clamped down on him with those tiny inner muscles and his moan filled her ears. She was pretty sure they heard that one back in DC, but she didn't care. She wanted this and didn't care who knew.

Words and thoughts raced through her head. She couldn't grab on to any of them. She opened her mouth to say something—anything—and drew in a deep breath. When his fingertips touched her, swirled over her as he pressed and retreated inside her, something broke. The tension snapped and the building inside her let go.

She pressed her hand over her mouth to keep from screaming his name as everything exploded. Her body bucked and her hands tightened into balls. A heel dug into the back of his thigh. She didn't have control over any of it. He'd set off a frenzy inside her and all she could do was ride it out as she came.

When she felt him stiffen and sink deeper into her, she could barely see. She wanted to watch his release. See it race through her, but she could only find the strength to lift a hand to the back of his neck and bring his face tighter against her neck. A shiver moved through him as his elbow gave out and his body fell harder against her.

She hugged him close as the last pulses of his release moved through them both. When he relaxed against her again with his hands curled under her body and his mouth pressing against her neck, she thought she could stay like that forever. He'd drained the energy out of her and he didn't look any stronger. The thought that she did that to him, that she could make him lose control and concentrate only on her, filled her with a sense of feminine power she planned to hold on to.

"I can't move." He mumbled the comment against her skin.

For some reason she found it hysterical. She laughed, a giggle at first, then full-on laughter. She tried to get control but she couldn't after everything. Not when this perfect moment meant everything to her.

He lifted his head and watched her with eyes filled with amusement. "You okay there?"

Her shoulders stopped and she put a hand over her mouth. She wanted to say something but went with nodding.

"I need to get back out and see what they've found. Get Ellery back," he said.

Reality kicked her in the gut. Hearing him talk sucked the life right back out of her. A desperate clawing sensation started deep inside her, as if she had to hold on now or risk losing this feeling forever.

Still, she kept her voice calm and steady. "Okay."

"But not yet." He rested his head on her chest and wrapped a hand around her waist. "I want this for just a few more minutes."

Relief filled her. That made two of them. She couldn't imagine a time when she wouldn't want this. It could be the adrenaline rush or the danger, but being with him shifted her world into perspective. She'd been searching for so long. Now that she was so close, what she really craved was this quiet time with him.

In this dream world Ellery was safe and Benton was in jail. In here she could pretend. But the world would intrude and she understood that, too.

"Do you think you can save her?" Sutton needed the reassurance. Needed him to act like it was no big deal.

"I have to."

Not the answer she expected at all. Her hand froze in the middle of brushing her fingers through his hair. "Meaning?"

For almost a full minute he didn't say anything. He lay on her. She could see his eyes were open and a bit glassy. He hadn't tried to sit up or move.

"My mom was killed when I was still in college." He used his finger to trace a circle pattern on her stomach.

She didn't say anything because she feared any question, even a hum, might stop him. The idea of knowing more about this man with the bone-deep protective streak, of seeing the man behind the gun, suddenly meant everything to her.

"I was home and my father and I were fighting because we always fought." He exhaled, blowing a breath of hot air across her skin. "We were standing right at the front door and he was yelling. Telling me what a disappointment I was to the family name because I'd had too much to drink the night before and acted like an ass in front of his powerful friends."

She kissed the top of his head. "As twentysomethings do."

"He wouldn't stop. He trotted out every sin I'd ever committed, because he never forgot anything. I snapped." His voice grew louder as if he were reliving every minute.

She winced, fearing what he'd say. "Did you punch him?"

"Worse, I humiliated him." He flattened his hand against her, cupping it just below her breast. "I started talking about his mistress and how everyone knew and how they all talked about it, and how she wasn't the first."

She didn't know what to say to that. Her mom raised her alone and they fought, but normal mother-daughter stuff over friends and clothes. "I don't think—"

"My mom was right there."

"Oh." Sutton closed her eyes on a wave of pain for him. For that poor woman.

"She ran outside to the waiting car. See, my father is an ambassador now but he was far more powerful in government back then. The war in Iraq was going on and there were protests and bombings." Josiah closed his eyes then. "She got in the car and started it . . . and it blew up."

Everything inside Sutton stopped. Her mind zipped to that video of his uncle. It had to stand a reminder of the horror of seeing his mother lost, of being right there and not being able to save her. That would kill a man like Josiah. She now saw what shaped him and why he operated the way he did. It all became so clear but all she wanted to do was hold him close and help him ride out whatever emotions churned inside him.

"My father blames me. It didn't matter what I said or that I went into intelligence work or came to the Alliance to try to make amends. He liked that I changed my name for the job, so he could pretend I no longer existed, but nothing made up for that one moment."

There were no words to fix or soothe this, but she tried anyway. "The bombers did it. Your father's bad decisions made her run. You didn't do anything."

"I told his secret."

"Oh, Josiah." She cupped his cheek as the horror of all the guilt he lived with washed over her. "Did they find out who did it?"

"They? I did." He lifted up and balanced on an elbow over her. "I handled it."

She could guess what that meant but it didn't matter. All she saw was the pain stretching across his face and darkening his eyes. "Of course you did."

"But every time, right before the shot goes off or the bomb explodes or the knife slices in, I see her face." He rubbed a hand over his mouth. "Just for a second. Because she was the one I couldn't save."

Her heart ripped in half for him. "You'll save Ellery."

He looked at her again. "I have to, Sutton. I can't fail."

"*We* won't."

17

BENTON WALKED around the back of Ellery's chair. The ties holding her hands behind her back dug into her wrists. More bands secured her legs to the hard wooden seat. He didn't see blood, and she appeared to be able to sit up. He regretted not doing more damage, but in this case a healthy bargaining chip worked better than one near-death.

He continued stalking around until he stood in front of her. With her head down and her auburn hair falling over her shoulders, her face stayed hidden. No matter, since he could see her chest rise and fall. He accepted the breathing as evidence that she was fine.

But the time for hiding had come to an end. "I assume you're comfortable."

She didn't move. Kept her breathing steady and even. She'd been well trained. Kudos to Tasha and her crowd for teaching the tech girl survival skills. She was going to need them.

"Ah, silence. Lucas would be pleased . . . if he were alive." As expected, she flinched. Love, such a stupid emotion. It made smart men simple and tough women weak.

Benton had no idea if that were true. Reports of his death could be faked but Frederick's description of the wound gave Benton hope that he'd taken an Alliance member out. Not that it really mattered. He'd flown in especially for this moment and had not been disappointed. Frederick did not let him down, which proved a nice change after failing to inflict enough damage on the Alliance at Iselwood.

"The silent treatment is not going to save you." Benton folded his injured arm and held it close to his stomach, cursing the Alliance as pain shot down to his fingertips.

She lifted her head and pinned him with a furious stare. Gave him the full treatment, flushed face, thin lips. "You're disgusting."

"You don't even know me."

He was the survivor. He escaped the lab explosion and rain of bullets that took his brother years ago. Since then he'd lived through countless attempts by rebels and warlords to steal his goods without paying. He even walked away from the missile Harlan shot right at him. Long after the Alliance ceased to exist and its agents were buried in pieces in the ground, he would thrive.

She tugged on her arms and winced.

"If you keep doing that you'll slice through your wrists." No cheap zip ties here. The Alliance would know how to break those. This job called for sharp wire.

She slumped down in her chair. "What do you want?"

"The complete and total destruction of the Alliance." Seemed simple enough to him. "Your group annoys me."

"You sound like a petulant child."

"That kind of talk is going to earn you a bullet in your brain." In reality, he refused to let her anger him. He had work to do and a plan. Calls for his head over the botched toxin auction needed to be handled. The Alliance would unwittingly help with that. "But maybe that's your hope. Get me to end this fast." He treated her to a tsk-tsking sound. "I think not."

"Stop talking about it and just do it." She leaned forward and gasped. Tears formed in her eyes as her mouth dropped open.

"You're tied to the chair around the waist as well." He frowned. "I bet that one hurt."

She groaned but didn't say anything. Didn't fight back.

"So tough." He shook his head in reluctant admiration. This group didn't whine. He looked to Frederick for his reaction. "Impressive, isn't she?"

Frederick nodded but didn't bother to uncross his arms. "Very."

He stood at the door to the warehouse. The same warehouse that sat just one mile from the one they'd blown up so they could grab Ellery. Benton loved the poetry of that. Send the Alliance scurrying and hide right in front of them.

"Harlan, Mike, and Josiah. They need to go first. I'm thinking I need something big and bold. An incident that leaves it impossible to even identify their bodies." He walked around her again, stalking his prey and moving in closer with each round.

"Go to hell."

He didn't touch her because he didn't have to. His words sliced deeper than any knife. For someone like her, someone who cared about her coworkers, hearing about what was about to happen and knowing she couldn't stop it should rip her apart. "Unfortunately for you, you were in the wrong place on this assignment. Though convenient for me and what I need."

"Which is?"

"I just told you." And that was all he planned to say. She'd been searched and checked for trackers. He had wi-fi, cell, and GPS jammers. Nothing could get through. Still, he didn't believe technology answered everything, and he didn't take for granted that devices could stop the Alliance.

"Pakistan." She didn't ask. She made a statement.

A huge mistake. Just mentioning that assault brought the memories storming back. He'd been so close to perfecting the toxin delivery system. That's what happened when you held brilliant scientists hostage and threatened to kill their families. Then the Alliance came to town. Led by West Brown, Harlan, Josiah . . . Mike. They'd all pay.

"This is your revenge." Her chin jutted forward. "Right? Your big play."

He was no longer satisfied with evening the score. Alliance had to be eliminated. "Every time I turn around, there you are."

She smiled at him. "Good for us."

Frederick took a threatening step forward but Benton waved him back. Hurting her now wouldn't help the cause.

"Why Sutton?" she asked.

Benton debated avoiding this subject. Thought about letting her believe Sutton worked for him. But a part of him did want to brag. "She found me but now I'm afraid she's a loose end that must be cut."

"What does that mean?" As she spoke, Ellery moved her foot. Benton suspected she looked for ways to escape. Enterprising though not enough.

No more. If he started talking about Sutton and that bitch of a mother his temper would rise. He would not give Ellery that satisfaction.

"You should be more worried about how connected she's become to Josiah." Benton laughed at his own observation. "The men in your group are so predictable. They swoop in and rescue."

"Sutton doesn't need rescuing." Ellery continued to shift. Every time she talked, she moved. She likely thought the sound of her voice drowned out the creaking of the chair.

Benton played along, pretending he didn't see her fidgeting. Continued to stand there, looming over her. "But she does. So do you. The only question is if they'll be willing to trade you for her."

The color drained from Ellery's face. "Never."

Interesting. He could tell she said no but she feared yes. "Not that I would actually follow through with my end of that bargain since I intend to kill you both. Killing the women weakens the men, you see."

"You don't understand the Alliance at all."

But he did. He'd studied them and counted on them to act in certain ways. They rarely disappointed him with their gung-ho, rush-in-first attitudes. So tiresome. "Don't underestimate your value to them. Their connection to you makes then weak and I'll capitalize on that."

Frederick laughed. A low and menacing grumble that grabbed her attention.

"Who are you?" She stared at Frederick with confusion sounding in her voice.

"He's the one who knocked you out and killed Lucas." Benton saw that every time he mentioned Lucas's name she stiffened. She did an impressive job of acting as if she didn't care but she clearly did. "I'd have him apologize but I told him to do it."

Frederick gave a little bow. "With pleasure."

Nice touch. "See? You're not the only ones who hire men who kill on command."

"My team has a conscience."

"Such do-gooder bullshit. Sell that line to the widows of all bodies you've left on the ground from country to country." He opened and closed his fist to keep the circulation moving. "See, your type always is so convinced you're on the right side. There is no nuance for you."

"Stealing toxins and blowing up people with bombs is nuanced?"

"Necessary."

Benton saw the blood. A thin line dripped down from behind her wrist. All that fidgeting resulted in an injury. Not that he cared, but her bleeding out wouldn't help him. He gestured for Frederick to move behind her. "Check her."

He stepped around and pulled on something that had Ellery gasping again. Frederick stood up again and shook his head. "She cut herself, but it's fine."

Benton doubted that. He eyed Ellery again. "You're lucky I like you or I'd strap a bomb to you."

"I feel lucky."

"That's how you should see it." Benton flexed his arm to fight the coming numbness. "From the test runs and Josiah's uncle I would say that's a pretty vicious death."

Her eyes narrowed. "This is all about money."

"No, I have plenty of that." Benton glanced around at the room. Bare walls and nothing to give away its location. "This is about leveling the playing field."

"I don't understand."

"Of course you don't." Benton nodded to Frederick. "Cover her mouth and make the call."

Josiah stood across from Mike at the farmhouse's dining room table and stared at the laptop on the seat in front of him. Ellery usually handled this part. He ran his hand over the keyboard but she didn't come running, warning him not to mess with the equipment as she usually did. The possessiveness usually bugged him but he'd pay to have her there now.

He glanced around the small room. They were all congregated in there, squished with each one taking a side of the square table. Ignoring protocol and clearance issues, Sutton paged through the file they'd collected tracking Benton's whereabouts after adding in her intel. Tasha and Harlan went on and off the phones, talking to team members and intelligence officials as they moved satellites and scanned the area. Mike studied surveillance photos and maps.

Josiah took in the energy in the room. Watched Sutton as her gaze scanned each page. He looked at her and his mind flashed back to the bedroom. To her expressive face and the way she begged him to enter her. For a man who spent his adult life closed off and on the run, she had the impact of welcoming sunshine. Determined strength wrapped up in this beautiful package that stole his breath.

His hands tightened on the back of the chair as the memories rolled through him. Touching her had been so good, so right. He'd had sex with other women, sometimes required by the job and sometimes not. Lots of sex. Some great and some drawn out in hotel rooms for days while he celebrated a successful mission.

But the *after*, that part when he wanted to confide in Sutton, hold her, feel her hands soothing him, that belonged only to her. He never talked about his mother, had never told another woman. She filled a hollowness inside him he didn't even know was there.

And the sex had been smoking, leaving him exhausted and wanting more.

His computer screen blinked to life in front of him. "What the hell?"

They all rushed to his side of the table. Harlan took the seat. "It's a password."

Sutton leaned into Josiah as her hair fell over her shoulder. "For what?"

He inhaled her scent. Gave in to the urge to touch a hand to her back. "Dark Web."

She kept staring at the screen. "What's that exactly?"

"A system of unsearchable, unreachable network hosts on the Internet." Mike grabbed another computer and started typing. Lines of what looked like gibberish that really amounted to encrypted messages to the team members. "Sites can only be accessed by invitation and with specific passwords that rotate and change at timed intervals."

Sutton grabbed Josiah's arm. "I've heard rumors but had never seen it in action."

How did he explain that some of the worst horrors of humanity played out on the Dark Web? The new screen kept Josiah from having to answer. "There's the invitation."

"This can only be Benton, right?" She put her hand on the back of Mike's chair and leaned in further.

She shot back when Benton's face popped up on the screen. Josiah caught her before she stumbled. Not that he could see anything except a red haze of fury. That smug face haunted his nightmares. The only consolation was the burn scars. Next time Josiah would set the guy on fire and watch him burn.

"We meet again." Benton's voice, deeper and more gravely now. The ends of his sentences dragged. He still radiated a cocky confidence but the injuries told another story. "Since some of you now know what I look like and won't be around long as a group anyway, I figured it was fine to fully show my face."

Tasha moved Harlan out of the seat and sat down, facing off with the Alliance's nemesis. The world's nemesis. "Where's Ellery?"

"Right here." Benton turned, keeping his body stiff, and nodded to the area behind him. "See? She's fine."

Josiah got a quick look but he saw Mike had captured a still and studied it on the computer in front of him. No visible injuries and calm. Good for Ellery.

"Let us talk to her," Tasha said.

"I'm not stupid." Benton exhaled as he massaged his scarred hand with the other one. "Hello, Sutton. I hope you're enjoying your temporary lodgings."

"You're a sick fuck."

Mike grumbled the comment but the mic must have picked it up because Benton's head turned. "Since your boyfriend is alive, you should thank me."

Mike's hand tightened into a fist on the table. "You tried to grab him."

"Certainly you know by now that would have been a bonus but his capture wasn't necessary at this juncture. Soon, but not now. I merely wanted your attention while I set your building on fire." Benton's gaze zipped back to the center of the screen. "You have to be running out of those by now, Tasha. How many safe houses can one group afford to have?"

Josiah couldn't stand still any longer. He pulled out

a chair and sat down next to Tasha. Let Benton see him and know killing his uncle hadn't broken him. "What do you want?"

"So serious." Benton kept opening and closing his hand. The movement barely made it on screen but now and then he'd lift the arm higher and they'd catch a peek. "How is your family? Precious things, aren't they? You should try to make amends with your father."

No way was he engaging in this conversation. Josiah would sooner walk into Benton's lair and meet him one-on-one. Then he'd see just how smarmy and confident the guy was.

"Get to it, Benton or whatever the hell your name is." Josiah knew not to tip their hands on that piece yet. Let Benton wonder if they'd put it all together.

The amusement vanished from Benton's face, leaving behind a dead expression and dead eyes. "This is a one-time offer. Ellery for Sutton."

"Forget it. Take me. I'm more valuable," Tasha said.

"Tempting." Benton barked out a harsh laugh. "I can only imagine how crazy that would make Ward, which would be a bonus.

Before Josiah could stop her, Tasha nodded. "Good, we'll—"

"No," Benton snapped out. "We're not negotiating. I have other plans for you. Ones that will rip Ward to shreds and since he's not on this continent, you will need to wait. This round belongs to Sutton as a punishment for her meddling."

The words screeched across Josiah's brain. He had to fight not to shout. "No."

Benton tried to shrug but only one shoulder lifted. "You know what I want. You have twenty-four hours to decide or Ellery dies."

"What are—" The screen went dark. Tasha slammed the keyboard, pounded on the keys, but nothing brought Benton back. "Damn it."

"Ellery is alive. She looks unhurt," Harlan said as he started to pace his side of the table. "That's something."

Sutton glanced up at Josiah. "Why does he want me so badly?"

Mike answered. "He's probably hoping to grab you, figure out what you know, and stop you from leaking too much of it to us."

The look of confusion in her eyes tore at Josiah. Despite her training and skills with a gun, she didn't sign up for this. She'd been thrown into this life by a madman and hauled around by the team, Josiah had no idea how she kept it together, but he did know she wasn't going anywhere. "You're a loose end."

She exhaled. "Okay, well, the guy you could see hovering in the background by Ellery was Frederick."

"We know all about Frederick now. Benton might not pop on checks but Frederick does." As soon as she provided the name earlier, the team had gone to work. Josiah thought about the material they collected and of Frederick's obvious lack of a conscience.

A new wave of worry for Ellery swept through him. Frederick would kill her without thinking. And God knew how many of those damn bombs they'd made and had ready to use.

"He's a sick motherfucker." Mike called the guy

a few other names. "Seems to enjoy his little games, maybe as much as the actual killing."

Harlan cleared his throat. "About this offer . . ."

There it was. Josiah saw it coming. He knew Harlan would be the one to broach the issue, the by-the-book jackass. "No."

Sutton slipped her arm under his elbow. "Josiah."

She sounded . . . "Sutton, fuck no. That's not even a question. We don't use innocents to lure targets."

"I'm in this. I've been tracking him." She sounded so reasonable. So sure. "I touched all of this off by taking the information from his file and tipping you guys off."

Mike shrugged. "Technically, Benton was aiming for us long before you landed in Paris."

"We're not doing this the way Benton wants it." They all had to see that. Josiah looked around the room for any sign of sanity and came up empty. Anxiety sucker punched him in the gut. He felt the walls closing in and vowed to hold them back.

"Isn't it my decision?" Sutton asked.

"No." He turned and blocked her gaze from the rest of the room. She could stay at the farmhouse while they searched. Hell, he'd put her on a private flight and somehow get her back to Ward and Ford and the safety of the U.S. if he had to. "Don't even think about doing this."

Tasha stood up. "I need to speak with Josiah."

"About me?" Sutton pushed around Josiah to face the woman in charge. "If so, I'm staying."

Something softened in Tasha's expression and in her tone. "About the job."

"Sutton." Mike held out a hand to her. "Come with me."

She hesitated.

He smiled at her. "Really, it's okay."

They all started moving. Sutton walked outside with Mike before Josiah could stop her. He wanted to grab them all and shove them into seats. Lecture Sutton on the insanity of even considering this plan.

"Harlan, you stay, too." Tasha nodded toward the chair she'd just left.

They could play musical chairs all night. It didn't matter. The answer would not change. Josiah would say it a thousand times if he had to. "This is not happening."

Harlan sat down. "You sure you're thinking with your head here?"

Fury slammed into Josiah out of nowhere. It wrapped around him and launched him straight into fighting mode. "Do you want me to kick yours in?"

"Gentlemen, that's enough." Tasha pointed to the chair across from Harlan and didn't speak again until Josiah sat in it. "Ellery is vital to operations."

No, no, no. "Tasha, come on."

"Sutton is not a novice." Tasha made a clicking sound with her tongue. "She came looking for a fight and I think she's prepared to take it on. Not at our level, but with enough expertise to assist us."

"Benton is going to kill her." A vision of her bound to a chair with a bomb strapped to her chest flashed in his mind and Josiah had to blink it out. Had to concentrate. "This is all a joke to him. He has no intention of giving Ellery back to us."

Tasha frowned. "I know that."

Josiah knew better then to let the relief flood in. There was no way these two would give up on an argument or a plan that easily. "Okay, then why are we even talking about this?"

"We can work out a plan to get Ellery and keep Sutton." Harlan sounded so reasonable, as if this kind of operation didn't require days of planning and time studying the intel to pull off.

Josiah knew better and he wasn't the only one. "Tell that to Lucas."

"Benton can try whatever he wants, but this time we'll be ready." Harlan sounded so sure. So positive.

Josiah couldn't call up a scrap of evidence to support that theory. "You're insane if you believe that."

Tasha held up a hand. "Okay, yes. This is dangerous, but it may be our only chance to get Ellery and grab Benton."

No way was he falling for reason or emotion of whatever Tasha was aiming for here. Josiah shook his head. "No."

"We'll leave it to Sutton. She's a grown woman."

Something in the tone started a stabbing sensation in his gut. "You can't feed her to that animal."

Tasha's voice rose. "I said she decides."

"Fine, then I'll go tell her." And he meant "tell" because there was no way he was running through a pro/con list with Sutton. There was nothing to debate. He was going to tell her this assignment was not happening.

The idea of her being in danger tightened something inside of him. He barely knew her but all of a sudden he dreaded the idea of losing her, either to getting on a plane and flying to safety or to Benton.

Images bombarded his brain. Seeing her body sprawled out on the ground or bleeding out in the grass. Being so close and not being able to resolve the situation again would kill him. He couldn't even think about what Benton might do to her, about her being injured in any way.

He got around the table and headed toward the kitchen before Tasha's voice stopped him. "Josiah, I know you care about her."

"Understatement." The word slipped out but he couldn't call it back or erase the stunned expressions on the faces staring at him. He put his hands on his hips and glanced at the floor. "Shit."

A second passed before Tasha spoke again. "Maybe you're not objective enough to be in on this plan."

"When it comes to her I'm not, but you aren't locking me out." He had no idea when or why it happened but he was all in when it came to her. And that meant protecting her even if she insisted she didn't need him shielding her. "And she's not going."

18

SUTTON WAITED until Josiah sat on the bed to join him. She'd run through the particulars with Mike about what would happen tomorrow if she did nothing. He'd been reluctant and kept mentioning Josiah but he finally spilled that Ellery would die. That she was prepared to die on the job. They all were.

Sutton had never heard anything so awful in her life. Here they were, putting their lives on the line every day, and the expectation was one day they wouldn't return home. The thought made her heart ache. The idea of Josiah in a coffin. Of Ellery . . .

That couldn't happen without her trying to help. She didn't claim to be a hero, but she wasn't someone who sat back and stayed safe while others walked into danger. She'd been raised by a strong woman who put herself through school and made a home out of nothing. Set an example by how she lived her life.

Sutton's one thought, one target, had been the man she now knew as Benton. A laser-guided focus consumed her. Now she stood on the cusp of making him pay for all he'd done and she couldn't back down. Now she had to convince Josiah.

Before she could touch him, he fell back against the mattress with his arms covering his face. "The answer is no."

"What if the question was sex?"

He lifted an arm and stared up at her. "Really?"

The hopeful puppy expression almost did her in. It certainly switched the pain in her side to a fluttering in her stomach. Looking at him tended to do that for her. "Just wondering."

His hands fell back against the mattress. "Are you trying to change the subject thinking I will forget that you're talking about becoming a target?"

Sutton put a hand on his thigh. "Ellery is alive and looks okay and I want to celebrate that."

Sure, they needed to talk this through, but she did want him. Something about the idea of facing death made her want to experience as much of life as possible; that meant him. He'd come to take up so much of her life and thoughts in such a short period of time. She was sure he'd chalked it up to the adrenaline rush associated with danger. That's why she didn't ask. For her it went deeper.

She glanced at him and he scowled back. Any other time it might tick her off but she found it pretty cute right then as he visibly struggled not to lose his temper.

"What's with the look?" she asked as she smoothed her hand up his leg to rest on the waistband of his jeans.

He rested a hand over hers. "I'm not going to change my mind."

As if he got to make the decision for her. *Men* . . .

She slid an arm along the covers and lowered her

body until she lay next to him. "How do we get her back?"

"I knew it." He sat up and moved to the edge of the bed. Then he stood. "You are brave and this fearless thing is hot, but having a PI license doesn't mean you're trained to handle someone like Benton. He is the worst of the worst."

The name now made everything inside her clench with hate. "I was trained enough to help at the school."

Josiah's scowl only deepened. "That's not the same thing."

She didn't see the situation that way. "I've always been a step behind Benton. Now I know why. I wasn't just following the guy I thought killed my mom. I was actually tracking a guy no one could track. He's—"

"—a fucking animal."

She'd seen the aftermath in that video of Josiah's uncle. Felt the pain thrum off him as he talked about his mom. "Yes."

She struggled to find the right words as she sat up. This sort of thing was so far out of her understanding. Her mother had never talked about cases. She'd protected and probably overprotected, but Sutton never heard the specifics. Never ran into someone like this Benton guy in real life.

"What has to happen to create a man like that?" she asked, when Josiah stayed quiet.

"We're not sure yet. Some people like to see the world fall into chaos. Light the torch, then whip it into a crowd. Others are believers or greedy or sick. So far we're thinking greed motivates him."

She thought about how her mother would claim to be full and skip a meal right before payday just so Sutton would have enough to eat. "How much money does one person need?"

"Good question."

She'd looked into Josiah's background. On that damn tablet that caused so much trouble. She'd used the bombing to trace his past. She knew he came from a connected family. The articles talked about titles and estates. Things so far outside her world.

But they didn't seem like him either. She hadn't seen him pull rank or act as if his money and background put him above the rest of the team. If anything, he stepped up to sacrifice as much as, if not more than, the rest.

That sort of selflessness intrigued her. "And I'm not, you know."

His head shot up. "What are we talking about?"

"Fearless." Not even close. "I'm not Tasha."

He came back to the bed and sat next to her. Took her hand in his. "No one expects you to be."

"The idea of going back to Benton or being traded or whatever scares the hell out of me. Like, I can barely say the words without throwing up." The thought of facing Benton and seeing Frederick made her dizzy with fear. Part of her wanted to hide in a closet until all of this was over. "Sure, I can shoot but I'm human. I know how terrifying that man can be and I've always been careful. Walking right to him kind of violates that."

He squeezed her fingers. "You're not going, Sutton. I can't be clear enough on that."

"But you need Ellery back." Sutton got that. Ellery provided the tech support they needed and acted as the emotional center. More importantly, she was their friend. The guys treated her with respect but teased her like they would a baby sister. All but Lucas, who definitely didn't look at her as his relative.

Josiah's expression went blank. "Do you think I'm that bloodthirsty? As if I see you and her as commodities we can just exchange?"

"I think you're practical because you have to be. There's evil and you fight it and sometimes you don't fight fair." She used both hands to grab on to his now, willing him to hear her. "I'm not judging. That all makes sense to me."

"I don't want you to go. Okay?" He tilted his head back and stared at the ceiling for a second before looking at her again. Let out a long groan of what sounded like frustration before dropping his head again. "The idea of something happening to you makes me physically sick."

The words lit something inside her. They cleared out the darkness and flooded her with a sense of calm. Suddenly the scary seemed so much less scary. "Josiah."

"I've treated you like shit since the first day we met and said awful things to you. Didn't believe you in the beginning."

She put a finger over his lips. "That's over."

With a sweet loving touch, he held her hand to his mouth and kissed her palm. "I'm sorry."

The touch soothed the worries away, but the words

stunned her. She sat back a bit on the bed as she turned them over in her head. "Do you say that often?"

"Never."

This man. "That makes me feel special."

"That's the point." He turned until her leg slid up and over his. "You are. I don't want you to be, but you are."

Other women might be offended, but not her. She felt the same way. It started as a reluctant attraction. Now it was a pull she could not break. She was falling for him and that might be scarier than anything Benton could do to her. "Believe it or not I find that sweet."

Josiah smiled as he slid her fingers through his. "Hard to believe you're the same woman I kidnapped a few days ago."

The comment hit like a punch to the chest. "Oh my God. Was it only days?"

"Yup."

She sat there and watched him. His attention stayed on her hands. He didn't throw her down. Every action told her she meant more to him than sex. She loved that. "I still want to, you know."

He glanced up at her. "You lost me again."

The man was not exactly picking up the clues she kept dropping. So she'd be less subtle. With a hand on his chest she pushed him back on the bed. On her hands and knees, she crawled up his body, stopping at his waist.

"Oh, now I'm getting it."

"Finally. Good God, man. Keep up." Her fingers

went to the front of his jeans and danced across the material.

While he watched her, she lowered the zipper. Careful even though her insides screamed to hurry, she slipped his erection out of his boxer briefs. The warmth of his body heated hers. His excitement sparked hers.

She slid her hand up and down. Followed with her tongue. "This."

"Sutton." His hand went into her hair and held her close.

When she put him in her mouth, they stopped talking.

Josiah knew he was alone the second he woke up. He couldn't believe he'd even slept. He came into the bedroom to talk some sense into her. Thought a few minutes of a nap might not be a bad idea before he ventured out to do battle with the rest of the team again. Somehow he'd slept two hours.

He sat up and the blanket dropped to his waist. He wasn't wearing much more than underwear but he had no regrets about that. Just thinking about Sutton and that hot mouth made him smile. The way she . . . His blood went cold.

"Shit." He jumped out of bed and scooped his jeans off the floor. He had them in his hand when he threw the bedroom door open and stepped into the hall. He'd worked up a fevered fury by the time he turned the corner and hit the main living area. One step into the room and all conversation ceased.

Sutton sat at the kitchen table with Tasha and Harlan.

Mike hovered nearby eating a sandwich and spied him first. He stopped chewing and visibly swallowed. "Uh, dude. This is not a clothing optional establishment."

"You forget your pants?" Harlan asked as he sat back in his chair.

"No." That's all Josiah got out. Anger clouded his head and the rest of the words wouldn't come.

Mike winced. "Technically. He's holding them."

That did it. "I meant no. She is not doing this assignment."

Sutton gave herself a visible shake and finally blinked. "You didn't get dressed before coming out here?"

He was not playing this game. "They all know we're sleeping together."

Mike snorted. "We do now."

All of a sudden everyone cared about his wardrobe and the sleeping arrangements. That was fucking great.

"Fine." He practically ripped the jeans tugging them on. He had a flannel shirt in his hand and put that on without bothering to button it before holding his arms out to the sides. "Happy?"

"I can't unsee it, so no," Mike said before taking another bite of his sandwich.

Josiah ignored that but he couldn't ignore the sight of Sutton sitting there, talking with the two people who would set up the strategy for any operation. He pointed at her. "Get up."

Her eyebrow lifted. "Excuse me?"

He was not in the mood for the battle of the sexes

right now. This wasn't about her being a woman. It was about her mattering to him. Pure and not even a little bit simple because his life was a shit storm, but there it was.

He skipped over all that and got right to the point. The one he kept saying even though no one listened. "The answer is no. We are not putting you in danger. Whatever happens in there is not going to change my mind."

Mike's eyes widened. "Whoa."

For the first time since he entered the room, Tasha lifted her head from whatever she was reading. "Josiah, maybe you should take a breath."

"She is not one of us." Why couldn't they see that?

But the room had gone silent. They all looked around. Most stared at Sutton as if waiting for her to blow.

"You need to work on your tact," she said in a quiet voice.

He wasn't in the mood to whisper. He wanted to yell and hit things. "Yeah, I get it. I'm not good with comforting or tact. I'll work on those, but that doesn't change my position now."

Tasha sent him a sad smile. "It's not your decision."

She made the rules, so if she thought this mission could work and Ellery had a chance she'd talk Sutton into it. That's why Josiah needed to cut this off now. "Tasha, no. Ellery is not more important than Sutton. We are not going to make those distinctions. It's sick."

"Ellery has operational significance," Harlan pointed out.

"Shut the fuck up." Josiah switched from frustration to rage. Harlan was right but that didn't make the words any less infuriating.

Heat flushed through Josiah's body and he felt a knock in his head. Likely stress, which was fine. He understood anger. The rest of the emotions, no.

"Josiah." Sutton came over to him. Put her hands on his forearms and stared him down. "I can't live with the idea that I could have done something to help Ellery and didn't."

The feeling, noble but misplaced, didn't change his mind. "And she is not going to be okay with you sacrificing yourself to save her. And then there's the part where Benton is going to perform some sort of double cross and try to kill you both."

"We can protect them," Harlan said. "That's the point."

Josiah didn't bother to look at him. "You can't guarantee that. Hell, we couldn't even guarantee Ellery's safety when she was with us. Benton got her, didn't he?"

"But we can say with some certainty that Ellery will die if we don't try."

The sound of Mike's voice had Josiah turning around. "You don't agree with this, right? You know having Sutton out there is dangerous for her and could be dangerous for us."

Sutton snorted. "Thanks."

"It's a fact. I will be so busy protecting you that I could . . ." Josiah wouldn't go there. He refused to say more on that score. "No, we're not doing it."

"Which is why you won't be protecting her." Harlan nodded. "I will."

"No." Since he was two steps from launching across the room and beating the hell out of Harlan, Josiah stopped there.

Mike threw the rest of his sandwich on the plate. "They're doing it with or without you. I'm going to be there and do everything—and I mean everything—to make sure Sutton stays safe and Ellery comes back to us."

In his head Josiah knew Mike was right. This call made sense, but he wasn't leading with that part of him right now. "It's not enough."

Sutton grabbed on to his hands and tugged until he looked at her. "Trust me."

"This isn't about trusting you." God, that wasn't it at all.

She trailed the back of her hand down his cheek. "No, it's about trusting them, and you do. So, end of discussion."

"Then it's settled." Tasha stood up. "Be ready to move in ten. That should give everyone time to get fully dressed."

19

THE CALL with the details for the exchange came hours after the blow-up at the house. Since then Sutton had wavered, changing her mind and going back and forth about the sanity of this whole operation about six or seven hundred times. Not that she told them or warned Josiah. He was a bundle of angry nerves and she couldn't add to that.

But it was too late to turn back now. They were on the way. Harlan and Tasha sat in the front seat but tension zipped around the utility truck, threatening to choke them all. Benton had insisted only Sutton enter the building, but Harlan made it clear he was going along. The building in question sat close to the site of the fire, which meant Benton likely had been close by that night. Josiah had sworn for hours over that one.

She slipped her hand over his thigh as she sat next to him. She expected him to nod or even stay quiet in response. He surprised her by leaning over and kissing her. Right there in front of Mike across from them and within viewing range of the mirrors in the front. All while he disassembled his gun.

He was a complex guy. Just when she thought she could read him, he did something unexpected, like a slow lingering kiss.

"Will you kiss me next?" Mike asked.

Sutton looked up and laughed when she realized he was looking at Josiah.

"What would your professor say?" Josiah asked, not skipping a beat.

"Probably something like, 'You can do better than the guy with the gun' but I'm only guessing."

The easy camaraderie helped to calm her jumping nerves. They joked and gave each other crap but they'd die for each other. She loved that about this group. They might be the best of the best and all that, but they held on to their humanity. Maybe just barely some days, but she saw it on every face. The dead emptiness in Benton's eyes didn't reach here.

Tasha turned around in her seat. "We all clear on the plan?"

They'd run through it so many times that Sutton had it memorized. Just when she got it down they informed her that once in there all hell would break loose and to just use common sense. She was starting to wonder if she had any.

"Any sign of trouble or a double cross, we yank Sutton and leave." Josiah stared unblinking at Tasha.

She nodded. "Yes."

Not that he bothered to ask her. Sutton swallowed a sigh. He still didn't get that she had signed up for this . . . sort of. She didn't have a death wish and planned to be stuck to Harlan's side, but she knew in her heart this was the right answer. No way could she travel through life, go back to her real life gathering evidence on the supposed bad guys in her small world, while she knew her choices and fears damned Ellery.

Besides, she was ready. In a way. She had a knife at her side and the gun. At Harlan's request, Mike had run her through a series of quick tests with the gun. Thanks to the pair of contacts Tasha had picked up from God knew where, perfect prescription and everything, Sutton had passed them all. He also told her not to use the knife, which she assumed meant she sucked at those skill tests.

When the van came to a stop a moment of panic took hold. That quick the shaking started and something clogged her throat. She had no idea how these guys walked into this level of extreme danger every day.

As if he read her mind, Josiah gave her the out. "You can still say no."

She glanced at Mike. Thought about Ellery in that chair.

"You can, Sutton," Mike said. "No one would blame you."

He was wrong about that. She would. "I'm ready."

Her voice sounded firm and confident. She hoped her legs would hold her when she jumped to the ground. Mike saved her from a rough answer to that question when he opened the door and slipped out, then turned to help her. Her hands stayed on her waist for an extra beat as she forced her knees to stiffen.

"Thanks," she whispered.

"We all get scared. Courage comes from plowing ahead anyway." He winked at her.

Then Josiah was in front of her. That drawn expression and severe frown. She wanted to brush her fingers over those lines and kiss him stupid. She settled for smiling.

Josiah glanced over at Mike. "Did he just give you a pep talk?"

"He's a good guy."

Josiah nodded. "The best."

"I know you don't want me to do this." She rested her hand on his waist because not touching him wasn't an option. She needed the connection, even if it was just this one last time.

"No." He cupped her cheek with his palm and let his thumb brush over her lips. "I want you safe."

"I will be." With him, like this, she felt as if she could conquer anything.

Tasha appeared next to them with Mike at her side. "I'll ride this out in the van with the equipment."

Mike chuckled. "Which you hate."

"I do, but with Ellery gone, the tech and logistics parts fall to me." She checked her watch before looking at them again. "No one goes in until I check for heat signatures and Mike runs a wire in there."

"Benton has to be expecting both," Josiah said.

Tasha waved off that concern. "Probably not the heat signatures. I had to borrow that equipment since he destroyed ours."

Even Sutton understood that tone. "Borrow?"

"I'll give it back. Eventually."

"Another thing to blame on Benton." Mike sounded ready to kill. "Fucker set our building and our equipment on fire."

Tasha sobered as he turned back to Sutton. "Do you remember the commands?"

"Yes." They'd been pounded into her head. She been quizzed until she had to beg for something to stop the headache. Sutton appreciated the importance of it all but if bullets started flying the last thing on her mind would be what she should do if Tasha yelled, "Scramble" over the comm.

Tasha started to turn away then came back. She held out a hand to Sutton. "It takes a lot to impress me. You do."

Sutton shook it without thinking. She was too caught up in the stunned expressions on the men's faces and how that vote of confidence from someone like Tasha chased away some of her doubts. "Thank you."

Josiah didn't move as the others started to shift. "That's huge."

"People, it's time," Harlan said in a voice that boomed over all the others.

The words sliced through her. She blocked how she could see her breath in a smoky film on the cool night air. Lights bobbed above her on long wires and every building stood dark yet protected by high fences and elaborate security systems.

Their target sat eight buildings down on the right. They had the van and Tasha stashed another vehicle just outside the main gate into the complex. Backups and redundancies and protections. They had it all covered.

The only wildcard was one horrible man. "Will Benton actually be in there?"

Josiah shook his head. "I doubt it."

"So, there's no way to catch him today." The thought deflated her. Through all the prep and speed courses in every skill they thought she'd need, she missed that big part.

Harlan launched into lecture mode. "This is about bringing Ellery home. Nothing else."

"Live to fight another day," Mike said at the same time.

"Exactly." This time Harlan pointed at his watch. "Let's go."

Josiah took off without saying a word. The dismissal, intended or not, started an ache deep inside Sutton. This could be it for them, and he walked away.

Fine, so would she. She got two steps before she felt a hand on her arm. The world spun around her as she turned.

Before she could talk, his mouth landed on hers. Swept her up in a searing kiss. She held on as sensations battered her and the world flipped right again. When she opened her eyes, Josiah's face swam in front of her.

"Do not play the hero." His voice broke as he said the words.

She'd never heard a better sound. "You either."

Josiah and Mike followed the fence line around the west side of the buildings. Harlan and Sutton lagged behind at a safe distance, then branched off to skim the opposite side of the buildings. They'd see each other from a distance as they passed from building to building, but they'd stay separate. A smart choice but Josiah hated that part of the operation.

"You okay?" Mike asked.

"Not really."

They continued to walk while scanning the area. The "clear" signal hadn't come in from Tasha yet. That meant he and Mike had to get close enough to the target building to take a peek inside. Josiah hated the idea since the whole scene smelled of a setup. No way was Benton going to hand over Ellery without a fight.

It struck Josiah as equally implausible that Benton would let them all walk away today. He had a surprise in store for them and Josiah worried they were walking right into it. No matter what, he wouldn't let him touch Sutton. That put them at an impasse, and knowing Benton, he'd try to kill his way out of it.

They passed two sets of buildings before Mike spoke again. "She gets you."

Josiah understood the comment. He'd thought the same thing. Sutton didn't get all clingy and beg him to quit. She accepted the job and the risks. She knew the story of how he landed there and why it mattered. He sensed she respected that. "She sure does."

God, a police officer's daughter. An American. His father would have a heart attack if he knew. Maybe it was a good thing they never spoke to each other.

They came up on the third building. Josiah spied the

problem and held up a fist to stop their progress. The cut fence. He glanced up at the top of the fence posts. The video cameras didn't move. To test them he picked up a small rock and tossed it. Nothing happened and that was not a good sign.

"Coincidence?" Josiah wanted to think so, but didn't.

"No such thing."

"Glasses." He held a hand out to Mike, who handed over the binoculars.

It didn't take much adjusting for Josiah to close in on the building's door. He spied the new locks and the security panel. A chain lay on the ground, probably cut, which suggested someone tampered with the system.

The place might look beat-up and run-down, and the break-in could be unrelated, but Josiah doubted it. This would be the perfect distance for Benton's men to set up for an ambush. Hide here and wait. Which meant if Josiah and Mike could wipe them out now they'd increase Harlan's chance of success.

That thought sent his mind zipping back to Sutton. Josiah forced the memory of her face from his head. She needed him to succeed and he would.

"I guess we're heading in," Mike said as he took a turn looking through the glasses.

"You know this is going to turn into a fucked-up mess, fight?" Josiah was pretty sure that was going to happen any second now.

"Our specialty." Mike continued to cover the area. "I hate going in dark."

"Benton could pick up our transmissions. No talk on the comm means no chance of being overheard." But they would be able to hear the click Tasha sent over the line if she picked up heat signatures in the target building, hopefully one of those belonging to Ellery.

Until then, they were on their own without cover. And with nothing from Tasha yet, they had to check this out first.

Without saying a word, they slipped through the open fence. The warning gunfire Josiah expected never came. That kept them moving, low and fast. He wanted to pick a different door, one not obviously used. Anyone could be on the other side of this one.

"This feels wrong." That felt like the understatement of the decade but Josiah whispered it anyway.

Mike nodded as he dropped to one knee on the side of the door closest to the opening and the lock. Slipping a thin wire out of his pocket, he attached the tiny, almost invisible camera to the end. The equipment qualified as state of the art but that wouldn't help them if someone opened fire. Josiah kept watch just in case.

Adrenaline whipped through him as Mike put the camera away and motioned for them to slip inside. Keeping their steps quiet and movements to a minimum, they filed in. Darkness greeted them. Josiah took a minute to adjust. He could make out a small room with a wall of windows. It looked like an office space that opened to a larger warehouse but the treated glass blurred everything beyond.

The bigger issue was the lack of anything. The place looked empty. Not so much as a stick of furniture or a piece of paper. Josiah couldn't think of a good reason for someone to pay top dollar for security to guard this place . . . or why anyone had broken in unless it related to Benton.

He signaled for Mike to move. They approached the door to whatever came after. The small, barely audible click behind them had them both spinning around. Josiah's finger touched the trigger as an open hand appeared in the open doorway. Then Harlan's face.

Mike held up his hands as if to ask what the hell was going on.

That's what Josiah wanted to know. He mouthed Sutton's name and Harlan stepped inside with her at his side.

Talk about a plan gone wrong. This was exactly what wasn't supposed to happen. All four of them pinned down in a building about which they didn't have any intel. Just thinking it through made the nerve at the back of Josiah's neck pinch. His gut told him to usher Sutton out, but now that they were in there anyone could be outside waiting. Even now they could be surrounded or sitting on a bomb or any number of terrible scenarios.

Time for Plan B . . . or D, or whatever the hell kept them all alive.

Josiah lowered his gun and glared at Harlan. "Why?"

"There's movement at the next building. We circled back and saw the fence." Harlan's voice barely registered above the sound of the wind blowing against the side of the warehouse.

"We've been funneled in here for a reason." An effective strategy. Josiah had used it more than once himself. He didn't like being on this side of the plan.

Sutton's eyes grew even bigger. "Then we should leave."

Harlan shook his head. "The idea might be to pick us off as we go back out."

"We go through." The only option. Benton wanted to play this game, so they'd play. The one upside was being able to watch Sutton firsthand. Josiah pointed at her. "Stick close."

He went first. No way was he sacrificing anyone else on the team. If anyone fired, he'd handle it. He touched the knob, and the door opened under his hand. He listened for any sound and heard a thumping, like something hard hitting against concrete. A little wider and he saw it. Saw her. Ellery tied to a chair in the middle of the room. She shifted and with each move lifted the legs and smacked them against the floor.

Spreading out, they moved along the long empty room, heading for her. Her head popped up and she froze. She strained against the tape covering her mouth and shook her head. Her gaze darted behind them as she tried to warn them off.

Fuck that. They were grabbing her no matter what.

Harlan slid along the far right side and turned around, aiming his gun behind them. Josiah used the cover to run to Ellery. He had the tape off as Mike

and Sutton worked at cutting the wires around Ellery's legs.

She gasped as her frantic gaze traveled over each
one of them. "It's a trap."

"No shit." Mike released one leg then the other.

"There's a bomb and a gunman."

Ellery barely got the words out before the shooting started. The bangs echoed off the scaling walls as
Josiah tried to get a handle on the shooter's location.
Shots pinged and kicked up divots in the wall. The guy
had to be missing on purpose because with nothing to
hide behind, they were open targets on the floor.

Josiah slid in front of Sutton and pushed her down
behind him. Mike stood in front of Ellery as Harlan
came up the side firing.

They had to spread out and move. "Mike, take
Sutton."

She yelled something and reached for his hand, but
Josiah pushed her in Mike's direction. That left Ellery.
Harlan exchanged gunfire, shooting in rapid succession as Josiah slid to the floor and tore at the wire binding Ellery's hands to free her. She moved and tried to
spin around, which only cut the wire deeper into her
wrists.

One bang and Harlan spun to the side. He swore as
his shooting hand dropped.

Josiah recognized the signs and his gut clenched.
"You hit?"

"Get her out of here," Harlan yelled back as a dark
stain spread on his shoulder and he switched hands. He

fired from the left. He could do it but wouldn't be as accurate.

Josiah refused to leave anyone behind. "Let's move."

With Mike providing covering fire from his position at the far end of the room by the office, they took off and headed for him. First handle the inside, then they'd take on whoever loomed outside.

A few steps and Harlan stumbled. Josiah hustled Ellery forward, then pushed her ahead. When he turned back to grab Harlan a good ten feet separated them. Josiah had no idea how that happened. He took one step and got sucked out of the room. A wall of air smacked him in the face just as Harlan staggered to his feet. A loud boom sounded. The floor bounced and Harlan went down.

The roof exploded. Wood and chunks of cement fell, blocking Josiah's path to Harlan. Glass shattered around them in a deafening crash. Tiny shards rained down. Josiah put an arm over his head as he struggled to see through the smoke and falling debris.

It all happened in slow motion yet so fast. He blinked as he tried to get his mind to catch up. He could make out a lump on the ground and a figure in the distance. He looked around for Mike and the women. They came running toward him.

The second boom rang out. The force of the pressure knocked him down. His head bounced against the floor and a shower of what felt like small boulders pummeled him. He heard his name and thought Sutton might have screamed.

The pain in his head blinded him as he wrestled with the weight on top of him. The edges of his vision blinked out. He had to get up and tried to move. He got as far as his elbow before strong hands linked around his chest. Smoke swallowed up the light and sirens wailed in the distance as someone dragged him.

Then he breathed in the cool night air. He opened his eyes and Sutton hovered over him, concern evident in her eyes. He closed his eyes as he tried to remember what happened and what else he needed to do.

It hit him . . . "Harlan." He said it soft at first with a scratchy voice, then louder as he looked around for Mike.

Tires screeched and a black van pulled up. Not the one they came in. The other vehicle. The one Tasha had hidden just in case. Josiah looked from her in the driver seat to the building caving in behind him.

Jesus, Harlan was in there.

"We can't—" His protests cut off when Mike slipped an arm around his chest and lifted him off the ground.

Josiah saw Sutton and Ellery. Relief filled him that they were safe but reality chased the confidence away. They had one missing. "We have to go back in. We don't leave people behind."

A mix of stark pain and anger raced across Mike's face. "He's gone."

Josiah refused to believe that. He repeated the denial in his head but couldn't get the words out. Before his brain could kick back into gear, he was in the backseat of the van with his head on Sutton's lap. He had no idea how he got there but he had to sit up.

He shifted and pain screamed through his head. Bile raced up his throat and he choked it back. When the van smashed through the locked gate to the complex it lurched and they were thrown around inside. One more bounce and the darkness claimed him.

20

BENTON WALKED in a circle around the spot where Frederick knelt in the middle of the garage floor. He held his gun in his hand and debated shooting Frederick in the head. The price for failure should be death. Unless Frederick started begging for an alternate solution, it would be. But he didn't say anything. Benton saw no trace of fear, and that pissed him off.

He stopped right behind Frederick and leaned in close to his ear. "Explain."

Frederick kept his eyes forward. Didn't so much as flinch at having a word yelled in his ear. "Josiah grabbed the woman."

"Sutton." The one Benton wanted because it was time. Her life expectancy had expired. He'd allowed her to live far longer than he ever should have.

Killing Olivia Dahl years ago had been easy. Death by ambush. Benton had liked the sound of that and it fit in with her job. Just as he enjoyed watching the news a year later and seeing the FBI agent assigned to his brother's case killed along with his family in a home invasion. And that car accident that wiped out the other agent's family? Pure brilliance.

Benton was especially proud of how he wiped them all out without suspicion ever mounting. Nothing traced back to him. No one saw the three deaths as connected. But he knew. He'd gotten the vengeance for his brother. He'd ignored Sutton back then because she was a stupid kid and not on his radar. The newspapers showed her grief stricken and ruining her life had been enough. Then, not now.

Benton moved around to stand in front of his supposed assistant. The man whose training could not be argued. "You had the element of surprise on your side."

"They changed course and then the explosion happened too early."

Benton tightened his hand until the scars pulled and his arm ached. "It happened on schedule."

He knew because he timed it all perfectly. Lure Mike and Josiah in and let the fire consume them. Take Sutton and Harlan and make them watch before taking them out. By the end of the night Tasha should have been in a ball in a corner somewhere, wallowing in grief over her massive failure and the loss of her team. Then Benton would go after the rest of them.

Simple and expedient. He'd planned it out for maximum impact. Destroy his enemies, the only people who had ever found him, then get back to work. His customers kept grumbling and they needed a show of strength. A reminder that he, not they, was in charge. But Frederick's failure delayed all that.

"You don't—"

"Your instructions were clear." Benton talked right over the man who silently begged for a bullet in his brain without even knowing it. "Bring me Sutton and hold on to Ellery. But do I have either? No."

"I didn't expect Harlan to walk into the building. They should have remained separated. It's standard protocol in these situations."

"*Should* have." The computer clicked to life as an emergency call came in. Frederick glanced at it, then at him. In a night of failures and disappointments, Benton did not need another distraction. "Ignore it."

"Some of our clients are—"

Benton put the end of the gun against Frederick's temple. "Our?"

"The whispers are growing louder."

With his size advantage and his skills, Frederick could have overtaken the threat but he didn't. He knelt and took every last humiliation. Maybe there was an ounce of worthwhile loyalty in Frederick yet.

More importantly, maybe there was a way to salvage this. Regain the upper hand on his revenge and over his clients. Benton lifted the gun. "Then we'll appease them."

"Sir?" Frederick moved more than his eyes for the first time since being ordered to kneel. He turned his head and followed Benton as he backed up.

Benton had been thinking about a possible solution for days. He needed to rebuild the toxin program, as promised. His clients had waited long enough. He stared at the computer and thought about how much his clients were willing to pay for their toys. They seemed to have a never-ending supply of cash and a willingness to do harm. His favorite combination.

Sometimes they wanted information. Sometimes they needed information. Either way, for the right prize the cost would skyrocket. So, why not take advantage of that and let other interested parties help him with his pest problem.

He turned back to Frederick and gestured for him to stand up. "Make sure Harlan lives."

Frederick's eyes narrowed. "Why?"

"So I can kill him." The more Benton turned the solution over in his mind, the more he liked it.

"Sir?"

Frederick lacked vision. Benton saw that now. "If my clients want proof of my superiority, a spectacle of sorts, I'll give it to them."

Sutton watched Mike finish wrapping the bandages on Ellery's wrists. She thought of him as this big, tough guy and here he was playing nurse. Of course, the gun strapped to his side reminded her of his role as bodyguard.

Weeks ago she would have been twitchy being around someone so clearly comfortable killing when she worked so hard to uncover the evidence to resolve cases. Maybe not in one person's favor, but to end them. Josiah could be even colder. Mike liked to joke. Sometimes she'd stare at Josiah and he seemed so lost in his head. He didn't talk about guilt but it wrapped around him and he dragged it with him.

She tried to soothe and comfort, used her body and words, but in the quiet she could hear the wheels turning in his mind. Of course, she'd take that over his current questionable state. She was pretty convinced he had a concussion he refused to recognize. No stubbornness issue there.

The door banged open as Josiah and Tasha walked into the farmhouse kitchen from their secret meeting in the barn. Sutton hated to ask what came next. She'd spent the early days with the team locked in a room not knowing. Now they spoke in front of her as they joked about twisting the need-to-know requirements until they broke.

Ellery peeked around Mike's broad shoulders and looked at Tasha. "How's Lucas?"

Sutton fought off a wince. In the middle of the fighting and fear she'd forgotten about Lucas and how the not knowing must be tearing Ellery apart. If Josiah were the one in the hospital bed far away . . . Sutton couldn't even think about that.

"He came through surgery fine." Tasha dropped a stack of papers and her laptop on the table next to where Ellery sat on top. "West and Lexi are flying to meet him at a neutral location."

Sutton remembered all the rules about staying put and no reinforcements. "Where?"

Tasha didn't look up from her paperwork. "Undisclosed."

Of course. Josiah explained how Tasha could be curt but that it was her way of protecting them all. If no one knew where to find team members, they couldn't cough up the intel.

She watched him walk around the table now, all tall

and hot and focused on the job ahead. Even without her glasses she noticed every little thing. When he sat next to her she had to refrain from curling into him and trying to forget the last few hours. Instead she sat still, but she did smile when he put his hand on her knee.

She relaxed into the touch and dropped her voice to a whisper. "Who's West again?"

"On Bravo team," Mike said. "Lexi is his girlfriend."

"West took the lead on the Pakistan operation that wounded Benton." Josiah squeezed her leg, then reached up for a water bottle in the center of the table. "Lexi has medical training."

More bits and pieces. Sutton tried to remember all the names and how they fit together. Bravo and Delta. It was a lot to take in. Very cloak and dagger, more like an action movie than reality to her. But these guys lived it. They sometimes talked in code and half sentences while she rushed to catch up.

Tasha sat down and stared at Ellery. "What do we need to know?"

"Benton specifically wants Mike, Josiah, and Harlan." Ellery glanced at Sutton. "He also referred to you as a loose end."

At first Sutton couldn't believe Ellery kept all that straight through the horror of being attacked. Then her words sank in and something inside Sutton clunked. She felt the hard stop and the hollowness in her stomach. "Because of my mother."

Ellery shook her head. "I don't know what that means."

"I'll fill you in later. Basically, Sutton's mom drew out Benton, then using another name and seeming to be innocuous, when she touched off an investigation that killed off Benton's half brother." Mike smiled. "Oh, forget later. There it is."

"That would explain why he wants you out of the picture. You can tie him to his past, which may mean I can find him. Finally get one step ahead of him." Ellery tightened her hands over the bandages, then jumped off the table.

Tasha grabbed a thick file and put it in the middle of the table. "We'll need that advantage with Harlan . . ."

Another death. More destruction. It all piled around Sutton until she couldn't breathe.

A resolved silence fell over the room. Josiah finally broke it. "What about your dad?"

"Gone before I was born and died while driving drunk shortly after." Sutton spit out the biographical information like it didn't matter. To her, it didn't. Glenn was out of his life and never really in it. Her mother described him as irresponsible and insisted she learned a lesson about men from him and little else. "Benton doesn't have anything to do with him."

"So he was a loner. No real ties," Josiah said, filling in the rest.

The bloodless explanation echoed inside her. She slowly turned to look at him. "I'm not sure if I should be impressed or ticked off that you know all that."

She inhaled and tried to remember who the people around the table really were. They dug around and looked for connections. She did, too, but not on this level. Not with their resources and the wide net they cast. Looking at every possible lead made sense to them, and that could mean invading her privacy. She didn't fight it. For now.

Josiah shoved some of the files around. "We know anything else about Benton's brother?"

Mike smiled. "You mean the dead one."

"Is there another?" Sutton asked, suddenly worried there were more nutjobs out there blowing people and buildings up.

Ellery typed, mostly with one hand. "Just the half brother, Ronald."

Tasha looked at Ellery. "Rip that family's life apart. I want to know who they know, where they ever lived. Where every last penny is kept."

"Right." Ellery kept typing. Never looked up.

"Then dive into Olivia Dahl's personal life."

Energy whipped up around her. Sutton didn't know what she'd said or why they all seemed to be moving and reacting, but they were. "Wait a second. Do you think my mom was involved in whatever happened with the toxin back then because—"

Tasha held up a hand. "No."

The denial sucked some of the spiraling out of Sutton's anger. "Then why?"

She didn't realize her nerves were jumping or that her foot tapped against the floor until Josiah put a hand on her thigh again. "Benton went after her. She was collateral damage. Just as you are. Just as others could be."

She'd been down that road as well. Too many deaths littered the ground when Benton blipped off the map. She'd been locked in this battle so long that having people step up and help her, believe in her, threw her off. She came out fighting. Went on the defensive.

She shut all of those instincts down. With her elbows on the table, she sat there unmoving as the weight of all they said crushed her. All good news, but still. Emotions whipped up. She seemed so close to getting what she wanted, but still she thought about Harlan and the danger. The simple fact that this wasn't over.

"Ellery?" Tasha handed Ellery a piece of paper with a series of numbers written on it. "I borrowed Benton's trick and used air surveillance."

"What does that mean?" Sutton's real question was *how* she did that.

Mike must have gotten it because he laughed. "You don't want to know."

"Look at the feeds and track every car, bus, or plane out of that warehouse area and find out where it went," Tasha said. "One of them will lead us to Benton, or at least his associate."

"I'm on it."

Sutton looked at Ellery's bandages and the dark circles under her eyes. "Don't you need time off?"

"Not until we find out exactly what happened to Harlan and make sure Benton is dead," Mike said.

Josiah sat up straighter. "Oh, we're going to kill that fucker. After we recover Harlan."

Sutton's head kept spinning. In her heart she'd started to think of him as gone. She was pretty sure that's what Mike said back at the warehouse. "Wait, are you saying he got out?"

"We think he may have been dragged out," Josiah said on a deep inhale. "There was someone else in that room."

Mike nodded. "I saw him, too."

"I've had some of our assets check the building now that it's safe to go back in." Tasha's mouth flatlined. "There's no body in it."

Assets . . . body. Sutton turned it all over in her head. "What does that mean?"

Josiah's jaw tightened. "Benton likely has Harlan."

One horrible thought screamed in her brain: That might be worse than being dead. "Which means?"

Josiah looked at her then. "Something big is coming."

"Harlan, though that's not your real name, is it?" Benton took great pride in standing in front of the man while holding his top-secret work file in his hands.

The guy looked like hell. The bullet had torn through his shoulder and had his arm hanging at an odd angle. Without painkillers or anesthesia, Frederick had sewn Harlan up enough to get him through this next part. Said he never even flinched. Now he wore a bandage where the red soaked through in spots.

Then there were the cuts from the glass and the way his eyes stayed unfocused thanks to Frederick nailing him in the head. Any other man would be unconscious.

"Nothing to say? I must admit, Tasha has you all very well trained."

The silence continued for a few more beats. Harlan sat tied to the chair and stared first at Benton then past him to where Frederick leaned against the far wall. "Go to hell."

"Interesting thought." The sensation of almost being burned alive was not one Harlan should discuss. Benton had experience in that area. Now Harlan would, too. "It turns out you will be beneficial to me after all."

"I'm not helping you."

Benton ignored that. "See, some very nasty people are upset about what happened in Pakistan."

Through the cuts and bruises Harlan smiled. "How did it feel to catch on fire?"

"Oh, you'll know soon enough." Then he wouldn't be smiling. He'd be too busy screaming, and Benton couldn't wait to tape every minute of it. "See, I've decided to hold an auction. The winner gets the prototype of the bomb vest, but the real gift is you."

Harlan's swollen smile faded. "No one knows who I am."

"That's the beauty of this. Thanks to Pearce I know who you are, who every member of the Alliance is, and about many of the operations you've undertaken. That information is valuable. There are a lot of people who would like to see you all pay for your interference."

Frederick laughed. "Now they can."

"And you pocket the cash and go hide in a cave in Pakistan." Harlan spit a wad of blood on the floor by Benton's feet. "Good luck with that."

He refused to show any reaction. He would not give Harlan the satisfaction of killing him too early. Not when there was so much fun to be had in waiting.

"No, those days are over. I picked out this lovely spot on a pile of rocks that used to be a fortress. Now it's home." When he inhaled he could almost smell the orange blossoms. One of the oldest towns in Spain, with the bullfighting ring and the mosques.

Frederick cleared his throat. "Sir, we should—"

Caution usually proved to be a wise decision. Benton exercised it with ruthless efficiency, which explained why no one had seen him or could identify him until the Alliance came knocking. But Harlan's time was almost over. He should know there would be no more hiding. And it didn't hurt to rub his nose in his complete failure. "Warm breezes through the villa. Ruins to explore. Good food and wine. Just me and the tourists."

"Boss." Frederick came off the wall and walked toward Harlan.

Benton held up a hand to stop any lecture Frederick might be stupid enough to give. "Seemed only fair to give the man something since he'll be dead tomorrow and won't be able to tell a soul."

"True."

"But I do want you to know that you won't be the last. I'm going to take particular pleasure in sending Josiah home to his daddy in pieces." Benton had been living for that day and now it had arrived.

"You're going to fail."

Harlan sounded sure but Benton knew better. He had not survived this long on luck. "Never."

21

JOSIAH HATED being right. He stared at the laptop screen and the new password blinking in front of him. Another message from Benton via the Dark Web. Every fiber and every cell called on him to walk away and not sign into the link. But he'd never been a coward and he wasn't about to start now.

"Are you okay?" The fresh floral scent from whatever Sutton used in the shower followed her into the room.

Her husky voice stopped him from touching the keyboard. He wanted to lie but she'd be the one person who might be able to tell if he did. "No."

Scrubbed clean of makeup and the grime from the explosion, she looked bright and sunny. Wore a genuine smile. One that said she was happy to be alive and realistic about what could happen next. Her shiny hair fell over her shoulders and those dark pants hugged every sexy curve.

She walked in and thoughts of death fell away. For the first time in years he saw something other than the job. With her he didn't need to justify or lie. She knew the story of his mother and didn't rush to fill in the silence with empty words. Forget the family trappings and the titles and the land, she wanted him as he was— scarred and riding the thin edge of sanity.

After everything they'd been through he knew she'd be able to handle this, too. He pointed at the screen.

She watched him as she walked around the table to stand at his side. "That looks like—"

"Yeah."

Her hand landed on his back as her cheek rubbed against his. "Josiah?"

He debated saying more. His job depended on him being strong and confident. Kick down a door to a gun-runner's warehouse, infiltrate a human trafficking ring, rescue a journalist held by militants. He'd done it all. But losing someone on his team had the potential to lay them all out. This business almost guaranteed an early death. That didn't mean Josiah accepted the end. He fought it with every breath. Which made typing in that password so damn difficult.

Her hand lay on his arm and he covered it with his palm. "I'm going to open this site and Harlan is going to be dead or worse."

"A week ago I would have asked what could be worse than death." She sighed. "Now I know."

"I wish you didn't." He'd do anything to hide that truth from her, to let her live in happy denial like most people did.

She glanced at the keyboard, then back to him. "You can't save him if you don't look."

If only it were that easy. Harlan always had an uneasy relationship with the other men in the Alliance. About ten years older and accustomed to being in the field and acting a certain way, Harlan often disapproved of the way Josiah and Ford ran the individual teams. Harlan could best be described as British old school intelligence officer. He fought when necessary but ran over every plan ad nauseam, trying to cover every contingency.

Sometimes he forgot that real-life scenarios didn't come with a playbook. But he was a solid man and he didn't deserve whatever end Benton intended to give him.

It all played in his mind but Josiah didn't say any of it. Not out loud. But somehow she knew. The awareness hummed through her body. Refueled his energy reserves.

She pressed her nose against his neck. "Don't do that thing where you take on more guilt."

"He wasn't supposed to be in that building." That fact kept replaying in Josiah's mind. The man so devoted to plans and protocol broke both, and now . . . who knew where Harlan was now.

"Actually, it was supposed to be a bloodbath. A bit of a show. One that Benton could enjoy over time." When he started to congratulate her on her reasoning she wiggled her eyebrows at him. "What, you think you're the only one who could figure it out? I'm somewhat trained, remember? Being around you guys has only increased my skills."

"Impressive woman." And he meant it. She nailed it all. That's exactly what he and Tasha had figured out.

Sutton shot him one of those heated looks that promised more than a life with a gun. "Sexy man."

Much more of that and he'd forget about every responsibility. He had to compartmentalize his feelings for her, tuck them away, to stay on track. The throbbing in his head and seeing the exhaustion tugging at her eyes brought him back to reality. "I hate the idea that you could have been grabbed."

"But I wasn't and now you need to be the Josiah I know, or whatever your real name is, and do your job." She tapped the table right in front of the keyboard. "Save your friend, and if that's not possible avenge his death."

"I like the bloodthirsty side of you." And he liked the way she handled him, steering him where he needed to go. He was man enough to admit her getting a little bossy turned him on. "Benedict."

He clicked a button on his watch to send a signal to Tasha, Ellery, and Mike to come into the room. They needed rest and time to prep, but everyone needed to see this . . . even if none of them wanted to.

When he started to sit down, Sutton put a hand on his arm and stopped him. "What did you say?"

Oh, she knew, but he did like stunning her. "My real name."

"Are you allowed to tell me that?"

"I wanted you to know." That was the truth. He didn't disclose it to anyone because despite his issue with his father Josiah didn't want to put him in danger. But he trusted her. The days of looking for things to find wrong with who she was and how she got there were long gone.

"What's going on?" Tasha walked out of the room she was using as a bedroom and slipped around to their side of the table. "Ellery thinks she knows where . . ." Tasha leaned in closer. "A password."

"Damn it." Mike delivered his assessment from the doorway to the kitchen. "Just enter it. We need to know."

Tasha sat down and started typing while the rest of them crowded around her. The screen flipped. At first a gray box appeared, then the picture focused.

Except for Sutton's sharp intake of breath the room stayed quiet. No one said anything. All eyes stayed forward as if they waited for the next horrible moment to arrive.

The image hit Josiah like a slam to the gut. It was happening all over again. A live feed he couldn't stop. Even yelling wouldn't help because no one on the side of the screen could hear. No, this beamed into their lives for Benton's sick entertainment. They could only listen and watch in horror.

Harlan, beaten and injured, his shoulder wrapped and bleeding. But that was the good part. No one could miss the bomb strapped to his chest or the wires leading to his arm and to a cut in his chest. Tied to the chair and wearing a gag in his mouth, he stared into the camera.

Josiah could see Harlan swallow. Watch him breathe. The unwelcome sensation of being one step behind hit again. He'd tried to block the video and the memory of his uncle so he could get through this assignment. Now it all came rushing back. The bomb. The countdown. The reality that he could not fix this.

Harlan's gaze followed something or someone in the room. Then those same legs from the video of Josiah's uncle came into focus. Benton, but not showing his face. Standing right there in the middle of everything.

"Can we get a reading on a location? Shadows, directions of the sun, type of building—anything to go on?" Tasha asked.

Ellery opened a second computer and started typing. "No. This still could be the airport. A hangar, maybe over where the private planes leave."

"Airport?" Josiah didn't expect that answer.

"That's where she traced the car that took Harlan away. His implant tracker had blinked in and out, likely due to a jammer," Tasha said.

Mike slid into the seat next to her. "Benton knocked out our equipment but he underestimated Tasha's ability to call in favors and get air support as backup."

"This is Harlan Ross, real name Daniel Buckingham. Formerly of the British Army and, to be specific, the Special Reconnaissance Regiment." Benton's scratchy voice boomed through the speaker. "He carried out operations in Northern Ireland, Somalia, Iraq. And the list goes on."

Mike wiped a hand over his face. "Jesus, he just blew Harlan's cover."

"Why is Benton still hiding from the camera and saying stuff we know?" Sutton asked.

Josiah hated the answer but he said it anyway. "Because we're the only ones who know what he looks like but we're not the only ones watching this. This isn't even meant for us, except as an emotional torture device."

"He is a member of a group called the Alliance, with its roots in the CIA and MI6." Benton's voice droned on while the camera focused on Harlan, showing only Benton's legs. "The winner of this auction will receive the prototype for this very special bomb as well as the identities and operational information for the Alliance."

Mike shot out of his seat and stood up again. Started pacing the space behind the table.

"How does he have all of that?" Sutton asked.

"Jake Pearce." The guy who screwed up everything. Joshua never hated anyone as much as he hated that traitor. "Every time I think about that guy I want to kill him again."

"Let the bidding begin." Benton opened the auction, then left the screen.

Code names and numbers started running along the right-hand side of the site. Josiah didn't recognize any of them, but that was the point. Evil preferred to stay anonymous.

The bids ran up. The price ticked past three million

dollars in less than ten seconds. Josiah should have been surprised but he wasn't. "Good to know our lives are worth a few dollars."

But he picked up on something else. Despite the injuries and what had to be a bone-chilling sense that his life was almost over, Harlan kept moving. Not obvious. Just a small tap of his fingers.

Josiah moved in closer and pointed at the screen. "What is he doing?"

"I don't . . . The code." Tasha turned around and stared at Mike. "What is he saying?"

"I'm on it." Mike brought the laptop closer to his face. He watched and every few seconds wrote down a letter.

Sutton shook her head. "I don't get it. What's happening?"

"We have a modified version of Morse code. Something Mike developed for this type of situation when we had to get the information out any way we could." Josiah had never been so happy about this group's rampant paranoia and driving need to be ready for anything. "Well?"

Mike put the laptop back on the table and smiled. "Airport."

"Okay, we're going to assume the same airport where Ellery tracked him." Tasha stood up. "We've got four hours to launch an operation to save Harlan and stop this auction."

Mike kept watching then started shaking his head. "Ellery was right. Harlan's not at the private airport right here. He's at Charles de Gaulle, one of the busiest airports in the world."

Some of the wind rushed out of Josiah. "We're talking a quarter of a million people a day passing through." He thought about the crowds and the potential for damage. "That's a lot of opportunities for Benton to show off his new toy."

"Which is why we need to assume he has something bigger planned." Mike tucked the pen behind his ear. "This auction is about getting attention as much as it's about killing Harlan."

"Either way, Harlan dies." Josiah didn't mean to say it out loud but when everyone looked at him, he knew he had.

Tasha glanced at the auction bid. Up to fourteen million and climbing each second. "Make sure that doesn't happen."

A half hour later Sutton found Josiah just standing in the middle of their bedroom. Theirs, not hers since he'd joined her beneath those covers every night. The first time together had turned into others in an unspoken agreement that they not sleep alone. She had no idea what it meant long term or how to even separate out the man she found so compelling from the one who walked into such unrelenting agony every day.

She couldn't speak to his feelings. They had to be jumbled from all the death unfolding around him and rage simmering within. But she knew what she felt.

How her heart raced when he walked into a room. How his smile opened something inside her.

Some people would tell her she'd been on an adrenaline high since they met. Maybe. She probably needed distance but right now she didn't want it because she was too busy falling for him. And too busy worrying that this might be the only time she'd ever get. She'd come to Paris seeking revenge. She'd found love and now all she could do was ride it out.

Debating whether to give him space, she decided against it. She needed to touch him. Making sure she stepped loud enough to announce her presence so he didn't reach for a weapon, she walked into the room and slipped her arms around his waist.

His hands covered hers and he pulled her in tighter. "What's this for?"

"I got the impression you didn't get hugged very often." She kissed the back of his neck then rested her cheek against his broad back. "You missed out."

"Mike won't hug me no matter how much I ask."

She heard the smile in his voice. She loved that he still could. Over the last few days she'd lost the ability to separate out the terror from the calm. Even as they planned or conducted research her mind wandered all over, from the death and threats to the utter pleasure of what he did for her in bed.

That mouth. The gentle scratch of that scruff around his chin as it rubbed against her inner thighs. He'd let his fingers linger and made her beg for release. She found everything about him so damn hot.

But they had to survive, and not just them. She couldn't stand to lose any members of the team, even those she knew only by name and had never met. "Tell me we're going to save him."

Josiah didn't ask any questions. He just lifted her hand and kissed it. "I don't know."

Figured he'd pick this one time to feed her the unvarnished truth. "That's not really what I was hoping for. I kind of depend on your confidence."

"Me too."

She loosened her hold and walked around, skimming her hand around his torso, until she faced him. "Promise me something."

"What?" He put his hands on her hips and closed the gap between them.

She knew he'd hate the rest but she had to say it. "Tell me you won't trade places or put your life at risk."

He closed one eye and frowned at her. "That's basically what I do."

"I don't want you to get hurt." The simple sentence didn't come close to summing up her feelings. The words hung there when she wanted to say so much more. "When this is over . . ."

He stopped her words with a kiss. A quick one that continued on. When he finally lifted his head his frown remained. "I can't make any promises."

"When you bring Harlan back I'm going to give you a hero's reward." She would say anything, do anything, to keep Josiah safe. It sounded ridiculous with his skills and his size, but she would fight to the death for him. "But you have to come back in one piece to get it."

"I'll try." His lips danced over hers. "For you."

She put her hand on the back of his neck and treated him to a kiss filled with promise. One that let him know she would wait. When her breath grew heavy, she lifted her head and stared into those dark eyes. "Just come back."

22

JOSIAH HATED everything about this plan. The auction ticked on with less than a half hour left. At last check Harlan's life and the team's private information carried an eighty-million-dollar price tag. That was a hell of a lot of incentive. Benton couldn't back away now. He needed to preview the bomb and hand over the intel. Make an example of Harlan.

That meant he needed to die, and soon.

They'd skipped the main terminals and main body of the airport and headed for a series of garages at the outskirts of the property. A supply and maintenance area used mostly by commercial flights carrying cargo and mail. Harlan had tapped out "garage" and this area fit. So did the amount of power being used here, or so Ellery said.

Josiah hoped like hell they were right. It wasn't as if he could dump Sutton in a hotel and retrieve her later. Dividing the group meant giving Benton a chance to swoop in. This entire auction, though Ellery insisted it was real, could be another way to grab them. One by one. To be safe, the rest of the team had scattered all over the world, ready to take on new identities if needed.

Ellery and Tasha waited in the van parked nearby. Ellery tried to work her tech magic, searching frequencies and video and figuring out a way to defuse that bomb. Tasha ran point. She'd balked at being out of the main action when Harlan's life was on the line, but she was the only one who could run this operation. The best Josiah could manage for Sutton was to leave her with Tasha.

Mike and Josiah headed in. They had one shot at this. The bomb tied to Harlan's heart rate but it had a kill switch. Benton could set it off at any time, and seeing the rest of the team would likely cause that to happen.

They headed for the garage Ellery had pinpointed, guided in without any sound of help from Tasha. She'd break radio silence, if needed. Otherwise, she listened and moved pieces around and called in resources where possible and tried to cut off Benton's access to the outside world. It was the role Harlan generally played while Tasha sat at her administrative desk in her nice office in the big building.

Josiah signaled for Mike to move forward. They took turns with the lead, one rushing the building and stopping to hide behind natural landmarks and anything else that might block gunfire while the other kept watch.

When Mike waited fifty feet out, Josiah used the binoculars. Scanned the rooftops for snipers. Checked the open field and every hiding area for shooters. He didn't see anything. Benton's men could be sophisti-cated and committed. Snipers could sit for hours, days even, in the same position and hold. Josiah didn't see any sign that Benton could buy that kind of loyalty but it had been that kind of operation. Every expected zig turned out to be a zag.

After what felt like hours of keeping watch but really only amounted to minutes, he dropped the glasses and shook his head at Mike. Josiah tried to justify Benton's decision to go without cover. The lack of movement made Josiah edgy. Still, they needed to move if Harlan had any shot at surviving this.

Going in cold carried risks. Benton had picked up a love for blowing up things. He'd gone over the edge on this revenge. Ellery had even started picking up Inter-net chatter about Benton's unhappy customers.

Time to go.

Josiah gave Mike the signal and they went in. They met up at the wall close to the building's side door. They both stood with their backs pressed against the cool siding.

Mike never took his eyes off the horizon. "No shooters?"

Tension bounced between them. They'd done enough of these to know when an assignment was about to go sideways. In this case, Josiah suspected it was about to be flipped upside-down. "A bad sign."

"Very."

He thought about Sutton and that smile. Called up

the vision of Harlan tied to that bomb. So much to lose and it could all go in the next few minutes. "Time check."

"Twenty-two minutes until someone wins this auction."

That's all the information Josiah needed. "Let's get this done in ten. I like having time to spare."

Mike nodded. "Agreed."

They slid along the wall to the door. No need to worry about cameras or lock picking or any of those cool tech devices Ellery handed them to beat a password-protected system. The door was open. Not much, but enough for them to see light streaming from inside and to hear the steady hum of a machine of some sort.

Josiah slipped inside first and stopped. He wasn't sure what he was seeing. The back of a computer operation of some sort. Banks of equipment set up on tables and thick cables lining the floor. Ellery specifically told him not to shoot the computers or he would have. Seemed like the logical way to stop the auction but she claimed it would make tracking impossible.

With that avenue closed, Josiah went with the next obvious plan. They stalked around the setup. A sheet blocked their path and view of the rest of the room, so Josiah ripped it down.

There was the fake studio. Harlan in the chair. Benton standing right behind with a gun to Harlan's head. Frederick aiming at Mike.

Fucking perfect.

Since Josiah had no intention of surrendering, he

went for the big play. Adjusted his aim and shot Frederick's hand. When the man yelled with rage, Josiah hit him in the side and dropped him to the ground.

Mike took a turn and shot out the camera. Not both, because Tasha was tuned in and watching. Harlan could send another message. They weren't closing any avenue here.

Benton looked at his man thrashing around on the floor as he made a sound half like a cough and half choking. Then his gaze went to the shattered twist of plastic and metal.

"Well." He made a humming sound. "Neither of those actions seemed necessary."

But it felt pretty great. So would the next round Josiah planned to put in Benton's forehead. "Your turn."

He made an annoying tsk-tsking sound. "Careful, gentlemen."

The guy acted as if he made the rules. He was outnumbered. There could be shooters lingering out there. Josiah suspected that was the case. But he had Tasha and her perfect shot and pissed-off attitude to hold them off for a while.

"Put the trigger down." Josiah started a countdown in his head. If he got to five without this bomb being defused he was shooting Benton's kneecap.

"That won't help you." Benton reached over and removed the binding covering Harlan's mouth. "Do you want to tell them?"

"This isn't the only bomb," Harlan said in a rough voice between hard swallows.

Josiah couldn't remember ever hearing the man sound defeated. Angry and disappointed, yes. He liked to lecture and gave a knife-training session that taught them all a few things, but the man in the chair acted as if he was going to die today.

"I don't believe it." But he did. One look at Harlan's eyes and Josiah knew the truth.

"The one you really need to worry about is in Terminal 1, along with thousands and thousands of passengers and airport workers. Those people working the coffee shops and restaurants. All that fuel nearby." Benton actually smiled as he laid that all out. "Think of the damage."

He'd planned this down to the second. Took them to a place where he could escape easily and have plenty of decoys to cover his tracks. Josiah couldn't exactly play games with that many lives with something like fifteen minutes left to maneuver, which gave Benton the upper hand.

He touched Harlan's shoulder. "If his bomb vest doesn't explode, the much larger terminal bomb will."

Mike didn't ease his shooting stance. "Bullshit."

"Ever the farm boy." Benton shook his head. "Swearing or not, you'd be wise to listen to me. This vest will take care of Harlan and most of you two. The terminal bomb will knock buildings to the ground. There will be nothing left. I'm not sure even dental records will help you identify all the bodies."

"We shoot you and defuse the bomb." Seemed simple enough to Josiah, which was why it likely wouldn't work. But that wasn't the point. He was stalling, trying to give Tasha time to get word to someone. Bring in the bomb squad, or whatever the French equivalent of that was.

"Not possible." Benton moved until all but his upper body and head hid behind Harlan's slumping form. "You touch his vest, it explodes and the one in the terminal explodes. Death all around. If I trigger the explosives in the vest, I can still determine if I should also set off the one in the terminal, which I would. And, of course, if his heart rate accelerates, the vest goes off."

So many ways to die. Josiah glanced at Harlan then. Looked for signs of panic. Didn't detect any sweat or fidgeting. Even his breathing stayed steady.

As if he heard the thought, Benton commented. "I do have to commend him for staying calm in the face of certain death. That was training money well spent by the British government."

Enough talking and showing off, or whatever the hell Benton was doing. Josiah couldn't stand the sound of his voice and the brief hesitation between each word. "What do you want?"

"Revenge."

What Josiah had come to see as the most useless of motivations.

"And money," Mike added.

Benton shrugged. "I should get paid."

Josiah's gaze traveled around the room. The auction continued to play out and the video ran. Out of the corner of his eye he could see Frederick moving, trying to crawl along the floor, and Josiah raised his gun.

"Stop," Benton said, cutting him off. "Don't shoot him again."

"You're telling me you care about someone other than yourself?" Josiah didn't see it. That sort of emotion didn't fit the profile.

"Hardly, but one shot was enough." Benton walked over to Frederick and put his foot on the discarded gun before Frederick could touch it. Bending down with jerky movements, Benton picked up the weapon. Winced as he lifted with his injured hand.

"You're a crazy motherfucker." Mike's slight accent slipped out as his gaze moved over the room.

And seriously hurt. Sutton had been right about Benton and her description of his wounds accurate. Josiah made a note for later.

"I'm practical." Benton checked his watch and then the auction clock.

Ten minutes to go. Ninety-two million dollars on the table.

"In fact there are two things you two should do for me," Benton said.

"No."

Benton talked right over Mike's answer. "I assume Tasha is listening. She would be wise to leave that van and join us . . . unless she wants to die in a fireball."

No wonder he didn't have shooters. He had bombs set

everywhere. He could command them at will, though Josiah doubted the story about the one in the van was true. Hitting that trigger was much more accurate and assured than depending on some random commando to get the job done.

Still, the airport sat in a huge metropolitan area that served as the gateway to the rest of Europe. Brining in explosives would not be easy. There were security measures in place. Locks and guards. Benton might know people and be able to pay money, but this qualified as a huge undertaking. "We're supposed to believe you have all these bombs planted at a major airport."

"He does." Harlan tried to nod, then closed his eyes as his face went pale. "He dragged me along and set up a video so I could watch the setup in the terminal. I don't know about the rest, but he has people everywhere."

"See?" Benton sounded far too pleased with himself. "Now, I do have a one-time deal for you." A smile stretched across his face as a noise echoed at the side of the room. "Well, there they are."

The women walked in. Josiah had to assume they'd tried every other door and couldn't open them, which left this one right on top of the action. He didn't want to take the chance they knew the tale Benton had been telling. "Don't shoot."

"He's lying." Tasha made the comment as she moved farther into the room, with Ellery and Sutton armed and right behind her.

"Test me and then you can explain to the relatives of fifty thousand people why you made that choice."

Benton put a hand on Harlan's arm, making his eyes fall shut for a second.

Causing pain would raise Harlan's heart rate and end this before they could figure out a solution. Josiah couldn't let that happen. "Guns down."

Mike shot him a stunned look. "What?"

"We need everyone calm." Josiah saw the minute the comment registered in Mike's brain.

"Now, as I was saying." Benton moved his hand off Harlan's shoulder. "There is a way out of this."

Josiah's mind flipped through different scenarios to end this. "What?"

"Easy. You shoot him." Benton used the end of his gun to gesture toward Harlan.

Tasha slowly lowered her weapon. "What are you talking about?"

"If you shoot him, I won't set off the other bombs. Well, so long as I leave this property unharmed." Benton explained his compromise with all the emotion of reading a grocery list. "Harlan dies, but the rest of us live. And I leave, of course."

"Benton." The small sound came from the floor. Frederick held a hand to his stomach as he tried to lever up with the other elbow.

Benton didn't even look at the man who supposedly had served him for years. "You deserve an honorable death, Frederick."

Before the guy talked, Josiah had forgotten he was even there. He had shot him to neutralize the situation and take out the extra weapons. "No deal."

"Fifty thousand people." Benton looked at Tasha. "You couldn't evacuate the place if you wanted to. And that call that you think went through to issue a warning actually came to my phone." Benton slipped one out of his pocket and held it up. "But good try."

Josiah let the anxiety churn inside him. He needed the energy. Whatever it took to get his body primed for battle worked for him.

Benton looked at his watch again. "You have ten seconds."

"No." But Josiah checked the auction clock. They had more like three minutes than the ten seconds Benton called out.

"He dies anyway, along with some of you in here and half of the airport."

Before Benton could finish his newest threat, Harlan opened his mouth. His head lolled to one side as he shifted his weight in his seat. "Do it."

At first Josiah thought he hadn't heard him. Then he saw the determination on the older man's face. He'd spent a lifetime saving others and now he stood in the middle of a disaster that promised death to at least some.

Josiah couldn't do it. "Harlan, stop."

Harlan started to shake his head and winced instead. "You don't have a choice."

That couldn't be true. Harlan's career—the man— could not end this way. "You will not die today."

Josiah looked at Ellery and realized she held a gun not a laptop. She couldn't run programs and look for loopholes in here. Getting her to watch the show had been one more brilliant move by Benton in a long line of them.

"I'm going to die anyway. I knew that when they grabbed me."

Josiah remembered it differently. Harlan had stepped up and rescued them, then sacrificed his body. The bravery made Josiah more determined than ever to get Harlan out of that chair.

"As I said, the man is practical." Benton tapped his watch this time. "And you have seven seconds."

Killing Benton moved up the option list. Josiah turned slightly, but not enough for anyone to notice.

But Mike knew. "Don't take that shot, Josiah."

"Listen to the man. Killing me is definitely not the right answer unless you like the idea of this airport bursting into flames." Benton tightened his hold on the trigger.

"Josiah, you know I'm right." Harlan was pleading now.

The words slammed into Josiah. He fought off the pain rolling through him and the memories that threatened to drop him to his knees. There had to be something else. Anything else. "No fucking way."

Harlan shifted his attention. "Mike?"

"Jesus," he said under his breath.

"Five seconds until Terminal 1 explodes." Benton looked back and forth between Josiah and Mike. He didn't appear concerned that the countdown put him within explosion range. "Someone step up."

Josiah had other ideas on how to end this. "Take me with you. You want revenge; you'll get it with me. You know my family. It will cause a huge splash."

Benton just shook his head. "Three."

Harlan turned in his chair and the legs clanked against the floor. "Josiah, do it!"

"There's no way." Josiah kept shaking his head.

"Two." That voice rang like a gong.

Benton moved back, a slow step by step as he counted. Josiah hadn't even noticed until he realized how far away Benton now stood from the destruction zone.

He raised his gun again. "Do not move, Benton."

"Your time is up." Benton smiled as he looked around the room. "Anyone?"

Harlan thunked the chair against the floor again. "Shoot me now!"

Josiah shook his head as he tightened his fingers on the gun. "Harlan."

"I am begging you. Do it!"

The words still rang out as Josiah fired. One shot that vibrated through him. His muscles froze and he stood there. The blood drained from his body as Harlan's head fell forward.

As if in a slow-motion trance, Josiah fell to his knees. Hit the ground hard. The shot rattled in his bones.

Everyone moved. He tried to get up and check Harlan but the sidewall opposite blew out and off. Josiah couldn't move. Could only bend his head forward to evade the shock of air that punched through the room. His mind went to Sutton but he couldn't see her. Couldn't hear anything. The bang had blocked his ears.

He didn't see flames but smoke billowed. The shouting started right after. Looking down, Josiah saw the gun still in his hand and dropped it. Then he sat back on his heels. Activity buzzed around him and someone called his name. Not that he gave a shit.

He'd killed Harlan.

23

SUTTON TRAPPED the scream inside her. She rotated between wanting to heave and wanting to fall on the ground. Harlan's begging. Josiah's pain. It all had been too much. She wanted to shut down. Crawl into a corner and not come out.

Then she saw Josiah. Tasha rushed around giving orders. She had her phone and talked about the bomb. Ellery focused on the parts of the computer the targeted explosion hadn't destroyed. Mike went to Harlan.

Josiah hadn't moved. He sat back on his heels staring into space. She followed his gaze. No, he stared at Harlan's still form. Sutton joined him, concentrating and hoping that Harlan would open his eyes. That this had all been some elaborate plan and Benton didn't win this round.

But Harlan didn't move.

Everything inside her crashed. She felt raw and ready to burst. She might have if Josiah didn't just sit there. Forcing her legs to move, she went to him. He already had a concussion and bruises all over him. That didn't even cover the emotional battering.

She didn't know how much he could take. Anyone else would have reached the breaking point long ago.

She used the toe of her sneaker to move aside some of the debris. The rubber scratched against the floor, but still he didn't move. Careful not to add any more cuts to her already substantial collection, she knelt beside him.

"Josiah?"

"He's dead," he said in a flat voice.

The lack of emotion and the pale face scared the hell out of her. She wrapped an arm around his shoulders. "Can you get up?"

"Yes." But he didn't move.

"We should get out of here. Get some fresh air." The suggestions sounded ridiculous in her ears but she needed to try something.

He closed his eyes. His body swayed a bit but then he regained his balance. Maybe he needed rest. His brain could use a break while his body took a few hours to heal.

Then his eyes popped open and his attention shifted. He turned his head and stared at Frederick. Tasha hovered over him now. Patted him down as she checked his pulse.

Sutton heard a rumbling sound. A deep winding groan, half roar, from inside Josiah. She looked around for a truck. Feared another explosion. The sirens moved closer but this was something else. She touched a hand to the back of his head. She wanted to check for injuries but tried to be satisfied with just touching him.

Not that he saw her. She didn't even think he noticed her there. He moved on some sort of autopilot. One second he sat there, unmoving and glaring. The next he jumped to his feet, leaving her sitting in stunned fascination.

He scooped up his gun and stalked over to Frederick. Gone was the cloudy look of horror on his face. Rage moved through him. He practically vibrated with it. He stopped right over the body, right next to Tasha.

"What are you doing?" she asked.

Sutton scrambled to her feet and ran over to him. She didn't touch him. Anything could set him off. He seemed to walk right on the edge.

Josiah aimed the gun at Frederick's head. Somehow the guy stayed conscious. He lay in a curled ball on the floor until Josiah stepped near him, then Frederick tried to crawl. He dragged his body using one elbow. A streak of red followed him. Blood covered his hand and soaked his shirt. Still, Josiah loomed with his gun ready.

He lifted his foot and jammed it into Frederick's back. The man sprawled to the floor with a groan.

"Stay down." Josiah pressed harder.

Tasha stood up and faced him. "Josiah, think this through. Why do this here?"

"Tying up loose ends."

"Man, no. Not like this," Mike said, the pain evident in his voice.

Josiah didn't appear to hear any of the protests. He stood with his foot on Frederick's back. Listened to the guy's heavy breathing and met him stare for stare. "You're going to die."

"Do it."

Josiah's gun started moving and so did Sutton. She reached his side and touched his arm. "Not in cold blood."

"Josiah, listen to Sutton." Tasha's voice bordered on pleading.

He continued to stand there. The blood rushed out of Frederick and his eyes started to close. He needed medical attention. Even then Sutton wasn't convinced he'd make it.

All of a sudden Josiah turned his gun around and handed it handle first to Mike. Dropping down on his haunches, Josiah leaned in close to the man bleeding out on the floor. "You may not die yet, but I will make sure you don't walk away from this."

Frederick's eyelids flickered and he looked at Josiah. "I . . . won't talk . . ."

Josiah got down even closer. "Yes, you will."

Josiah's blood was on fire.

Tasha and whatever medical doctor she knew well enough to bring in had to save Frederick before Josiah could kill him. And that was going to happen. But not until the guy talked. He was the one person who knew something about Benton's real operation, probably knew where the animal hid now, and he would talk.

Sew him up, make him coherent, and get him ready. That was the deal he made with Tasha. The side deal with Mike was a bit more elaborate. Men like Frederick didn't talk easily. He'd been trained to withstand torture and could tolerate a lot of pain. He didn't have anyone close to him. All of that made the usual ways of gaining intel tough. But Josiah had an advantage. A threat that might shake Frederick enough to make him talk.

But Josiah couldn't concentrate on any of that now. He'd walked into the bedroom in time to see Sutton walk out of the connected bathroom. She wore a bathrobe, and from the long line of her leg peeking out of the slit, nothing else.

Seeing her set off something primal in him. He knew she wanted to talk it all out and comfort him. That's not what he needed. He'd stayed away from her for the last hour because all he wanted to do was strip her bare and get inside her. Lose himself in the feel of her until he couldn't think.

He didn't have a psychology degree but he was sure the driving attraction and unrelenting need for her right now had to do with his survival instinct. Something inside him reacted to her. He wanted to be with her, touch her, taste her. Not sweet. Not making love. Fucking.

He had to get out of there before he scared her. "I'll be in the kitchen."

He'd almost made it back out when she stopped him. "Josiah."

The whisper of his name made him hard. That's all it took. He slammed a palm against the door and exhaled. Counted down from ten.

Then she was there. She didn't stay across the room or hide in the bathroom. Either would have been smarter than standing so close that he could smell her.

Her hand swept up his back and she leaned in. Her soft hair brushed against his cheek. The touch woke his nerve endings. Revved them up.

"I should go." Had he said that already? He couldn't remember. It took all of his concentration to keep that hand on the door.

Not to be ignored, she ducked under his arm and stood up, wedged between him and the only way out of there. He should back up. Maybe jump out a window. The cool night air might do him some good. He needed a jolt to get his mind back on track.

She looked up at him. "Come here."

No, no, no. "Not a good idea." She had to see it. Feel it. His attraction went wild. This need inside him pulsed and flexed and screamed to get out. "I'm not feeling . . ."

God, he couldn't even find the right words. How did he tell her his humanity had crumbled, leaving behind only an empty shell. A shell he needed her to fill. With her, the world shifted and things made sense.

The nightmare of last night. Harlan ordering him. Josiah closed his eyes. Tried to block it all out. He drew in deep breaths.

Her mouth touched his and his eyes flew open again. She slid her hands up and under his T-shirt. Kept going until she lifted it off his shoulders and threw it on the floor.

"What are you doing?" Probably the dumbest question a man ever asked, but it was out there now.

"Helping." Her mouth went to his neck. She trailed a line of hot kisses down his throat, then across his collarbone.

"You do that by breathing." But the kissing . . . holy fuck. She didn't tease. She dove right in and wound him up.

The vibration spun through every part of his body. His erection pressed against the fly of his jeans until he thought he'd tear the fabric.

Still, he didn't touch her. Didn't dare. "I'm not good for you right now."

"We need to feel something." Her hand snaked down to cup him. She treated him to a gentle massage that made his eyes cross.

"I'm angry." Though with every second it was getting harder to hold on to that emotion. Need swamped him. It took all his strength not to grab her and throw her on the bed.

He tried to think of math problems and do simple addition in his head. Nothing worked. He had to have her. There, against the wall. On the bed. He didn't fucking care. This craving came from deep inside him, on a primal level.

She shoved the robe open. She didn't move except to curl her bare toes under and into the hardwood. Unable to wait another second, he slipped it off her shoulders and let it fall to the ground. He'd hoped he still held on to some of his control but the fabric ripped under his hands.

He was about to apologize until he spied the inches of smooth skin. Realized she wasn't fighting him. Those breasts. High and full. The tiny bump of her stomach that he loved to kiss so much. The light hair and those long legs. Everywhere he looked he saw perfection.

A fever overtook him. His chivalry shriveled. With his hands resting on her waist, he threw her back on the mattress. Not gentle. Not hard. But enough to send her sprawling.

Without a word, she opened those long legs, silently inviting him in. Energy pounded through him. Need mixed with a desperation that scared him. He stretched her arms above her head. Her body reeled him in until he couldn't think about anything else. Every awful thought and horrible memory faded.

He broke records ripping his pants off. He shoved the jeans down. Stood up only long enough to step out of his boxer briefs and grab a condom. Kicked the material to the side. The mattress dipped under his knee as he fit his body between her legs again. He crawled up, not stopping for foreplay. This was about getting lost in her body. In her.

Then he was on her. Their bodies slid over each other and the friction had him gasping. When she lifted those knees and skimmed her hands down his back to cup his ass, his brain turned to mush. He went wild. His hands toured all over her. Everywhere his fingers touched, his mouth followed. He couldn't get close enough or taste enough.

"I need to be inside of you." All thoughts of touching

and lingering over the moment fell away. Need drove him. With a burst of force, he ripped the packet open and almost sent the condom flying. He let her roll it on while he traced a finger over her and sent a silent thank-you that she was as hot and ready to go as he was.

He lowered his body, and his chest rubbed over hers. With his hands hooked under her knees, he lifted her legs. Angled her body with his. And when he entered her he nearly sighed in relief. Every muscle grabbed on to him and her body tightened around his.

He wanted to sink in and stay there but his lower half had other ideas. He started to move. Felt the bite of her fingernails against his back.

God, he wanted this. Needed her.

She licked the outline of his ear. He felt her shiver even as his insides thumped. Whatever smoothness he usually had failed him. He pressed in deep, then retreated. Increased his speed as his body begged for more. When she tightened against him, he lost it. He pumped into her, desperate to merge with her in some way.

The bed frame shook. He heard a scrape against the floor when the thrusts moved the bed's legs. He ignored it all and concentrated on the warmth of her body and comforting hold of her arms.

Her mouth moved under his. The kiss consumed him. Her body pulsed. When she pressed her head back into the pillow, he let go of the last of his control. He came on a groan with his face tucked in her shoulder. It took another minute for the shaking to stop and his breathing to settle into a normal beat. Even after, his muscles wouldn't stop trembling.

That could only be described as a frenzied taking. Not his finest performance, but satisfaction hummed through him. He knew he should get up, or at least shift his weight off her. He had work to do and a hunt for Benton to conduct. All those tasks waited right there and all he wanted to do was hold her tighter and close his eyes.

"You okay?" She kissed his cheek.

He was starting to think he'd never be okay again. And without her . . . he couldn't even imagine that right now. "I will be. I have to be."

"Not with me."

He lifted his head and looked down at her. "You amaze me."

"Right now I just want to hold you."

"Sounds good." And for the first time in his life, it did.

24

SUTTON'S BODY still hummed hours later. She leaned back against the breakfast bar in the kitchen and watched them all work. The usual buzz and back-and-forth were gone. No one moved. No one talked. It was as if they made a silent agreement not to mention Harlan or Benton or the constant emotional and physical battering of the last twenty-four hours. Just thinking about those frenetic moments reminded her of how fragile their lives were right now.

Tasha walked in the back door from checking on Frederick. Her medical friends, and Sutton still wasn't sure who they were, had saved Frederick. They didn't discuss his condition. Only said he was alive and would be ready for questioning soon.

In the meantime, he stayed strapped down and locked down in a makeshift hospital room in what used to be the barn. Even if he managed to slide off the bed, motion sensors and the video Ellery had set up to watch him would cover his attempted escape.

"There was a bomb in the terminal. More than one actually." Tasha spoke as if she read from a report.

"They would have taken down the airport and killed thousands. The claim about the one in the van was a lie."

"To draw you out," Mike said.

"Right. Ellery?" Those were all the details Tasha offered before moving the conversation on.

"From what I can put together the auction stopped before anyone won or the Alliance information could be disbursed."

Tasha frowned. "I'd prefer a more definite answer."

"Truth is, Benton has the intel and can sell at any time." Mike had set up next to Ellery. They talked and passed papers back and forth. Now he leaned back in his chair with his hands folded behind his head.

Josiah stopped typing. "And he'll do it soon unless his customers are placated by the use of the vest and what they saw on the video."

Sutton's gaze roamed over him. Their earlier frantic lovemaking likely scared him but it gave her hope. Felt life-affirming in a way. Under the gun and the bluster lay the beating heart of a man. A man who'd seen horrible things and made a terrible choice. The right one, but one that would plague him. It would haunt her, but she feared it might destroy him.

"Sutton's information tied everything together." Ellery turned around one of the laptops in front of her for the rest of the people at the table to see. Photos and articles filled the screen. "Here is everything we have on Ronald Kirn, the man who started it all."

Sutton moved closer and tried to see whatever Ellery

saw. Without her glasses the print looked tiny but she noticed the dark hair. An objectively attractive but not really handsome man. Normal. Like men she saw in office buildings in Baltimore all the time. But he had turned out to be the one guy you didn't cross. Police or not, messing with him had cost her mother her life. Her mind raced on but Sutton tried to shut it down.

"And here is Rick." Ellery kept typing. "Now add some pounds, a lot of scarring, and probably a bit of surgery, and you get Benton."

Sutton filled in the rest. "International terrorist and the most wanted man on the planet."

"Rick was a guy who blended in." Ellery tapped a few more keys and the photos changed. Benton, a younger nonscarred version, filled the screen. "A financial genius who worked behind the scenes and never took credit. He went on a hike and fell to his death. There were witnesses and the case was closed."

Tasha sighed. "And Benton was born. I'd guess he left the country with a new identity. With material, money, contacts, business savvy, and a head full of revenge."

Mike nodded. "Apparently."

Sutton wanted to sit down, walk around . . . throw Benton off a cliff. All these deaths, all the destruction, tied back to a greedy businessman who took over his brother's terrorism trade. It seemed so simple, yet she could see how it worked so perfectly. No one would suspect. He didn't stick out.

Her case merged with theirs. One man. So much death.

"There's more." Ellery glanced at Mike and he nodded before she started speaking again. "Two of the FBI agents involved in Ronald's death also are dead, along with their families."

A winding started deep in Sutton's stomach. "I tried to connect those dots and no one at the FBI would listen."

Benton wrecked lives. He got angry and took it out on everyone. Went after what you loved. A chair scraped against the floor. She heard mumbling but the room blurred. She was thrown back into those days. Her mom's boss coming to get her. All the questions, and the coworkers who talked about how great her mom was. All that pain and the draining sense of loss. It backed up on her now.

"You okay?" Josiah whispered the question against her cheek.

"Would you be?" Reality hit her. He did know this kind of pain and shock. She rushed to explain. "Sorry, I just . . ."

"It's okay." He wrapped an arm around her and kissed her forehead.

The sweetness of the moment mixed with the news she thought she'd never hear—that someone believed her. That there was a way to solve it all. The knowing felt good but part of her wanted to plunge her body into a scalding shower and wash it all away.

"Benton has had a lot of years to reinvent himself."

Tasha put her thigh on the edge of the table and leaned in. "To stoke his rage."

Mike nodded. "It's been said before but he's pure fucking evil."

"Agreed." A firm resolve had moved back into Josiah's voice. Confidence flooded him and filled the rom. "And Harlan . . ."

"We are doing this for him. The rest of this." Tasha swept her hand across the room. "For Sutton's mother and Harlan and for every other person trapped by Benton. Harlan died so that we could solve this and we will."

Sutton's heart thundered in her chest. Part of her still didn't believe Harlan was gone. She waited for him to walk in. "Did he have family?"

Tasha nodded. "He did, and we will honor him with a service later. Right now we need to do this for him."

"We can't get sidetracked." Mike looked at Josiah as he talked.

"Revenge first. Mourn later." It sounded as if the words were ripped out of him.

Sutton felt a new wave of sadness. It threatened to drag her under, but Tasha was right. Now was the time for strength.

"Go question Frederick." Tasha folded her hands together. Looked calm while her voice rang with fierceness. "Wake him up and do whatever you need to do. I want to know exactly where we find this piece of garbage and we're going to dispose of him once and for all."

"Ooh-rah."

Josiah looked at Mike. "You weren't a marine."

He shrugged. "If the chant fits."

The room buzzed with a renewed energy. The costs of this operation had been so high. An hour ago they seemed demoralized, as if they had to push themselves to keep going. Now an adrenaline shot replaced the pounding tension.

Josiah stepped in front of her, shoulders back and that determined expression on his face. "I know this is a shock."

"Get him." Yeah, that was the right answer. It rolled through her, and her belief grew with every second. They needed to end this. "Leave nothing behind."

He stared at her with wide eyes filled with appreciation. "What?"

"Honestly, put a bullet in his head and stop the world's misery." She tried to swallow. Fought back the tears. "For Harlan."

He nodded. "Yes, ma'am. Mike, you're with me."

"I like her," Ellery said.

Mike laughed as he got up to follow. "So does he."

Sutton heard the banter and it comforted her. They worked best when they pushed each other. And she needed them at their best.

"Josiah?" Tasha called out right before Josiah stepped outside. "No loose ends."

He nodded. "None."

Frederick woke with a start. A shot of adrenaline did that to a guy.

He moved his arms and metal clanked against metal. He shifted and winced. Probably pulled stitches, or so Josiah hoped. He watched Frederick glance down his body then jerk. Josiah bit back a smile at the reaction. He thought the bomb vest was a nice touch. Whatever it took.

"Hello." Mike put a hand on Frederick's pillow. "Yeah, unfortunately for you, you're not dead."

"But you are wearing our version of the bomb vest." This one didn't contain any explosives or hook to his heartbeat but it sure as hell looked real. Josiah had to give Mike credit for fake bomb building.

Frederick shook his head. "You won't."

"He underestimates us." Mike looked at Josiah.

"Apparently."

Frederick tried to move his arms. When they didn't go anywhere a second time, he flopped back on the bed. "You need me."

They did but Josiah didn't care if they never heard a word from this guy. The ending would be the same either way. "For what?"

"To get to Benton."

Mike shrugged. "We found him before, we'll find him again."

The guy did disinterested better than anyone Josiah knew. He had that laidback country boy act that he dragged out now and then. It worked here. A touch of farmer with an edge that said he'd shoot without thinking twice.

"He is going to sell your private information." Frederick looked back and forth between him. His voice stayed calm but a frantic energy thrummed off him.

"Which is the only reason we brought you back to life." And that was the truth. Josiah didn't care if the guy lived two seconds, but he would live those two seconds so that he could be questioned. Since he looked like hell he might actually only have two seconds, so Josiah got to the point. "You have two options."

"No." Frederick smiled. He clearly thought he had the advantage.

Mike leaned on Frederick's shoulder until the man's mouth dropped open and he whimpered. "Now, just listen."

"You are either going to tell me where Benton is or I'm going to flip this switch." Josiah slipped the fake trigger to the fake bomb out of his pocket and held it.

"You won't do it." Frederick's confidence grew with each word. "You're the good guys."

Josiah had always found the line between good and bad to be a little fuzzy, especially right now. "Really?"

"I prefer this game." Mike took the gun from behind his back and checked the clip. Before Frederick could say anything, Mike fired and Frederick jumped at the click. "You won round one."

He tried to shift on the bed and move farther away from Mike and the weapon pointed at his head. "You're insane."

"Are you starting to see the problem here?" Josiah asked.

"Me dead gets you nothing."

He must have pulled something because a splotch of red spread on the sheet right below the edge of the bomb vest. Josiah had no intention of calling the medics back in. None. "Satisfaction."

"A shitload of that." Mike fired again and another click sounded in the room.

"Are you the one who beat up our friend Harlan?" Josiah leaned in close enough to see the guy sweat. To see those dead eyes dart around in panic. So much for all that training. "Nothing to say, Frederick?"

Mike aimed the gun again and fired. With each shot, Frederick grew jumpier. The blood wet the sheet now and all the thrashing around caused scrape marks on his wrists.

Time to bring this to a close. "You've had training. We appreciate that."

Mike nodded. "Yep."

"But you also know when you've lost. Did they teach you that in your scary German intelligence classes?" Never mind that this guy failed to make the grade. That he was so fucking scary the black-ops guys didn't want him.

"Maybe not." Mike sat on the edge of the bed, causing Frederick to shift, which made him hiss as the color drained from his face.

"I'm going to take a play from Benton's book. Give you a one-time offer. You tell me where he is right now and we let you go. We'll give you twenty-four hours to scramble away. You can go back and be Benton's lapdog."

Mike snorted. "But the guy did leave you to die. Have some pride."

"Good point." Josiah pressed on the mattress and Frederick rolled closer. "Where? There's no reason to have any loyalty to him. We take him out, and if you figure out how to survive this you can claim his kingdom."

Frederick stilled. He went from looking haunted and on the verge of screaming to listening.

Mike must have sensed it, too, because he picked up the thread. "You're the one dealing with the customers anyway. Why not be in charge?"

Frederick shook his head. "You'll hunt me down."

"Oh sure." Mike actually petted his gun.

"That's our job. But Benton evaded everyone for years. You'll have your chance." Josiah thought that sounded reasonable. "If you're smarter than he is, you'll be fine. If you stay out of our way and off our radar, you're good."

"We're giving you an option that doesn't include a bullet in your brain or your body being ripped into tiny pieces," Mike pointed out.

Josiah saw the blood and watched the heart rate monitor. This guy needed serious medical attention or this was it. "You have two seconds."

"Look." Mike aimed the gun again. "You know I'll do it, right? And there is a bullet in here. I promise you that."

Frederick closed his eyes. For a second, Josiah thought they'd lost him. That they'd pushed the sick guy too far.

Then he whispered. "Ronda."

That didn't sound right. "Spain?"

"That's a bit cheery for Benton, isn't it?" Mike asked.

Frederick reeled off what sounded like an address. He could hear Ellery typing through the comm. They'd been listening in and now they'd go to work. He needed minutes only. He was about to play with Frederick some more when Ellery came back on the line and said she'd confirmed the address and was checking footage. Josiah didn't know what that meant but the speed impressed him.

Now to finish this.

"We're good." He glanced at Mike, then back to Frederick. "Sounds like we have a deal."

Frederick settled back into the mattress. "When will you let me go?"

"If we untie you now you'll pass out." Mike took out the clip and slammed it back in again.

Frederick was too busy looking at the sheet covering him. "I need a doctor."

"Yeah, you do." Mike held the gun at his side.

Josiah would let Mike have this one. He'd had unloaded his weapon one time too many in the last few hours. The last time took out a good man who deserved better and he wouldn't follow Harlan's sacrifice with a bullet for this piece of garbage. "I'll leave you to recuperate."

"Wait." Frederick frowned as his back came off the bed.

"Right." Josiah held on to the door handle as he

glanced over his shoulder at Frederick. "Just one thing. We can't give you twenty-four hours to run. You have more like two seconds. Mike?"

Mike lifted his gun. "I'm happy to handle this one."

Josiah shut the door behind him and walked into the sunshine. He heard the yelling, then the bang. "No loose ends."

25

SUTTON SQUATTED near the entrance of the villa next to the one Benton supposedly lived in. The view was nothing short of stunning. A stone mansion perched on a rock plateau. The gorge below and the mountains in the distance provided a beautiful setting. She couldn't believe someone as dark and lifeless as Benton could appreciate the place.

They'd spent long hours going over a plan and reviewing intel. Every piece of information pointed to a Brit living in the building, someone from old money with strong family ties. A guy with houses in several places who came to Ronda for the rich history and view.

All a lie. Benton lived there. Sutton had seen the video, grainy but she knew. She was just surprised Josiah agreed for her to come along. He didn't kick up a fuss. No, he insisted she'd earned the right to be there. And the plan counted on all of them, the ones Benton purported to want the most, to move in. If all else failed, her presence was meant to act as subterfuge while someone else moved in and took him out. Dangerous, but so was leaving Benton alive.

She glanced at Josiah. He waited about ten feet to her left. He would lead. He and Mike would go in, take out any guards, then she would slip in after the way had been cleared. Tasha provided cover and backup, plus watched for unexpected guests.

Ellery listened in, relaying coordinates and information every now and then. She gave the signal now. A soft whisper that blended into the background. "Go."

Josiah stood up, tall and lean. If the concussion bothered him, he didn't show it. Harlan and his uncle, it all had to play in his head in some way, but she suspected he stored the horrors for later. Now he focused.

He pushed off, taking on the winding stone staircase at a slow speed. Waiting and watching around each bend. For every step he took, she took one, keeping far enough behind that a stray bullet wouldn't hit her, but close enough for him to watch over.

The wind whistled through the old building. Sutton could hear some street noise outside. People talking as they passed by. Their lives went on as normal while inside the walls a battle brewed.

They made it to the first floor without incident. Tasha, impressive as always, had created a diversion on her own to get the people out of the house and Ellery verified it was empty. No heat signatures but plenty of them next door. Guards near the entrance and on each of the three floors. It looked like Benton expected company, or at least trouble.

They stepped into what looked like a great room. A long space, divided into several sitting sections. Not fancy but refined. Paintings and tapestries on the wall. Vases and sculptures behind glass and lit with spotlights. It screamed wealth, but in an understated way. The house still looked like someone lived there.

Sutton took it all in as they swept along the hard stone floor to the far end, right before the open veranda. She knew right now Mike approached from the building on the opposite side. They'd meet in Benton's house and then the hunt would begin.

After a quick check, Josiah slipped onto the balcony area. She followed, momentarily blinded by the sea of lights below her. They sat so far up that she could see the entire valley below. She heard a snap and realized Josiah was looking at her. She shook her tourist excitement loose and concentrated. She'd need it for this next step. They had to jump from one building to another.

Memories of their first meeting in Paris floated through her mind. All that fear and the way she hoped he'd fall. Now she counted on his strength. The need to get to Benton fueled her. She would go across without trouble. Forget the height and the danger. Somehow she'd make it because they were all depending on her to make it.

Josiah moved to the edge of the balcony. "Ready?"

"Yes." She was about to give him a smile of reassurance when she saw the shadow. Something moved on the balcony next door.

He must have seen her expression because he spun around and fired. Nailed the guy with only a small sound and sent him flying backward. The thump of his body and rattle of his gun against the stone made more noise than the gunfire. Thank goodness for silencers.

He turned back to her as if nothing happened. "Thanks."

Before she could ask for what, he was up on the railing. It crumbled at one end where the rock had worn away, but he stayed away from that side. One long step and he landed on the railing of the balcony next door.

As she watched, he dropped down and checked the guy on the ground, then peeked inside the room they needed to enter. He turned back around and nodded. Held out a hand as he stepped back up on the railing on his side.

Anxiety took off in a wild dance in her stomach. She thought she'd conquered it, but standing up there, balancing on a seven-inch stone bar, her stomach tumbled and almost took her breakfast along with it.

He gestured for her to go. "Hurry."

She heard him and let trust take over. One step, then another, and she jumped. Arms flapping in the air and all.

Everything happened at once. A man in a suit came out on the balcony behind Josiah. Josiah spun around and his foot slipped. She reached for his arm to pull her through but came up empty. Her arms grabbed only air as her body fell. The night whooshed around her, and the ground, once so far away, moved closer.

She stretched and made it as far as the outside of the balcony. Her shoulder hit the stone with a thud. As she started to slide, she hooked her arms around the ancient railing. Her sneakers thumped against the intricate stonework below as she tried to get her footing. Feeling around, she found a ledge and balanced one foot there. The other kept slipping off.

A scream rattled in her throat but she bit it back. If she yelled, Benton could come running. His men would hear her. If she didn't, her hold would give out and she'd fall. The choices had her heartbeat pounding in her ears.

Minutes, which felt like hours, ticked by. She heard grunts and the shuffle of footsteps above her. The men fought. She thought Josiah battled more than one. If he died . . . She snapped her mind back. Tried to think of a song she could hum in her head. Anything to calm the raging terror that threatened to steal her sanity as her fear of heights enveloped her.

Panic rumbled through her as her arms began to shake. Terror gripped her now as her muscles weakened. She couldn't breathe, couldn't get her heart rate to slow. She imagined her body falling and closed her eyes to keep from looking down. It would be all over if she did.

She whimpered as she buried her face against the cold post. She peeked through the slats and watched one man go down, but Josiah had to deal with another. She couldn't even watch Josiah punch this guy. They wrestled and the guard backed Josiah into the wall. Choking each other. They were locked in a death match. She almost let that scream go when the guard banged Josiah's already injured head against the stone.

She tried to pull her body up and not just hang there

like dead weight. If she could get to the guard, she might be able to help. This wasn't just about her now. She had to help save him.

Josiah spun around with eyes wide with terror. He swore as he scrambled to get her. Right when the guard went to ram Josiah's head a second time his body stiffened. The guard glanced down, then slipped along the length of Josiah's body. That's when she saw the gun Josiah had wedged between them and realized Josiah had fired.

When he saw her, his eyes widened and filled with fear. In two steps he was there. Long arms reached over the railing and he lifted her to the balcony. Her legs wouldn't hold her and the shaking wouldn't stop.

"Christ." He wrapped her in a suffocating hug as his mouth went to her ear. "Are you okay?"

She could feel him tremble and rushed to soothe him. "Yes."

She brushed her hands over him as she regained some of her strength. She forced her mind to the present and off all the what-could-have-beens. The view swam in front of her eyes and Ellery yelled in her ear. She tried to block it all out and breathe.

Josiah stiffened and she pulled back to look at him. "What is it?"

He exhaled. "Company."

Then Ellery's warnings registered. They weren't alone. Sutton balanced up on tiptoes and looked past Josiah's broad shoulders to the man standing behind them. Benton.

"I would say welcome, but you aren't." Benton's scratchy voice filled the quiet night.

Josiah turned and stood next to her. That's when she saw it. The gun in Benton's hand. He aimed it at her chest.

Josiah didn't lower his weapon either. "Rick."

"Ah, I see you finally figured it out. Put Sutton's past together with your big operation. I must say that took you longer than I would have thought."

Josiah didn't blink. "Shut up."

"Of course, no other intelligence agency or group ever got even half this far, so bravo." He acted like he didn't care but his expression had pinched, just for a second.

"A sad businessman from DC? I have to say it was a bit of a disappointment."

Josiah's taunting had Benton's mouth flattening into a thin line. "A genius who could make money from nothing and encouraged his brother to do more than serve the whims of the government that took advantage of him."

Every word sounded drenched in ego. Sutton had known men like this her entire life. The blowhards and big talkers. Benton could back up his words with weapons but that didn't make him any less of a child in her eyes.

Josiah let out a dramatic exhale. "I've heard this sad poor-me speech before. Every nutcase with a small dick says something like this."

Benton's face flushed red. "Do those speeches usually end with you getting shot and watching a woman bleed out at your feet? Because that's what's going to happen this time."

Josiah laughed at him. Actually laughed. "I don't think so."

Sutton's heart lurched. Benton would do it, too. He would think he could shoot his way out of this, not caring if reinforcements came behind them or how many people died to save him. He only cared about himself and his business and all that money. He could spout off about revenge or his brother, but she just saw an empty worthless shell.

"Do you think I'm alone?" Benton tried to lift his arm but the injuries limited his movement. "I have men with guns trained on Sutton. They will unload on my command."

"Do you think I'm alone?"

"You have, what, Mike and two women with you?" Benton looked ready to spit in distaste.

Josiah shook his head. "I don't think you appreciate women."

"Wonder why," she mumbled under her breath.

Benton's focus shot right back to her. "Your mother was a meddling bitch. I told Ronald to steer clear, but he was intrigued. Something about dating a woman in law enforcement while working against it excited him."

That explained how her mom got tied up in this mess. All this sickness and she walked right into it. Of course, she recognized Ronald for who he was. And the good deed of turning him in got her killed. The whole thing made Sutton want to sit down and weep. So much waste at the hands of a man who barely qualified as a joke.

"I think he liked the idea of seeing her, then going home and building weapons." Benton tried to smile then, as much as he could around the scars. "Gave him a thrill."

"She figured him out." Sutton needed to say that. Even if she died today, she needed to make that point. The woman he mocked and treated with such disdain saw through him. "Tasha tracked you down. Ellery figured out who you really were. My mother stopped your brother. All women."

"Your mother was nosy. Like you." Benton shook his head. "And look what happened? You led us here. To Harlan's death."

That shot landed hard. He'd aimed well. She did start this round. As she listed off what all those strong women had done, she couldn't add her name to the list. But if he expected her to cower or cry, he had the wrong woman.

She was about to point that out when the countdown started in her ear. She could hear Ellery's voice, soft as a whisper, as she got to eight.

"What's the plan here, whatever your name is?" Josiah asked.

"Kill Sutton and let you watch."

Josiah shifted just a bit. Enough to wedge part of his body in front of hers. "Are you forgetting I have a gun? More than one, actually."

"I don't think you'll use any weapon if her life's at stake."

He would if he had to. She would make sure of that. No way would she walk away from this if it meant Benton went free and others died. She was done with that ending. "Yes, he will."

Josiah's gaze flicked to her for a second. It was the first time he'd looked at her since Benton showed his face tonight.

"So brave," Benton said in a mocking tone.

She ignored the singsongy quality to Benton's comment and turned to face Josiah. "Do it."

"It's like Harlan all over again." Benton did laugh that time. "That has to be eating at you, Josiah. You killed Harlan in cold blood. You took his life, not me."

He shrugged. "I still blame you."

"Come on. You're not a machine. I mean, look at you. You fell for the girl in what, a week? Very romantic. It's a shame this will have a tragic Romeo and Juliet sort of ending." Benton looked toward the balcony railing as if to make his point.

She got it. She heard every word. Truth was, she did love Josiah. Forget falling, she fell. The speed made no sense. Every minute filled with high intensity as time ran in fast forward. But Josiah stayed constant. He turned out to be exactly who he promised to be that first day. The bossiness, the controlling behavior, the hotness, and the decency. It all combined to work for her.

And if what she needed to let him know, to set him

free, was to guide him through this, she would. "Shoot him, Josiah."

"Ha! I like her fire."

"You a fan of fire, Benton?" Josiah asked in a quiet tone. "I know I enjoyed watching you go up in flames last time."

"I'm still here," Benton snarled back.

"For another few seconds."

Sutton hoped that was true. Then the silence struck her. Ellery had stopped counting. She said only one word over the comm. "Here."

No one had filled Sutton in on that command. She didn't know what it meant or what was about to happen. Whatever it was, Josiah didn't panic. Didn't show any reaction.

Benton relaxed his stance. "What do you think will happen?"

Mike's voice boomed over Benton's. "Move."

"Right now." Josiah fired, hit Benton in the shoulder, and had him falling back. The second shot hit his chest and he dropped the gun.

Sutton ducked, waiting for more gunfire to ring out. All those claims about men watching and waiting to kill her, but nothing happened. Benton stayed on his feet and Josiah aimed again. At the last second, his attention shifted to the doors to the villa. She followed his gaze and saw Mike fully armed with . . . she didn't even know what.

Josiah's arm banded around her. She moved on instinct, shifting with him as he turned and ran. They took off, hit the edge of the balcony, and kept going. Stepped right up on the crumbling ledge and took flight. They hit the hard floor of the next balcony on their sides with a bounce and started rolling.

She heard a strange noise and saw a long streak. Mike disappeared but something hit Benton in the stomach. Then the entire balcony blew off. The explosion had chunks of stone flying everywhere and pebbles pinging against her skin. The last thing she saw was the blood on Benton's shirt and his open mouth as he went over the side of the stone cliff.

The ancient house groaned and the ground shook. The steady beat of falling rock and screams of people watching filled the night. When the smoke cleared, Josiah got to his feet and pulled her up beside him. "You okay?"

She touched her head and looked down, amazed that she could stand. "I think so."

"I'm good, too." Mike looked out of the hole in the side of the house. Stood in the middle of it. The balcony was gone and rubble and debris littered the area.

Looking down, Sutton saw a sheer rock cliff and pieces of stone everywhere. "You blew up his house."

"You brought an RPG?" Josiah sounded amused as he glanced at Sutton. "A rocket-propelled grenade. That's a big boy weapon."

"You've got to be kidding." Tasha didn't sound quite so happy as she stepped out on the balcony behind Sutton, gun still in her hand.

Mike shrugged as he glanced down. "I wanted something dramatic."

"Is he dead?" Sutton knew the question sounded ridiculous. Josiah shot him twice and Mike blew the guy into a deep ravine. But still, she had to be sure.

Josiah walked to the edge and stared down. "No way he survived that."

After everything and her now raging fear of heights, Sutton stayed toward the back of the balcony. Close to the house.

"I'm not leaving it to chance," Tasha said. "I want to see a body. I'll be satisfied with seeing pieces."

"Works for me." Josiah looked up again and glanced over at Mike. "How many guards did you take out?"

"Ten."

"Show-off."

"No." Sutton shook her head.

Josiah frowned. "What?"

She couldn't do this. No more talk of death. She understood they joked to break the tension, to make it through the horror. She couldn't get there. Not now. Not after how close they'd come and how many lives were lost. "Please, stop with the killing talk."

Gravel and loose stones crunched as Tasha walked. She shouted over to the other balcony. "Mike, go do recon on that body. I need to lock this place down so we can clean it out, and I doubt the local police are going to take that well."

He nodded, then disappeared.

Tasha headed back to the main part of the house but stopped right before going inside and looked at both Josiah and Sutton. "Good job."

"It's done." He nodded. "This job anyway."

Sutton didn't like the sound of that at all. "Aren't you a ray of sunshine?"

After a quick glance at Sutton, Tasha looked at Josiah. "On to the next bad guy."

"Don't you guys take a break?" Sutton wanted to fall over. The idea of them mobilizing tomorrow to handle some new threat made her queasy.

Tasha just stared out over the balcony. "No, and why is that, Josiah?"

He didn't hesitate. "Because they don't stop coming."

26

TASHA'S WORDS echoed in Josiah's mind hours later. All the rubbish he'd been holding back rushed forward. His uncle, Harlan, hearing Sutton tell him to kill her. And if his head had been where it should be, on the job, he would have.

The right move was to take away Benton's bargaining chip and then kill him. But he'd hesitated. In that second, the idea of watching her bleed out weighed more on him than the lives of the countless thousands Benton would have taken. He'd lost perspective. He'd never felt this empty.

He just didn't have anything left. No energy. No desire to keep pushing forward. He didn't care about the next bad guy, about the next threat. Someone else could step up because he was ready to sit down.

He didn't know how long he stayed there on the edge of the bed with his head down and his arms resting on his thighs. His back hurt and his head pounded. He kept getting dizzy and the thumping just got louder. Damn concussion.

Soon he heard her come in. The soft patter of her feet. The scent of her shampoo.

He stayed bent over but slid his elbows closer to his body. Fingers slipped through his hair, and her soft body slipped between his legs. He wanted to lift his head and warn her away, but he balanced his head against her stomach and closed his eyes instead. Let her warmth wash over him, if only for a little while.

His hands went to her hips. He rubbed his cheek against her. She talked about comfort. Now he got it. It fed your soul and let you get up again. He just didn't know if he wanted to stand. He'd been taking his post and doing the job since he got out of college. His reserves had run dry.

His feelings for her, all mixed up and confusing, had gotten all wrapped up with his hatred for what he'd become. He'd been fighting this fight for so long. He didn't have anything left to give.

"I'm so tired." He whispered the words against her shirt.

She kissed the top of his head. "You should take a shower and crawl into bed. I can bring you something to eat. Snuggle up next to you for a few hours."

More comfort, but she didn't get it. This wasn't about sleep or even about losing himself in her as he'd done before. It worked then. He didn't see it working now.

He forced his head up. His gaze met hers. The worry lingered there on her mouth and at the corners of her eyes. Worry for him. He couldn't remember the last time someone cared enough to worry for him.

"I don't know if I can do this anymore." His words sounded harsh and grating to his ears.

Her hands froze in the middle of their gentle massage against his scalp. "What's the 'this' in that sentence?"

"This work breaks you." He tried to find the right words but his brain wouldn't function and the hollowness started to swallow him up. "There's nothing left of me and who I was. I don't believe in anything."

She slipped her hand around to cup his chin and lift his head higher. "What are you talking about?"

"I don't even feel human."

She treated him to a soft smile. "To mourn Harlan, to protect me when you should have just left me behind, requires humanity. My God, Josiah. You've been through so much. If you didn't feel lost and exhausted, I would wonder. You're human. You need to recharge."

She made it sound good. So logical and easy. But she hadn't seen all he'd seen. The losses on this job piled up but it was still only one job. For him the Benton mess was one piece in a lifetime of death. The first explosion took his mother but there had been so many since then that he'd lost count. He used to keep track of the killings, but the number got so high it scared the shit out of him.

She slid her hand through his hair again. "You need rest."

"I need a break." She smiled but he knew they weren't saying the same thing. "I need to walk away."

Her mouth fell. "You mean from the job? I'm sure Tasha would—"

"Everything." But he sensed she knew that. The relaxed woman who walked into the bedroom prepared to hold him and soothe him disappeared. She still touched him and stood close but a certain wariness washed over her.

He'd hurt her. He could see it in every line of her body. On top of everything else, he said and did things that hurt her. He'd yelled at her, put her in danger. He'd watched the light drain out of her before and he was about to do it again.

"You mean me." She moved back, breaking her hold on him. "You need a break from me. Already."

This wasn't really about her. She was the one thing that made sense. The one thing he could not have. "You deserve so much better than me. The things I've done . . . the compromises I've made."

She shook her head, in a slow movement that showed her pain. "Don't do this."

"I can't see anything in front of me." That was the soul-sucking truth. He was a man without any real future. If he stayed in, he'd die. If he got out, he'd be useless.

His past would always haunt him and there were people who might track him down. Forget the threats of disclosure by Benton. He'd spent a lifetime in the intelligence field and you didn't do that without making enemies. Serious enemies. The kind who would use her to get to him.

It all snowballed in his mind. The pieces wrapped together into one gigantic problem he didn't have the will or the strength to solve.

"I will wait and be here for you, but you have to tell me there's hope." She lifted her arms, then let them fall again.

She looked so beautiful standing there. So fresh and clean of all the filth in his life. "That's the point, Sutton. I'm all out of hope."

"You need time." She visibly swallowed as she shifted her weight from foot to foot. "Everything just happened. It's been this vicious roller coaster, and it started long before I got here. I can't imagine what goes on in your head."

The last place he wanted her was in there. She'd see the darkness and the anger, all the guilt and the doubts. She'd run screaming from him, just like she should. "I don't want to think."

She held out a hand to him. "Come away with me. The mission is over and Tasha said you could leave after some sort of review."

Temptation loomed right in front of him. He wanted to walk away with her and pretend. Put this behind him and act like none of it mattered. To go somewhere and be normal, whatever that was.

But he couldn't do it. He couldn't yank her down into the unknown with him. "I can't even stand to be with myself."

She drew in a deep inhale. "Would it matter if I told you I think I love you?"

He put a hand over the stabbing in his chest. "God, please don't."

That fast she looked away, but not before he saw the

hurt in her eyes. He stood up, meaning to go to her and say something, he didn't know what. "Sutton."

She waved him off as she stepped back, moved closer to the door. Wrapped her hand around the knob in a grip that turned her knuckles white. "I've fought for my mother. I've sacrificed so much. Now I want peace."

That sounded so good, but he shook his head. "I can't give you that."

"You can, but you need space and time to figure that out."

He couldn't let her hope. "Don't . . . death follows me. You need to get out now."

She stood there for a few seconds, not moving. Then she nodded. "Just remember you're the one who told me to leave."

Then she was gone.

An hour later Josiah walked around the barn. The place where they'd nursed Frederick back to life, then killed him. That could be the story of his career. Give people hope, then kill them. Made him a hell of a human being.

He heard footsteps. Heavy thumps that didn't belong to Sutton. Relief washed through him, and that added to his guilt. He just couldn't take another emotional showdown; he was already reeling from the last one.

Seeing her leave that room shredded him. Tore something away from him, a sort of protective shield that saved him when his father threw him out. She got in. She got close. And when she mentioned love everything inside him shriveled because he wanted it so much.

Mike came up to stand next to him. Joined him in staring at the barn. They didn't talk for a few minutes. Let the breeze blow through and the sound of the high grasses whoosh around them.

"I should have taken the shot." Mike continued to look at his boots.

The comment didn't really compute in Josiah's mind. He figured every conversation would be like that for a while. "What?"

"I was about to when you fired on Harlan." Mike looked up then with a stark look in his eyes. "I hesitated. You didn't."

He couldn't talk about this. Not with her and not with Mike. "It doesn't matter."

"Yes, it does."

Looked like he had to come right out and say it. "I don't really want to talk about this now. Maybe ever."

Mike shifted and leaned his back against the side of the barn. Faced Josiah head-on. "Too busy feeling sorry for yourself?"

Now that comment he understood. It shot through Josiah, hitting him in exactly the wrong spot. "Excuse me?"

"Save the polite British bullshit for someone else." Mike's gaze traveled up and down. "You're a fucking mess. I get that. We all are."

"I'm fine." Josiah almost laughed because that might be the biggest lie he'd ever told. He lived in a world that lacked truth and ran his entire life pretending to be someone else, but that one was the worst.

"Sure. You watched your uncle, who sounds like he was more of a father than that shit of a dad you got handed, get blown to pieces. You killed Harlan." Mike shrugged. "Who wouldn't be fine after that?"

"Shut the fuck up."

Mike threw up his hands. "Hell, you gave me the order to take out Frederick in cold blood."

Josiah felt something now. Heated anger and more frustration than he could handle. He liked Mike, trusted him and depended on him, but this came close to the one step too far. "What the hell is your point?"

"We do things, Josiah." Mile stood up and came closer. "Shitty things but for the right reasons. We do good, though I know it doesn't always feel that way. The Alliance, unlike anything else I've ever been involved in, makes a difference."

"I used to think so." That wasn't fair. If Josiah were being honest he'd admit he knew all that. The real question was whether it was enough. Right now it didn't feel like it was. Not to keep him going on this path.

"Without you, without this team, innocent people would die."

"I don't need a pep talk." Mostly he didn't want one because he might start to believe it and, yeah, maybe Mike was right. He needed to wallow. He'd been stuck in this cycle where he talked himself into believing. He didn't want to do that again.

"You need a kick in the ass." Mike looked half ready

to hand one out. "People can go on with their lives, never knowing the danger passing right in front of them. You give them that. And pay a steep price, but that's the job. That's what we signed up for."

Every word made sense but that didn't wash the blood off their hands. "What if I want out?"

"You want to crawl into the woods and lick your wounds." Mike smiled and gave a little wink. "That's an animal reference, London boy."

Josiah laughed because he couldn't help it. Mike did that to him. "I got that. Yeah."

"You want to feel sorry for yourself. Honestly, you've earned the right. This one sucked. I can't even think about Harlan and how that ended without wanting to kill someone. But you were successful." He pointed in the direction of the farmhouse. "And you have a woman in there who will heal you if you let her."

"She deserves—"

Mike groaned. "Stop that shit. There is no one better than you. I know because I've fought beside you."

"A teammate is different from—"

"—the man who loves her?" Mike's eyes widened and his voice filled with amusement. "If I can admit I'm hung up on a hot professor, you can admit what we both already know."

Mike's honesty egged Josiah on. "Enlighten me."

"It wasn't adrenaline or circumstance. What you feel for her was meant to be."

Josiah couldn't help but wince at that one. "When did you get so romantic?"

"Probably had something to do with seeing you sweep her off a balcony."

The memory came rushing back. He hadn't even thought it through. If he'd taken five seconds to think about her hanging off that railing he would have deemed it too risky and figured out something else. Though he didn't know what. "I impressed myself with that one."

"You want to take time and find your humanity again. I'm all for that." Mike clapped his hands together. "I want you healthy and focused the next time you have my back, but hiding isn't the answer."

"Not my style." And that was the truth. Josiah didn't sit around and stew. Hell, he rarely sat around.

"Then why are you trying to do it?" Mike leaned in with his hand behind his ear. He was in full dramatic mode today. "That's right. You are."

As far as pep talks went, that was a good one. The need to shove Mike took away some of the emptiness. Amazing how punching and shooting made him feel better. And Josiah kept thinking about Sutton getting on a plane and flying away. Seeing her go and knowing that was it.

He'd never thought about commitments or serious girlfriends in his life. Other members of the team made it work. He admired the skill but thought it would be exhausting to keep trying. But then it hit him. It wasn't hard with Sutton. All the pieces fell into place right from the start. Even when he doubted her, he couldn't let her go. With her he could be who he was, share parts of his past. She didn't judge. She didn't just fall in line either, which he found so hot. The whole standing-up-to-him thing totally made him hot for her.

Mike burst out laughing. "You should see your face."

"I'm thinking." But Josiah could imagine. He'd been looking in the mirror at a man in love for days and didn't realize it, dumbass that he was.

"The hell with that." Mike snorted. "Go get your woman before I give you that ass kicking you're begging for."

That sounded efficient but Josiah knew his brain wouldn't reboot on command. Not this time. "I need time."

"Do it fast because Tasha arranged for a private plane to take Sutton stateside to a hospital and get checked out then debriefed." Mike glanced at his watch. "I'm driving her to a hangar in an hour."

"What the hell is Tasha thinking?" That might be protocol, but come on.

"I think she wants you to man up and make a decision, too." Mike smiled. "We all do because watching you is pathetic."

All of a sudden everyone cared about his private life. Wasn't that just fucking fabulous. "The people on this team should mind their own business."

"That's what've been saying." Mike winked and started to walk away. "Get to your thinking."

"That comment doesn't even make sense."

Mike held up and hand and gave him the finger, but never stopped walking. "I can't stall her forever, London boy."

27

SUTTON COULD barely see the duffel bag on the edge of the plane seat. Not a regular seat. This was more of a couch, all plush and leather. She intended to use it as a bed as soon as they got up in the air. Between the delays getting to the hangar and the additional delays now, they were way behind schedule. They had to fly soon, except the quiet suggested otherwise.

The pilot and another man got off the plane to talk with Mike fifteen minutes ago and never re-boarded. She peeked out the window and couldn't see any of them. Figured. She wanted to escape and the men decided this was the perfect time to stand around and chat.

She'd been through an emotional hurricane. Every emotion whipped up around her. She'd muscled her way through fear and frustration, terror and sadness. She'd been dealing with the anger over the true cause of her mother's death for some time. Her hatred for Benton and men like him would linger even longer.

But all of that paled in comparison to the heartbreak. It was silly and stupid. Rational people didn't fall in love in a week, certainly not when the courtship started out with a kidnapping. She wanted to blame the adrenaline. Maybe once she got away from him and the team, this would all fade into a bad memory and she could move on.

She rubbed the ache in her chest. The damn thing would not go away. It lingered at first but now four long hours had passed since the blow-up and her pain only grew. This is why she wanted to be off the ground and gone by now.

But being in the air wouldn't fix anything. When she told Josiah she loved him and he basically begged her not to, the knot formed deep inside her. Now it kept tightening. She guessed it would strangle her by the time she landed in Baltimore.

"What are you doing?"

At the sound of Josiah's booming voice, she looked up. He stood in the entrance, ducked down to avoid banging his head as he stepped inside. Seeing him switched off her thoughts. She went blank. "What?"

He stepped inside. His long legs brought him down the short aisle until he stood in front of her, pointing at the bag. "That."

His cluelessness touched off her anger. "What the hell does it look like? I have a bag and am on a plane."

He leaned in and squinted. "That's one of Mike's, I think."

She clapped. Thought that was appropriate since he'd finally gotten something right after getting *them* so wrong. "There you go, genius. Maybe you can work for Ellery from now on."

"Wow."

She knew her bitchiness hit full power, but he had ripped her apart and now he stood there talking about nothing. "You need to leave. We were supposed to take off something like two hours ago."

She sat down and pretended to stare out the window. Really, she couldn't see anything. Her vision still blurred and her heart roared in pain just from seeing him. He looked wind-tossed. Had a bit of color on his face, as if he'd been hanging around in the sun. Must be nice to be able to move on and not care.

"Mike's gone."

For some reason that made her heart clench even harder. It was as if everything that happened got erased and forgotten, including her. "I'm sure he has work to do."

"I told him to get out of here." Josiah bent over and pointed at a car in the distance, leaving the private hangar. "And take the pilot and crew with him."

She heard the amusement in Josiah's voice and turned back around to face him. He actually smiled. The simpleton had the nerve to stand there and smile at her after giving her the brush-off and delivering that news. She had to clamp her back teeth together to keep from yelling . . . Actually, why bother.

"You are impossible." That was so much nicer than everything she wanted to say but she tried to remember there were other people in the house. Some of them actually liked him.

He stood with his hands behind his back and nodded. "I know."

That threw her for a second. Whenever he agreed she got nervous and that was fast. "I thought you needed time and space."

"I do."

There it was. Back to the nonsense.

"Then go find them." She waved him away and turned back to the bag. She grabbed it by the handles, unsure where she planned to take or how she could get anywhere. Finally she just scooped out the small wallet Ellery gave her, the one filled with cash and identification and left the rest. It's not as if any of the clothes belonged to her anyway. Tasha found them or bought them. The woman worked magic. Hell, she probably made the clothes.

The plan was to find some sort of travel agent or get to a bigger airport then she could—

Josiah's voice stopped her. "You are on a roll."

She glared at him over her shoulder. "Excuse me?"

When he stepped closer she turned around. Something about having her back to him made her twitchy. She had no idea what was going on. He'd been a mess just a few hours ago. Now he looked bright-eyed and ready to do battle.

Actually . . . she took a closer peek. He didn't look so great. He kind of looked like she felt, turned inside out and raw. His face was drawn and his smile forced. Those eyes, all sad with circles, made it seem like he hadn't had a good night's sleep in months. And that might be right. She knew from sleeping next to him that he only snuck in a few hours at a time.

Maybe he hadn't bounced back like she thought. The idea gave her hope. Not because she wanted him to suffer, though a small part of her did, but because he needed to work through all the pain. It wasn't normal to fight like that and get up and go at it again and again without a break. Never mind the man had a concussion.

He pointed at the seat she just left. "Sit."

Like that her goodwill and worry vanished. "Go to hell."

He stared at the ceiling and exhaled. "Please sit."

Better, but she wasn't ready to do anything he asked just yet. He had wiped her out. She tried to comfort him and he unloaded. She'd happily take on that burden if it relieved him of some of his, but he seemed determined to blow them up. Crash his career, wreck his life, and ruin them. She could take a lot but that was too much.

She glanced at the duffel bag then back at him again. "Why are we doing this?"

"I want to talk with you."

Yeah, they'd done that and it was awful. She'd be nursing those emotional scars for a long time. "Are you going to admit to being an ass?"

He nodded. "Basically."

She officially had no idea what was going on. "This feels like a trick, but I'll sit."

Standing became impossible anyway. Her legs wobbled and her heart hurt. She felt battered and broken and right at the edge of breaking down. She didn't want to become that woman. The one who cried and tried to guilt him into staying. She'd learned so much over the last week, some of it terrifying, but some pretty great. She truly was a survivor. Imperfect, with a serious fear of heights, but worthy.

Her mind raced and all he did was stand there. He continued to look at her. The longer he did, the more he frowned. She knew then this wasn't going to be good. But after all he'd already said, she couldn't imagine what sore he intended to find and press down on.

He finally shook his head. "You're not leaving yet."

There was no way she could hang around here and pack up and pretend everything was fine and act like she wasn't crumbing into pieces on the inside. No one was that good of an actress. "Why?"

"I canceled this flight. I'll cancel the next one you book and the one after that." He rocked back on his heels.

She thought about shoving him over. "Have you lost your mind?"

This time he laughed. "Most definitely."

Maybe he was as far gone as he'd said. Part of her thought he gave the whole speech as some big kiss-off. That the devastation gave him some cover. Now she sensed she owed him an apology . . . not that she planned to give him one.

"Okay, now you're starting to scare me." She got up and gestured for him to her spot. "I think you should sit down and—"

"I love you."

The words just hung there in the small, quiet plane. He didn't laugh afterward or smile. Just used a firm, clear voice and spilled it out like that.

"What?" She squealed the word. Said it loud enough to shake the walls.

"You sound horrified." He rubbed his chin. "Not exactly the reaction I'd hoped for."

He sounded so British right then but she didn't let the sexy accent derail her. Didn't let that hope bubbling up inside her continue either. She tamped down on all of it. "You gave me this big speech about needing to wander off to the desert."

He frowned at her. "I'm pretty sure I never said that."

"You made it clear you were leaving me." That's the part she heard. That's what walloped her and left her unable to breathe.

"I did."

He needed to stop agreeing with her. "Then what are you talking about now?"

"I love you." He said it stronger that time. Added a shy smile. Didn't fidget or rub his hands together.

Her brain went blank. "Stop saying that."

"I plan on saying it a lot." He skimmed his palms up and down her arms. "Wake you up saying it. Go to sleep saying it." Pulled her in a little closer until his mouth hovered over hers. "You should get used to hearing it."

Her brain cells misfired as light started to dance inside her. "What's happening right now?"

"Really, I mean it. This time please sit." He guided her back to the cushions. She dropped down, sure she would fall through some hole and disappear. None of this made sense. None of it matched with their conversation hours ago.

The hunt for Benton was over. Tasha had confirmed they found the body and he was dead. No one looked at her like she was one of the bad guys. So she couldn't figure out what trick he was playing and why. Didn't he know the words both cut her and gave her hope?

"Sutton, all those things I said about being confused and exhausted and needing a break. Those were all true." He sat down next to her with her hand in his. "I feel like someone ripped me apart and there's no way to glue me back together again."

She understood. She'd been walking around in the same state since he left the bedroom. Even though he caused her pain, her empathy won out. He was allowed to leave her, to not love her. She kept reminding herself of those facts.

But right now he needed comfort and she needed a few minutes with him. Despite what he said, the last minutes together, probably, but still. She put a hand on his leg. Light and just for a second, but she'd needed to touch him. Now she regretted it. Being this close, with him right beside her, all the shields came down. She didn't have any protection against him or how he made her feel.

"I don't . . ." Nothing else came to her. The words got lodged and stuck and wouldn't break free.

"I do love you. It happened fast, but that doesn't make the feelings any less real."

"Are you sure?" Because he looked ten seconds away from heaving. She might have felt worse for him if he hadn't shredded her insides with his big speech about needing alone time.

He visibly swallowed. "I knew that when I said all those things to you. Maybe that's part of the reason I did. So much loss and now with my feelings for you, the idea I could lose something even bigger . . ." He shook his head. "It's a lot to accept."

The words brushed over her like a caress. She shook her head to fight them off. This was like a dream, something she wanted to be true but wasn't.

He squeezed her hand. "Listen to me. Look at me."

She saw something. This spark of life inside him that had been gone before. Hope flickered inside her. Instead of blowing it out, she tried to understand what he was saying. Force her brain to reboot and catch up. "But you said—"

"When I said you were right before, I meant it but I missed the bigger part of what was happening to me. That I'm better when I'm with you. You take the sting away and give me a new focus. One that's about life and sunshine, not death and gunfire." He smoothed her fingers with his. "I can't promise that I can put my life back together, but I at least want to try. With you."

"You love me." She said the words, then repeated them in her head. Let them sink in.

He laughed. "Yes, baby. I do."

The warmth of his smile stole some of the darkness. "Say it again."

He leaned in and kissed her. Let his mouth linger over hers. "I love you."

The words erased the pain. That quick, the doubts

died and the dreams flourished again. He wasn't promising her perfect, which was good because she wasn't that. He was giving them a chance. That's all she ever wanted. A way to see if this, what had grown between them, could live outside the adrenaline rush.

She kissed his cheek and rested her forehead there. Just hearing him want to move on filled her with hope. Touching him tilted her world right again.

"You do these things. Important things." She lifted her head and let her gaze search that sexy face. "You amaze me."

"I don't scare you?" He rubbed his thumb over her bottom lip. "Maybe a little?"

At the beginning but not since. She'd seen him in terrible circumstances and he'd acted with dignity. He talked about his humanity but he'd never lost it. She saw hints of it every day. He didn't advertise it or make a big deal, but he was a good man. And she would spend a lifetime convincing him of that, if needed. "I worry for you. That's different."

"I didn't blink when it came to killing Benton." He glanced down at their joined hands. "I need you to know that."

If that were the test for humanity she'd fail, too. She'd wanted to shove him over the side, fill him full of bullets. Her rage and her anger swamped her when it came to Benton. Even now, when he was dead, she continued to hate. That made her human, not the opposite.

She smiled and it felt so good. "Haven't you heard there's evil in this world?"

He returned the smile. Added a bit of smoldering hotness to his. "I read that somewhere."

She looked around the small space before glancing up at him. "But not in here."

"No, not in here." His hand slid up her thigh.

"We are on a plane, you know?"

"Alone." He stretched the word out for several syllables. "Think of it as a beginner's version of the Mile-High Club."

Her breath bobbled. With the sadness gone, her mind moved on to other things. The things he could do with his hands and that sexy mouth. "So now what?"

"We figure out if we can recover, if I can. In the meantime, we start the rest." He started to lean back, drawing her on top of him as he spread out on the makeshift couch.

Her leg slipped through his and she moved her knee higher. "Subtle."

"Wait until you see me naked."

She climbed on top of him. "Forget about this being a plane, let's do that now."

28

THE NEXT morning Josiah could not stop smiling. After a few hours of seeing how hard they could make a parked plane shake, they'd headed back to the farmhouse. Josiah did not let that soft mattress go to waste either.

All his problems and doubts waited for him, just out of reach, and he'd get to them. But for now he decided to engage in some Sutton healing. Let her ease some of the pain away. Talk with her, listen to her.

Mike threw a rolled-up napkin at Josiah's head. "You're fucking annoying."

Leave it to Mike to bring reality crashing in. Even that couldn't spoil Josiah's good mood. A night rolling around in the sheets with Sutton? Perfection. "You're jealous."

"Hell, yeah!"

"It's not my fault Drew is back in DC. At least he's home now and you've talked with him." Josiah missed the conversation but he watched from the window as Mike paced back and forth, talking on the phone.

Mike winced. "Do you have any idea how much scrambling I'm going to have to do to fix this?"

"You're going to tell him the truth, right?" After the big speech outside that helped Josiah see his way through the emotional clutter, and the way Mike now dropped small bits of information about his personal life, Josiah assumed Mike was ready to move forward.

Frankly, he was relieved for Mike. The whole hidden-personal-life thing Mike had done from the beginning had begun to wear thin. It put him at risk, put Drew at risk. Now it was all in the open.

Mike gave him a blank stare. "About?"

Sometimes Josiah thought Mike liked being difficult. "The Alliance. What's really going on in your life? Those sorts of things."

"No." He followed the curt response by taking a sip of coffee.

Not the answer Josiah expected at all. "Really?"

Mike made a face. Looked like he debated just getting up and storming out. Wouldn't be the first time. He didn't talk about emotions all that well. None of them did.

He finally piped up. "When I leave a job I go home to him."

Josiah wasn't sure what the travel and living arrangements had to do with anything, but okay. "I get that."

He laughed. "No, you don't."

Josiah didn't see the big deal. "Explain it."

"I walk away from this. I put down the gun . . . well, metaphorically, since I actually have a weapon on me at all times." Mike waved the words away and kept talking. "My point is I'm not a killer when I'm with him. I don't have to scale buildings or defuse bombs. I can be Drew's boyfriend."

Josiah tried to imagine that. The Mike he knew was always *on*. The idea of him going on dates and making dinner, sitting around watching a movie, didn't fit with anything else he knew about the guy. The idea of two different lives intrigued him. "How do you turn the killing gene off?"

"Practice."

Josiah guessed there was some joke in there about how he kept a huge part of who he was a secret from the Alliance for so long. Josiah didn't want to get into that now. As his boss, they'd have to talk about it and deal with it. Not today. Not even this month.

But Josiah still couldn't fight the feeling that he was missing something. "I'm serious."

"So am I. I compartmentalize the pieces of my life to keep Drew away from the shit."

That sounded so easy. Josiah tried to think of a world where he could go back and keep his relationship with Sutton clean, not clue her in and play at being normal, if it would work. As soon as the idea came into his head he discarded it. He didn't want to close her out of pieces of his life. He wanted them both all in, all the time.

Part of him wondered if Mike really wanted that, too. "What if he needs to know?"

Mike shrugged. "Then I'll tell him."

Then the truth hit him. "You think he'll leave you. Mike, you can't think—"

He emptied his coffee cup. "I'm not taking that chance."

Suddenly his friend's life and choices made sense. Josiah could see why Mike picked the road he did. But Josiah didn't have to. Sutton knew and accepted the job and the life. He didn't have to play games and worry that if she saw the wrong thing she'd go. She'd seen the worst and didn't blink. That was the kind of luck he didn't intend to take for granted.

Tasha walked in and threw her car keys on the table. "I put Ellery on a plane to go and watch over Lucas."

"He'll love that." Josiah tried to imagine that reunion. They both acted as if they didn't care, but the looks . . . Damn, they were so obvious it actually hurt to see them together. All that pretending not to notice each other. It was exhausting.

"He will. It's my recuperation gift to him." She looked around. "Where's Sutton?"

"Sleeping."

"Rub it in," Mike mumbled as he got up and threw his mug in the sink.

"That's enough sex talk." Tasha's voice had turned serious.

Josiah didn't want to hear bad news or talk about a job, so he performed a fast forward. Let her know he was done with business for a short time. "When do we leave?"

"Tomorrow." She leaned back in her chair and stretched her legs out in front of her. "I need to plan Harlan's service. You're both going and speaking, so don't try to—"

"Fine," Mike said with a nod.

"Absolutely," Josiah said. Being there, standing

up for the guy and making sure people knew his life counted was not a question. It would be rough and heart shredding but Harlan deserved at least that much. "Sounds good."

"Thank you," she said in an uncharacteristically soft voice.

"We owe him, Tasha. We get that." Josiah would never deny that.

She picked at a worn spot on the table. "I know he could be difficult, but he was damn good at this job and in the end . . ." Her voice cracked.

Mike held up a hand. "Pure hero."

That about summed it up for Josiah but the words clogged in his throat. He pushed out the only one he could say. "Yeah."

Then he looked at Tasha. Really looked. She was the toughest woman he knew. Hell, she could take down most of the men on the team if she wanted. Her shooting, her determination and stamina. But right now sadness moved through her.

He had forgotten until this minute that Tasha and Harlan had served together on and off for a long time, including well before the Alliance. She brought him into the group. She fought for him to have a position equal to Ward in administration yet be able to go into the field when needed. She was his champion and, at heart, his friend.

She cleared her throat. "So, service, then I'm going to tell Ward we're getting married."

The news skidded across Josiah's brain. "That's interesting."

Mike's eyes bugged out. "Whoa."

"Yeah, he doesn't know yet." She shrugged. "He will soon."

"Shouldn't he ask you?" Mike drew out each word of the question, as if waiting for her to unload.

She snorted. "Oh, please."

Josiah didn't know how to take that reaction. "Too traditional?"

"He asked ten days after I met him. The ball has been in my court ever since." She shot them both a big smile. "Besides, we need a party. We all need to celebrate. Harlan would appreciate that."

But Josiah's mind kept spinning. He tried to imagine Ward waiting while she waded into danger. Ward's hand injury kept him sidelined, but Josiah couldn't imagine the frustration that came with being in the control room while the love of his life took so many risks.

"We can probably have one without the wedding," he said, choosing his words as carefully as Mike had.

She snorted. "I want the wedding."

"There you go." Mike grabbed some glasses and clunked them down on the table. "We should do a toast."

"To weddings." Josiah glanced at Tasha and smiled. "And to Harlan."

The tears welled in Tasha's eyes that time. "Someone find some wine."

Two weeks later Sutton stood on the balcony wrapped in a heavy sweater as she watched the snowfall. She lifted her head and let the first few flakes of the first snow of the season land on her cheeks.

Strong arms came around her and snuggled her close. Josiah's scent, kind of woodsy and musky, washed over her. He'd showered and piled on the clothes. She preferred him without but he insisted the heat stay off and they light a fire.

She'd let him get right on that after a few more minutes of holding.

He kissed her hair. "I promised you a vacation. Some time away from worrying and the job."

She looked at the harbor. The lights of the marina cast the boats bobbing in the water in shadows. The steady clang of metal on metal sounded out in the darkness.

She laughed and could see the steam from her breath.

"Yes, you did." And he needed time to heal.

His lips traced the outside of her ear. "Told you we'd travel for a few weeks."

"Uh-huh." His tongue tickled and his erection pressed against her back. This guy could go and go. Pretty soon she was the one who'd need lots of rest. "I didn't think we'd end up back in Baltimore."

"It's a nice hotel."

Understatement. He'd insisted they skip her place in favor of a fancy boutique hotel made out of an old maritime museum. It was warm and cozy and the room service worked round the clock, which they'd taken advantage of for every meal.

"You're lucky I love you." She joked but the reality

was she didn't care where they went. She just wanted to spend time alone with him. To wipe away some of the hurt and double back, get to know each other like normal people do. Not that anything about him or his life qualified as normal.

"Yes, I am." He licked that spot right below her ear. The one that drove her wild.

"You're impossible." And she loved him. Every mixed-up, flawed, strong, heroic part of him.

She pushed her hips back against him and he groaned. A long, low growl that echoed in her ear. It sounded so delicious, she did it a second time.

He nipped her ear. "Naughty."

"You love that, too."

"I so do." He turned her around to face him. His nose had turned pink and the tops of his ears looked red thanks to the cold. "Would it help if I told you I had two tickets to Australia in my pocket?"

She didn't want to get excited but her stomach had taken off in a happy dance. "Is it for work?"

"For a beach vacation with you. It's summer there." He made a face. "Well, almost."

"Just the two of us?" She still didn't quite trust this planning. He talked to his team daily. She wouldn't put it past him to set up some sort of group getaway.

That would be fun, but she wanted him all to herself. Just them lounging on a beach, drinking fruity drinks . . . thought she wasn't sure if that happened in Australia. She didn't really care.

"Well, I rented a house but there will be people outside, I assume. I can't really control who goes in and out of the country." He winced when she pinched him. "Hey."

He was so much more than she ever dreamed. She hadn't been the little girl who sat and dreamed about weddings. She didn't think she needed a man to be happy. But then she found him and the world opened up to her. She could trust and love and hope and dream, and he would stand next to her. It was a pretty humbling thing.

She slipped her arms around his neck and cuddled against his chest, trying to steal some of his warmth while she got close. "You did this for me."

"I will refrain from making a smartass remark—"

"That's wise." She glared at him, but she knew he was kidding. So was she.

"You said you'd take me, warts and all." He kissed her nose.

"Don't use that as an excuse to be jerky." She snorted. "Not that it would matter."

He pulled back and stared at her. He sounded amused and a tiny bit confused. "Why?"

The poor guy still didn't understand how much he meant to her. How he filled in those gaps. How being with him was so much better than being stuck in airports and on planes. "I love you just as you are."

"And I'm enough?" He shuddered. "That makes me feel bad for you."

He said it as a joke but she sensed the underlying fear. Not that he would admit it. She'd accidentally used the word "fear" with him a week ago and got treated to a five-minute lecture on how he pushed through fear.

Men.

"You are enough. You're everything." And she meant it.

He got that soft, going-to-kiss-you look. Then he did. A hot, wet, going-to-take-you-to-bed kiss. "I love you."

Every word filled her with happiness, but still . . . "But we're still going on that trip."

"Understood." He nodded. Looked all serious all of a sudden. "Any chance you want to practice for those beaches by getting naked?"

This playful side of him made her heart thud. "Always."

He lifted her off the ground. "You really are perfect for me."

"I keep telling you that." And she would forever.

ACKNOWLEDGMENTS

A HEARTFELT THANK you to May Chen, my incredible editor. You never cease to amaze me . . . and I'm not just talking about when you're right about revisions, which is always. Your guidance and support on this book were invaluable.

Thank you to my agent, Laura Bradford, for your hard work in selling the series and in keeping me sane while I wrote it.

Also, thank you to everyone at HarperCollins and Team Avon for all your hard work. You've made me feel welcome from day one, and that is a gift I do not take for granted.

As always, much love to my husband and thanks to my fantastic readers who make it possible for me to do what I love for a living. I am so grateful.

Next month, don't miss these exciting new love stories only from Avon Books

Shattered by Cynthia Eden
Criminal psychiatrist Dr. Sarah Jacobs is all too familiar with bad boys, but the dark, dangerous man she meets in the New Orleans underworld is irresistible. Jax Fontaine doesn't claim to be a good guy, but he's loyal to his own code and honest about what he wants. And when a deranged killer targets Sarah, Jax will do whatever it takes to keep her safe. . . .

The Wrong Bride by Gayle Callen
Shaken from her sleep during the night and bundled off to the Highlands by a burly Scot, Riona is at first terrified, then livid. Hugh McCallum insists they were promised to each other as children to ensure peace between their clans. The stubborn laird refuses to believe he's kidnapped the wrong Catriona Duff. Instead, he embarks on a campaign of slow-burning seduction.

Scandal Takes the Stage by Eva Leigh
Playwright Maggie Delamere shuts down aristocrats with a flick of her quill. But when writer's block and an enemy from Maggie's past simultaneously strike, Cameron, Viscount Marwood, proposes she should stay at his manor. There's something behind the relish with which she skewers her "gentleman" characters, and Cam intends to unlock her secrets—one delicious revelation at a time.

At Avon Books, we know your passion for romance—once you finish one of our novels, you find yourself wanting more.

May we tempt you with . . .

- **Excerpts** from our upcoming releases.

- Entertaining **extras**, including authors' personal photo albums and book lists.

- Behind-the-scenes **scoop** on your favorite characters and series.

- **Sweepstakes** for the chance to win free books, romantic getaways, and other fun prizes.

- Writing **tips** from our authors and editors.

- **Blog** with our authors and find out why they love to write romance.

- **Exclusive content** that's not contained within the pages of our novels.

Join us at
www.avonbooks.com

AVON

An Imprint of HarperCollins*Publishers*
www.avonromance.com

*G*ive in to your Impulses!

These unforgettable stories only take a second
to buy and give you hours of reading pleasure!

Go to *www.AvonImp*
have
Available where

AVON

IMP 0811